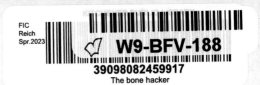

ALSO BY KATHY REICHS

Adult Fiction

Déjà Dead

Death du Jour

Deadly Décisions

Fatal Voyage

Grave Secrets

Bare Bones

Monday Mourning

Cross Bones

Break No Bones

Bones to Ashes

Devil Bones

206 Bones

Spider Bones

Flash and Bones

Bones Are Forever

Bones of the Lost

Bones Never Lie

Speaking in Bones

The Bone Collection

Bones Buried Deep (coauthored with Max Allan Collins)

A Conspiracy of Bones

The Bone Code

Cold, Cold Bones

THE
BONE
HACKER

A TEMPERANCE BRENNAN NOVEL

KATHY
REICHS

PUBLISHED BY SIMON & SCHUSTER
NEW YORK LONDON TORONTO SYDNEY NEW DELHI

SIMON &
SCHUSTER
CANADA

A Division of Simon & Schuster, Inc.
166 King Street East, Suite 300
Toronto, Ontario M5A 1J3

This Simon & Schuster Canada edition August 2023

SIMON & SCHUSTER CANADA and colophon are trademarks of Simon & Schuster, Inc.

For information about special discounts for bulk purchases, please contact Simon & Schuster Special Sales at 1-800-268-3216 or CustomerService@simonandschuster.ca.

Manufactured in the United States of America

10 9 8 7 6 5 4 3 2 1

Library and Archives Canada Cataloguing in Publication

Title: The bone hacker / Kathy Reichs.
Names: Reichs, Kathy, author.
Description: Simon & Schuster Canada edition.
Identifiers: Canadiana (print) 20230191134 | Canadiana (ebook) 20230191150 | ISBN 9781982198701 (softcover) | ISBN 9781982198725 (EPUB)
Classification: LCC PS3568.E476345 B66 2023 | DDC 813/.54—dc23

ISBN 978-1-9821-9870-1
ISBN 978-1-9821-9872-5 (ebook)

For my infallibly wise and ever steadfast ensemble,
les Grandes Dames of Forensic Anthropology:
Leslie Eisenberg
Diane France
Madeleine Hinkes
Elizabeth Murray
Marcella Sorg

"Yes, to dance beneath the diamond sky with one hand waving free."

—Bob Dylan, 1965

THE
BONE
HACKER

PROLOGUE

The man was dead before he tumbled from the bridge.

Before his body hit the water.

Before propellers flayed his flesh like a deli meat slicer.

Earlier knowledge of these facts might have made a difference. Or not.

I'll never know.

1

The monster barreled in unannounced, a dense black predator devouring the unwitting summer night. Ruthless. Fire-breathing. Intent on destroying all in its path.

I was in its path.

I was going to die.

Boom!

Snap!

Thunder cracked. Lightning burst overhead and streaked toward a bobbing horizon, turning narrow swaths of sky a sickly yellow green.

Boom!

Snap!

Again and again.

The air smelled of ozone, angry water, oil, and mud.

I was hunkered low on the deck of a nineteen-foot Boston Whaler, wind whipping my jacket and hair, rain pounding my hunched shoulders and back. With all my might, I clung to a steel upright, desperate not to be flung overboard. Or electrically fried.

The boat belonged to Ryan's buddy Xavier Rabeau, never one of my favorites. Ryan was in the stern. Rabeau was under cover in the center console. Of course, he was.

Rabeau's twentysomething *blonde*, Antoinette Damico, lay in a fetal curl beside me. Though not yet hysterical, she was moving in that direction.

We were heaving and pitching in the middle of a roiling St. Lawrence River. The outboard was dead, overwhelmed by the ceaseless waves hammering it.

Later, meteorologists would speak of the climatic phenomenon in near reverent tones. They'd talk of microbursts and tornadoes. *La microrafale et la tornade*. They'd name the storm Clémence, either appreciative or ignorant of the irony in their choice. They'd explain in two languages how the impossible had happened in Montreal that night.

But a full postmortem was still in the future.

At that moment I could only grasp with all my strength, heart pounding in my chest, ears, and throat. All that mattered was staying aboard. Staying alive.

I knew little about boats, less about restarting an ancient Evinrude whose one hundred and fifty horses had all fled the stable. Badly wanting to help, I was helpless. So I cowered between the rear seats, bracing with my feet and white-knuckling the upright supports. Inwardly I cursed Rabeau, who'd been so focused on loading into the boat sacks of supermarket snacks and a cooler of iced beer—only beer—that he'd left every life jacket behind in the trunk of his car. Bastard.

I also cursed myself for failing to ask about safety vests before leaving the ramp. In my defense—not his, he owned the damn boat and should have been more responsible—when we boarded, the air was cool and dry, the few passing breezes as gentle on my skin as the brush of butterfly wings. A billion stars twinkled in a flawless sky.

We'll have an incredible view of the fireworks, Ryan had said, excited beyond what seemed fitting for a fiftysomething ex-cop.

What could go wrong? Rabeau had said.

Everything.

When I lifted my head, drops sluiced down my face, watery javelins blurring my vision and stinging my cheeks. Never easing my grip, I raised up and pivoted on my toes.

Ryan was aft of me, tinkering with the rebellious motor. Though the downpour obscured most detail, I could see that his hair was flattened in places, wind-spiked and dancing in others. His long-sleeve tee was molded to his spine like the skin on a porpoise.

Snap!

Boom!

The boat lurched wildly. The cooler skidded, tumbled, then shot up and sailed over the starboard side. Easing back down onto my butt, I watched the perky blue YETI disappear, a cuboid shadow riding the ebony chop.

Around us, other boats were struggling to return to shore, their multicolored lights winking erratically through the veil of water. An overturned catamaran bobbed roughly twenty yards off our port side. Helpless. Like me.

Closing my eyes, I willed a safe landing for those on the cat. Hoped their captain had followed regs and provided life vests.

Beside me, Damico was alternating between crying and barfing, impressively, managing to do both simultaneously. She'd abandoned the first of the plastic Provigo sacks used to transport her boyfriend's munchies and brews and was starting to fill the second. Now and then, when the deck reangled sharply, she'd wail and demand to be taken ashore.

Rabeau was rocking and rolling at his captain's chair, feet spread, awaiting word from the stern. Each time Ryan called out, Rabeau tried the ignition. Over and over, the two repeated the sequence. Always with the same outcome.

Nothing.

Then the sound of Quebecois cursing.

Hostie!

Tabarnak!

Câlice!

Above the cacophony of wind and waves and male frustration, my ears picked up an almost inaudible sound. A high, mosquito-like whine. Distant sirens? A tornado warning?

I offered a silent plea to whatever water deities might be watching. Clíodhna, the Celtic goddess of the sea? Where the hell did that come from. Gran, of course. Christ, I was losing my mind.

The bow shot skyward, then dropped from the crest of a high wave into a trough.

Thwack!

A sound rose from Damico's throat, a keening thick with silvery-green bile.

I reached over and placed a hand on her shoulder. She lowered the Provigo sack and turned to face me, mouth an inverted *U*, a slimy trail of drool hanging from each corner. Lightning sparked, illuminating the skeletal arch of the Jacques Cartier Bridge behind and above her.

I felt tremors of my own. Swallowed. Vowed not to succumb to nausea.

Not to die. Not like this.

Death is inevitable for us all. From time to time, we ponder our passing. Visualize those last moments before the final curtain. Perhaps because I'm in the business of violent death, my imaginings tend toward the dramatic. A tumbling fall and fractured bones. Popping flames and acrid smoke. Crumpled steel and shattered glass. Bullets. Nooses. Toxic plants. Venomous bites. I'm not morbid by nature. The odds are far greater that the climactic setting will include pinging monitors and antiseptically clean sheets.

I'll admit it. I've considered every possibility for my closing scene. All but one.

The one I fear most.

I've viewed scores of bodies pulled, dragged, or netted from watery graves. Recovered many myself. Each time, I empathize with the terror the victim had endured. The initial struggle to stay afloat, the desperation for air. The dreaded submersion and breath-holding. The inevitable yielding and aspiration of water. Then, mercifully, the loss of consciousness, cardiorespiratory arrest, and death.

Not an easy way to go.

Point of information: I have a robust fear of drowning. Don't get me wrong. I'm not afraid of rivers, lakes, and pools. Far from it. I body surf and water-ski. I swim laps for exercise. I'm not afraid of going into the water.

I'm afraid of not coming out.

Irrational, I know. But there you have it.

So why was I there, in an open boat, about to die during the mother of all storms?

Fireworks.

And love.

Summer had taken its sweet time arriving in Quebec that year.

April teased with warm days that nibbled away at the black-crusted snow. Then April did what April does. The fickle mercury would plunge, encasing lawns, driveways, streets, and sidewalks in a mud-colored slick of frozen meltwater.

May offered ceaseless cold rain delivered in a variety of ways. Mist from velvety hazes. Drizzle from indolent gray skies. Splatter, big and fat from low-hanging clouds. Drops driven by winds disdainful of tempo carports, canopies, and umbrellas.

As the first official day of summer approached, the weather gods had finally smiled. The sun had appeared, and daytime temperatures had managed to inch above seventy. Just in time.

L'international des Feux Loto-Québec, also known as the Montreal Fireworks Festival, a Montreal tradition, is one of the largest fireworks festivals in the world. Or so its organizers boast. I've never fact-checked. Every year, the extravaganza kicks off in late June.

Second point of information. My significant other is Lieutenant-détective Andrew Ryan, a former Sûreté du Québec homicide cop. Sort of former. More on that later. Ryan is a sucker for pyrotechnics. On any level. Black Cats. Lady Fingers. M-80s. Roman Candles. Bottle rockets. If it goes boom or shoots pinwheels, the man is enthralled. Go figure.

L'international des Feux competition is a world apart from the little poppers and streakers Ryan purchases to detonate in parking lots and fields. Each country's performance is professionally choreographed, marrying music to the art exploding high above. The pyromusical presentations can be seen and heard for six consecutive Saturdays all across the city. Ryan loves them and rarely misses a performance.

I am a board-certified forensic anthropologist, practicing for more years than I care to admit. My career has been spent at death scenes and in autopsy rooms. I've observed firsthand the countless ways people harm other people and themselves. The follies in which humans engage to get themselves killed. One such folly is the mishandling of explosives. I am less of an enthusiast than my beau.

Face radiant with boyish excitement, Ryan had proposed viewing this year's kickoff performance from the river. Since the fireworks are launched from the La Ronde amusement park, situated on Île Sainte-Hélène across from Montreal's historic old port, the whole wondrous display would explode directly over our heads! *Magnifique!*

Next thing I knew, *Voilà!* We'd been invited onto Rabeau's boat.

I must admit, the experience was moving, listening to "Ride of the Valkyries" or "Ode to Joy" as peonies, crossettes, and kamuras exploded high above. Ryan named and explained each.

Until Clémence showed up to kick ass.

So here we were. Without a motor. Without life vests. Soaked. Pitching and rolling and struggling to stay aboard a vessel far too small for the conditions. Easy pickings for lightning.

Then, through the wind and the waves and the furious thrumming of drops on fiberglass, my ears registered a sound that I'd been frantic to hear. Gulpy and unstable at first, the watery glugging gradually blended into a steady hum.

The boat seemed to tense, as if sensing new determination in the old Evinrude.

The humming gathered strength.

The vessel began moving with purpose, no longer at the whim of the turbulent *rivière*.

The humming intensified and rose in pitch.

The bow lifted and the little Whaler thrust forward, leaving a frothy white wake as she sliced through the chop.

Ryan crawled to join me for the rocky return to shore. Arm-wrapping my shoulders, he held me tight.

For the first time since the storm broke, I drew a deep breath.

Clémence was living up to her name. Taking mercy on us.

Our little party would survive.

Others wouldn't be so lucky.

2

I woke early, feeling a bit melancholy and unsure why. Until I picked up my iPhone and noted the date.

Independence Day is my favorite American holiday. No feast to prepare or overeat. No baskets to fill and hide. No presents to wrap, ornaments to hang, or cookies to bake. Call me a grinch. But buy me a bucket of the Colonel's finest and light a few sparklers and I'm happy as a kid at a carnival. Although, that morning, my enthusiasm for anything pyrotechnic was still at rock bottom.

Five days after her wild theatrics, Clémence was still a topic of conversation. In that brief interval, I'd learned more than I needed to know about microbursts and how they differ from tornados. *Las microrafales et las tornades.*

A microburst is a localized column of falling air within a thunderstorm. That's the burst part. The plummeting downdraft is usually less than two and a half miles in diameter. That's the micro part. As for the speed of those zephyrs, I've no idea of Clémence's personal

11

best, but winds produced by microbursts can reach up to 100 mph, equivalent to those of an EF-1 tornado.

Guess where Clémence smacked terra firma? Yup. Right around Rabeau's little boat.

Some good did come from the whole debacle. Ryan agreed that we would no longer socialize with Xavier Rabeau and the vomitous Mademoiselle Damico.

By eight-thirty a.m., I was completing my third circuit of a network of small streets in Hochelaga-Maisonneuve, a working-class neighborhood just east of Centreville. Driving slowly, eyes alert, I passed a school, a small park, several convenience stores known in Quebec as *depanneurs,* and rows of iron staircase–fronted two- and three-flat buildings. Found not a millimeter of open curb.

On my fourth pass along rue Dufresne, I spotted the red flicker of a taillight halfway up the block, shot forward, and waited as a Ford Fiesta the size of my shoe maneuvered itself free. With much shifting and swearing, I managed to wedge my car into the vacated space.

Pleased with my small victory, and quite sweaty, I grabbed my laptop and briefcase and headed toward the Édifice Wilfrid-Derome, a thirteen-story glass-and-steel building renamed years ago to honor Quebec's famous pioneer criminalist.

Not unreasonably, or out of stubbornness, many locals still call the structure the SQ building. The Laboratoire de sciences judiciaires et de médecine légale, the province's combined medico-legal and crime lab, occupies the top two floors. The Bureau du coroner is on eleven. The morgue and autopsy suites are in the basement. All other footage belongs to the Sûreté du Québec, the provincial police. The SQ or QPP, depending on whether you lean francophone or anglophone. French or English.

Hurrying along the sidewalk, I could see the *T*-shaped behemoth looming over the quartier. Somehow, the brooding hulk looked wrong against the cheery blue sky.

And cheery it was.

Summer was in full command now, the days hot and muggy, the nights starry and sultry. After the long, bleak winter and the year's heartless spring, *les Montréalais* were delighting in their town's balmy rebirth.

Bare-shouldered women and pasty-legged men in Bermudas and sandals sipped endless iced coffees and drank pitchers of Molson at tables dragged onto walkways and patios by bar *propriétaires* and *restaurateurs*. Cyclists and rollerbladers filled the bike paths paralleling the city's thoroughfares and waterways. Pram-pushers, joggers, students, and dogwalkers formed colorful streams flowing in both directions along les rues Ste-Catherine, St-Denis, St-Laurent, and nearby boulevards.

Festivals had begun cascading in quick succession. Les Franco-Folies de Montréal. The Formula 1 Grand Prix du Canada. The International Jazz Festival. The Festival International Nuits d'Afrique. Just for Laughs. Montréal Complètement Cirque.

The season had been a long time coming. Knowing it wouldn't tarry, the populace was embracing it with a gusto lacking in my native North Carolina.

But there'd be no strolling, lemonade sipping, or picnicking for me today. I was heading to an autopsy room to examine dead babies.

Feeling melancholy. On the Fourth of July.

Don't misunderstand. I enjoyed Canada Day and Saint-Jean-Baptiste—La fête nationale du Québec. Great fun. But neither was a star-spangled birthday party like the Fourth.

Get over it, Brennan.

Entering the lobby, I swiped my security pass, swiped it again in the elevator, at the entrance to the twelfth floor, and at the glass doors separating the medico-legal wing from the rest of the *T*. Tight security? You bet.

The corridor was quiet early on a Thursday morning. As I passed windows opening onto microbiology, histology, and pathology labs, I could see white-coated men and women working at microtomes, desks, and sinks. Several waved or mouthed greetings through the glass. Marcel, one of the new technicians, might have said *"Joyeux quatre juillet."* Happy Fourth of July.

I returned their greetings with a quick wave and continued to the anthropology/odontology lab, the last in the row. After placing my laptop and briefcase on the desk and stowing my purse in a drawer, I slipped into a lab coat, collected the box of bones that I'd recently recovered, and carried it to my examination table.

Steeling myself for the upcoming task, and barring all thoughts of my daughter, Katy, when she was an infant, I arranged what was left of the first tiny skeleton. There was little to arrange. When finished, I began on the next.

I'd been sorting and rearticulating for almost two hours when I sensed, more than heard, a presence at my back. A skill I've developed over years of interaction, perhaps relying on the detection of olfactory cues, among them the faint smell of pipe tobacco. I turned.

"Bonjour, Temperance." LaManche greeted me in his precise Parisian French. Of all my acquaintances, only he insists on using the formal version of my name. No shortening to Tempe for him.

"Bonjour," I replied. *"Comment ça va?"*

"Ça va."

From the look on his face, things weren't going as well as he claimed. Maybe. The old man's hound-dog features whittled deep by vertical creases made him hard to read.

A word about my boss.

Dr. Pierre LaManche has been a pathologist since God invented dirt, *le directeur* of the medico-legal section of the LSJML for as long as I've worked there. I couldn't have guessed his age when we first met. Still can't. He's older now, obviously, a little more stooped, but still a man of impressive stature. And stealth.

Either by intent or habit, perhaps one having matured into the other, LaManche moves with a stillness that allows him to appear without notice. He wears crepe-soled shoes and keeps his pockets free of coins and keys. No squeaking. No jingling. Some find this lack of auditory forewarning unsettling.

"I'm about to begin on the infants from Sainte-Agathe," I said, assuming LaManche was there for a preliminary report on my previous two days' activities. Following a phone tip, he'd sent me with a team from Service de l'identité judiciaire, Division des scènes de crime, Quebec's version of CSI, to search the basement of a farmhouse in a rural area in the Laurentians.

"There are four in all, correct?" LaManche asked glumly, arms folded across his chest.

I nodded. "Each was buried in some sort of small container. Maybe a shoe box. I was able to salvage several scraps of what appears to be cardboard."

"Have you a rough estimate of when these poor babies perished?"

"My first impression is that the deaths occurred over time, with none being recent." I hesitated. "But—"

"Of course." Knowing I dislike being asked for an opinion before completing my full analysis, LaManche raised two gnarled hands, palms toward me. "I apologize. Take your time. I will not rush you."

"I'm seeing no evidence of trauma. I may not be able to determine cause of death."

"Such a sad business. But that is not why I'm here."

I waited.

"Witnesses have reported seeing a man struck by lightning while observing the fireworks last Saturday night. You may recall there was a violent storm?"

Oh, yeah.

"The man was watching from the Jacques Cartier Bridge. When struck, he pitched from the safety grating onto which he'd climbed and into the river. Although the crowd was dispersing hurriedly, many witnessed the incident."

"Does anyone know who he was?"

"No. Apparently, he was alone. Attempts to recover a body began on Sunday. The effort proved unsuccessful until today."

Merde.

I knew what was coming.

"First thing this morning, I received a call from Jean-Claude Hubert." LaManche referred to Quebec's chief coroner. "Monsieur Hubert said that his office had been contacted by an SPVM officer named Roland Plante. Constable Plante stated that at 0730 this morning he responded to a report of a body in the Bickerdike Basin. Do you know it?"

"It's a ferry dock in the old port?"

"It is some manner of dock. Constable Plante said that he drove to the basin and met with a boater named Ernest Legalt. Fairly certain that Legalt was correct and that human remains were present at the site, Plante called the coroner."

Again. Dragging corpses from water is one of my least favorite chores.

"I hate to send you to death scenes twice in one week, but . . ."

Dipping his chin and raising his brows, which resembled bushy gray caterpillars hugging his orbits, LaManche let the unstated request hang between us.

"Of course," I said.

"Assess the situation, *s'il vous plaît*. If the remains are human, and you suspect there is a possibility of recovering more, I will request a search boat and divers."

"I'm on it."

"Would you like transport?"

"No. Thanks. I'll drive myself."

Twenty minutes later I was back in my car. Passing under the Pont Jacques-Cartier, I thought of the man struck by lightning while standing on the structure. I wondered how he'd managed to get onto the overhead guard rail and fall into the water.

Heading west on Viger, I passed the Molson brewery that sprawled along the river to my left, then accelerated past the round tower of the Radio-Canada building. I followed signs toward Boulevard Robert Bourassa and the Ponts Champlain and Victoria. Montreal is an island, thus the abundance of bridges.

I exited onto Chemin des Moulins and, after a bit of *U*-turn maneuvering, was skimming along Avenue Pierre-Dupuy, a narrow strip of pavement bisecting a pointy spit of land ending at Dieppe Park. Ahead on the right were several high-end condo complexes, beneficiaries of the spit's large green spaces. I recognized Tropiques Nord and Habitat 67, an address that Ryan had once called home.

Ahead on the left was Bickerdike Basin, a man-made rectangle of water carved from the St. Lawrence River between the green spit and a massive concrete pier. Shoreward from the pier was another basin, shoreward of that the lower reaches of the old port.

The road ended in an expansive parking area surrounded by chain-link fencing. Eighteen-wheelers and smaller trucks waited here and there, some with cargo containers, some without. Ahead, on the basin's near end, a container-handling gantry crane rose high into the sky, a colossal and extraordinarily complex arrangement of cables and beams and other components I couldn't possibly name.

To the right of the crane, an opening in the fencing gave onto a strip of pavement that sloped downward, then continued as a single lane paralleling the right side of the basin. A sign warned: *Defense d'entre sans autorisation.* No entry without authorization.

Reinforcing the sign's sentiment, an SPVM cruiser sat blocking the narrow access point, light bar strobing the area red and blue. A uniformed officer stood beside his vehicle, gesturing with both arms that I reverse and proceed no farther. Rolling to a stop, I alighted and walked toward him.

The officer spread his feet and planted his hands on his hips. He was not smiling. He probably didn't want to be there, with the heat, the screeching gulls, the smell of oil, dead fish, and algae. Well, neither did I.

"You may not approach, madame. You must move on." A small brass badge above his shirt pocket identified him as *Const. Plante.*

"I'm Dr. Brennan," I said, pulling my ID from my pocket. "LSJML."

"You work for the coroner?" Dubious does not do justice to Plante's tone and expression.

I handed him the ID. "I am the *anthropologue judiciaire.*"

Plante studied the plastic rectangle for so long I thought he might be memorizing the contents. He looked from the photo to my face, back at the photo. Returning the ID, he nodded, still unsmiling.

"Have you seen the body?" I asked.

"Such as it is."

"Is Monsieur Legalt still here?"

"Yes. But don't expect much."

With those puzzling statements, Plante turned and headed down the ramp.

3

As in many locations, questions of jurisdiction can be tricky in Montreal. The city lies on a small hunk of land in the middle of the St. Lawrence River. The Service de Police de la Ville de Montréal, the SPVM, handles policing on the island itself. Off the island, the job falls to local departments, or to the provincial force, La Sûreté du Québec, the SQ. Though coordination isn't always great, the system works.

Bickerdike Basin sat squarely on the island. Thus, the SPVM and the less than genial Constable Plante.

Plante strode with a speed and determination that radiated his desire to wrap things up quickly. I followed, hauling my unwieldy recovery kit. The added poundage meant I had to struggle to keep pace. The heat—by then the temperature was in the mid-eighties—didn't help.

To our right ran a high concrete wall topped by a bike path and Avenue Pierre-Dupuy. At intervals, heaped tires cluttered the wall's base where it met the pavement. Between the heaps, here and there, parked vehicles brooded in the narrow strip of midday shade.

To our left lay the basin. We passed what looked like a floating boat launch, then a couple of barge-like vessels, a tug. Maybe a tug. As I've admitted, I'm less than an expert in nautical taxonomy.

Ahead, beyond Plante, a man smoked and paced beside a red-and-white cabin cruiser with two big outboards riding its stern. Even from a distance I could tell that *el capitan* wasn't big on elbow grease.

I assumed the pacing man was Ernest Legalt. Legalt's body language suggested that he, like the constable and I, would rather be elsewhere.

We'd gone a hundred yards when Plante raised a hand to his mouth and blasted one short piercing whistle. Legalt pivoted our way, sun flashing blue off his aviator shades.

Plante reached Legalt well before me and spoke words I was still too far off to catch. Legalt took a seriously long drag of his smoke, flipped the butt into the basin, and exhaled slowly.

A minute later, I joined the two men, not panting, but breathing much harder than I would have preferred. Setting down the cumbersome case, I swept damp bangs from my forehead.

Legalt eyed me for a full three seconds. Failing to find my appearance reassuring, or wishing to hide the fact that he was nervous as hell, he dropped his eyes to his shoes, a pair of flip-flops that had probably once been purple.

I couldn't blame the man for finding me lacking. Having dressed and coifed for a day with exhumed infant bones, I wore jeans and a tee that said *Science doesn't care what you believe in.* My hair was yanked into a structurally unsound topknot. The sprint at Plante's heels had done nothing to improve the already slapdash look.

But Legalt wouldn't be winning a beauty prize, either. My first impression: the guy looked like an escapee from a deep fryer. His skin was brick red, his hair the color of a week-old French fry, his body muscular in a ropey, sinewy way. His outfit—a dingy wifebeater over frayed jeans whose pocket linings hung below the point at which the legs had been scissored off—lived up to the low fashion bar that I'd set.

Before I could speak, Legalt jabbed a thumb toward the boat tied to a cleat beside us. Half a thumb. Everything past the proximal joint was missing.

"*Bonjour. Comment ça va?*" Hi. How are you?

Legalt did not return my greeting or query my health. "It's aft."

"You are Monsieur Legalt?" I phrased it as a question.

Tight nod. The aviators winked blue.

"I'm Dr. Temperance Brennan." I held out a hand. Legalt ignored it.

"My motors is probably fucked."

"*La madame* has come from the Bureau du coroner." I let the error go. Plante's intro was close enough to the truth. And more understandable to the layman.

Legalt said nothing.

"The *Grésillent* is yours, sir?" Up close, I could see the name in scrolly letters on the algae-crusted hull. *Sizzling.*

Legalt nodded again.

"May I ask why you chose to tie up in Bickerdike Basin?"

"I told all this to the cop." Head tip toward Plante, who'd distanced himself to speak into his mobile. "He wrote it down."

"I'd like to fully understand the situation," I said.

Legalt raised the mangled hand to harvest a fleck of tobacco from one lip. Flicked the fleck. Compressed the lips.

Above us, a motorcycle roared by on Pierre-Dupuy. A car door slammed, and an engine started up.

"Sir?" I prodded.

The cerulean lenses focused on me. Reluctant. "I was meeting a fishing buddy. Last minute, the bastard canceled."

Legalt's French was heavily accented, his word endings swallowed in the manner of the upriver Québécois. I had to listen carefully.

"Can you describe what you saw?" I asked.

Legalt rolled his head, probably his eyes. Hard to tell with the aviators.

"Sir?"

To my relief, Legalt switched to English. Mostly English.

"I'm moored twenty, maybe thirty minutes when a shit ton of gulls starts mobbing my outboards. Forty, fifty, maybe more. For a while, I ignored them. What the hell? Gulls is gulls. But these bastards was screaming and flapping and fighting like someone set fire to their balls. I'm bored waiting for Guillaume, *le connard*, so I go to the stern to see *pourquoi le fou.*"

Overhead, a gull cawed, perhaps disagreeing with Legalt's portrayal of Laridae behavior. Perhaps offended by his reference to the "asshole" friend. Or their genitals.

"And?" I prompted.

"A mother lode of crap was caught in my blades. Figuring it was the usual river shit, I start poking around trying to cut it loose. Then I whack something *lourd.*"

Lourd. Heavy. That didn't sound good.

Legalt pulled a pack of Player's from the pocket of his cutoffs, shook it, grasped one of the remaining cigarettes with his lips. Slipping matches from below the cellophane, he lit up, inhaled, and, with a twist of his mouth, blew the smoke sideways.

In my peripheral vision, I noted Plante checking his watch.

"Go on," I urged.

"What the hell? I go to poking some more."

Legalt paused for another round with his Player's. A long one.

"Yes?"

Legalt shrugged. "I figure maybe it could be my lucky day. Salvage from the sea, ya know?"

I didn't. "And then?"

"Eventually, I see that the thing inside is slimy and white. And it's reeking like a son of a bitch. I know what a rotting carcass looks like, so I reckon it's a dead animal or fish. I'm trying to flip it, when what do I see but a freaking foot!"

"Which you believed to be human."

"*Tabarnak! Les orteils* was pointing right at me!" Perhaps visualizing the moment the toes appeared, perhaps seeking divine protection, Legalt crossed himself quickly, ciggie still cupped in his hand.

"What did you do next?"

"What you think? I got off the goddam boat."

"That's when you called the SPVM?"

Legalt nodded, cheeks pinched as he drew another blast of carcinogen into his lungs.

"Did you touch or manipulate the remains in any way?"

"*Êtes-vous fou?*"

I took his "are you crazy?" as a firm "no."

"Can you show me what you found?"

Legalt looked as though I'd suggested he inject himself with polonium-210.

"May I have permission to board?" I asked.

"Knock yourself out."

Plante must have been listening. When I turned, he was already in motion.

"Monsieur Legalt prefers to remain ashore," I said.

"*Reste ici!*" Plante ordered Legalt, not at all gently. Stay here!

Positioning himself beside the *Grésillent*'s bow, Plante extended an arm. The swells were modest but with aspirations, the boat rocking some, so I took his hand. The last thing I wanted was to stumble in front of these two.

Straddling the gap maintained by a pair of rubber fenders, I swung my legs over the gunwale and hopped onto the deck. Rail grasped in one hand, I indicated my case with the other. After Plante handed it to me, I made my way aft, bracing against the cabin wall for balance.

The long-handled hook lay where it had rolled when Legalt bolted, a jumble of flora still caught on the working end. Flies had gathered above the jumble, darting and whining, sun iridescent on their blue-green bodies.

Though faint, the odor coming from the object of their interest was unmistakable. Mixing with the briny mélange of saltwater and decaying vegetation was the sweet, fetid scent of decomposing flesh.

I was flipping the clasps on my case when Plante joined me. He watched as I shot pics. Gloved. Masked.

When I squatted, the flies rose in a whining cloud of protest. Ignoring them, and the water bugs, snails, and occasional crab clinging to or scuttling from the knotted mess, I observed closely. And understood the source of the smell.

Caught in the slimy strands of kelp and seaweed were soggy chunks of varying shapes and sizes. Pale and bloated, they stood out in sharp contrast to the sea-darkened vegetation. I recognized them as scraps of rotting flesh.

Stomach knotted, I rose.

"Might there be a net on board?" I asked while shooting more photos.

"*Un instant.*"

Plante descended into the cabin. I heard rattling, a thunk, then he returned with a tool that appeared far too short for the job I envisioned. I eyed it skeptically but said nothing.

After freeing the boat hook of any remaining vegetation, I grasped the handle two-handed and moved farther aft. Plante followed. Together we peered down over the stern.

Legalt's description had been dead-on. A "mother lode of crap" jammed the space between the outboards, rising and falling with the movement of the water.

Lowering the long pole, I positioned the hook and began to lever as hard as I could. The gulls, clearly displeased, squawked and circled low overhead.

After much maneuvering and an abundance of perspiration and unspoken cursing, the cluster of seaweed, kelp, and branches reluctantly yielded and popped free.

There was little current in the basin. Still, I didn't want the tangle to bob off and be carried away from the boat. Or, worse, to sink. Reaching out, I snagged one sturdy-looking loop of stem.

The bundle rolled.

Four toes pointed skyward.

The flesh was mottled green and white, and bone showed where portions had been lost to scavengers. Still, Legalt was right. *Les orteils* were unquestionably human.

Wordlessly, Plante thumbed a button on the net in his hands. Its telescoping handle extended to full length.

Way to go, constable.

As I kept the seaweed snarl as still as possible, Plante tried scooping it into the net.

Sounds easy. It wasn't. It took at least a dozen tries to bring the slop aboard.

Plante and I watched murky water run outward from our catch and darken the deck. Even in the open air, the smell of putrefaction was almost overwhelming.

Overhead, the gulls screamed. Closer in, the flies flew into a frenzy.

Again, Plante descended into the cabin. This time he returned with a tarp.

I watched him unfold and spread the makeshift covering, knowing his effort might deter the gulls. But not the flies. I had no doubt that the dogged females would find a way in. That they would gleefully oviposit. That their eggs would render my upcoming task even less pleasant.

Pulling my phone from my pocket, I hit a speed dial entry.

LaManche answered immediately.

"*Oui*, Temperance. Things are going well?"

"Sizzling."

"*Pardon?*"

"Never mind. Send a van."

"*Alors*. The remains are human?"

"They are."

"Is it the man from the bridge?"

"Impossible to say."

"Is the body intact?"

"Far from it."

"Shall I redeploy the marine search team?"

"Without delay."

4

I stayed to oversee the transfer of the seaweed bundle and its grim contents from Legalt's boat to a coroner's van. While making sure that process unfolded properly, I also observed a team of divers as they searched Bickerdike Basin.

LaManche phoned at two and again at three. Each time I reported that nothing more had been found. On the second call, he encouraged me to return to the LSJML, but was persuaded by my suggestion that I remain on scene in case questions arose.

Good decision. In the next five hours the basin yielded seven additional hunks of algae-coated flesh. Three were human. Four were not, and of questionable species affiliation. Possibly the partial fore and hind legs of a pig.

Ryan rang at five. I told him I planned to hang in as long as the divers kept working. Said I'd text when leaving the port. He promised a home-cooked dinner. Other services of a much more personal nature.

At eight, the team leader, a tall skinny guy named Pen Olsen, ordered a halt until morning. I was disappointed that we'd recovered so little. Still, I was hot, tired, and grubby. Not really unhappy to call it a day.

I drove toward home in a thickening dusk. A perk of summer at the forty-fifth latitude north. The sun lingers late, often departs with the splashy brilliance of a Rothko.

Beyond my windshield, the city was turning itself over to night. Windows oozed yellow from the two- and three-flats in Griffintown, eerie blue from the Centreville skyscrapers rising beyond them. Neon beckoned its gaudy welcome from overhanging signs and tubes surrounding tavern doors and windows along the way.

Hooking a left onto Boulevard René-Lévesque, I sensed the usual thoughts and emotions coloring my outlook. I felt sadness for the person surfacing piecemeal from the river. But also hope that the new day would prove more fruitful.

A series of images flitted at the edge of my consciousness. A figure. A bridge. Ruptured webs of lightning writhing overhead and sparking tentacles earthward.

The body parts that I'd bagged and tagged—the foot, the segments of a leg and an arm—suggested a fully-grown adult. The bone visible below the bloated and mangled flesh looked robust, but not overly so. I was unsure if we were recovering a male or a female. Was it the man struck down during Clémence? Or was the river yielding some other unfortunate fallen from a boat, shoreline, or bridge?

I also felt compassion for those whose lives would forever be changed by news of this death. I knew how that would go. I'd witnessed—and at times participated in—the heartbreaking telling. I'd seen the initial look of perplexity, denial, or disbelief. Eventually, the widened eyes. With comprehension, the stoic silence, tears, or physical collapse. There is no proper or predictable response. Reactions to loss are as varied as the swirls and ridges on a human thumb.

Finally, I felt the resolve that comes with each new case. I didn't know this victim. Had no idea his or her appearance. His or her hopes and dreams, accomplishments, or failures. But already I was committed to unraveling the mystery of his or her passing.

As I plunged into my building's underground garage, my stomach growled at a pitch probably heard in the Carolinas. My thoughts shifted from corpses to cuisine.

Sylvain greeted me, epaulettes overreaching the span of his bony shoulders.

"*Bon soir*, Dr. Brennan. Long day, eh?" Like Legalt and many Francophone Montrealers, Sylvain speaks to Anglophones in a mélange of French and English. Franglaise.

"A very long day," I agreed.

Sylvain walked to a bank of elevators and thumbed a button. Waited the millisecond it took for a car to arrive. Smiled me through the immaculate mirrored doors.

I ascended to the fifteenth floor and crossed to our condo.

That last—a simple declarative sentence—is loaded with a double-barreled whammy about major changes in my life. Let's parse.

First barrel: Fifteenth floor. For decades I occupied a small, ground-level apartment with a shotgun kitchen and French doors accessing a courtyard on one side and a tiny lawn on the other. I am now co-owner of a three-bedroom condo in a posh new high-rise complete with marble-floored lobby and uniformed doorman.

Second barrel: Our. Except for my cat, Birdie, and the occasional encampment by my daughter, Katy, I've lived solo since separating from my ex some time back in the Neolithic. I now have a roommate on both ends of my geographically complicated life. That roommate is Andrew Ryan.

How did this happen, you wonder?

After years of ducking Ryan's pressure for greater commitment from me—including repeated marriage proposals—I finally succumbed and agreed to cohabitation.

As proof of my pledge to this new living arrangement, I gave notice to the landlord of my beloved wee flat. Ryan sold his pad at

Habitat 67. I undertook construction of an addition to the annex in Charlotte, and *le monsieur* and I began looking at condos in Montreal.

Endless condos.

After a multitude of fruitless realtor-guided outings, and swayed by the glorious floor-to-ceiling windows spanning the unit's entire south side, we purchased a property that significantly exceeded our agreed-upon budget. More burgers and fewer steaks, we told ourselves. Nights at home not out on the town.

As with my previous address, my current one is squarely in Centreville, a precondition upon which I'd been inflexible. No burbs for this uptown gal. But beyond that single commonality, the new digs are light-years distant in terms of amenities. Stainless-steel appliances. TV embedded in my bathroom mirror. Built-in espresso extravaganza. Smart panels that do everything but brush my teeth.

Lollapalooza view that is worth every penny.

And the available pennies have been more than anticipated. My income, though far from colossal, is solid. Ryan's PI business, formed in partnership with former Charlotte-Mecklenburg Police Department homicide detective Erskine "Skinny" Slidell, is doing quite well.

Life offers few pleasures greater than the aroma of simmering food when arriving home at the end of a grueling day. That pleasure greeted me upon opening the door of 1532. Garlic? Maybe oranges? Definitely bread.

"Honey, I'm home!" Dorky, I know. But Ryan and I never tire of using the weary old meme.

No response. Of course not. Atroce was blasting full force from every speaker in the condo.

"Hello!" I shouted over the screaming instrumentals.

Nothing.

"Bird?"

More nothing from the cat.

Setting my purse on the sideboard, I followed my nose.

Ryan was in the kitchen, wearing an apron and stirring something in a pot on the Wolf cooktop. Birdie was at his feet, eyes intent on the chef's every move. Neither acknowledged my entry.

I crossed to Ryan and placed a hand on his back. When he turned, startled, I gestured that he lower the volume of the music. Sort of music. I'm not a fan of death metal. Ryan and the cat love the stuff.

Ryan did as requested, returned, and wrapped me in a hug.

"*Comment ça va, ma chère?*" he purred into one of my ears.

Not awaiting an answer, he stepped back, nose pinched as though encountering a toxic odor. Which, undoubtedly, it was.

"Eau de dead flounder?" he asked.

"Hilarious." I was too tired for a clever retort. "What's for dinner?"

Ryan put on an exaggerated Parisian maître d' snob accent: "After la madame enjoys a shower, her meal shall await."

"Tell me it's not seafood," I said.

"It's not seafood."

Birdie looked disappointed.

Also among life's pleasures is the combo of cascading hot water and scented bath products. Wishing to avoid anything even hinting of a maritime theme, I went with amber orange shampoo, body gel, and lotion. Perhaps inspired by whatever culinary marvel Ryan was concocting.

Fifteen minutes later I was back in the kitchen, smelling like something that grows only on trees in Seville. Ryan gestured me to the dining room. The glass table—one of the very few items to make the transition from my old place—was set for two. Place mats. Napkins in holders. Side salads. Candles. Cat seated at the far end.

With a theatrical flourish, Ryan centered a plate on each of the mats. "*Voilà!* Chicken à l'orange with jasmine rice!"

Birdie's nose went into hyperdrive, but his four paws remained primly on the chair seat. House etiquette if he wished to be included at meals.

The food was delicious. The dessert, pistachio gelato, perhaps even better.

While eating, we kept the conversation light. No talk of violent death or putrefying corpses. Mainly we discussed options for an upcoming vacation. I wanted a destination featuring white sand and *beaucoup soleil*. Ryan was thinking mountains, and trails, and hiking boots. We agreed on one thing. The time was growing close. We had to reach a decision.

After a hasty cleanup, we made espresso and moved to the two leather chairs positioned to maximize the panorama that had so beguiled us.

And still did.

A nightscape of shadowy hills and valleys, tail- and headlight-streaked roads, and dimly lit quartiers spread from rue Sherbrook at our feet to the distant St. Lawrence, now an ebony ribbon dotted at intervals with inverted pink vapor cones.

Birdie dozed on the ottoman by my feet, belly full of chicken scraps and ice cream. Neither he nor Ryan had queried my day. I appreciated that. But, inevitably, the shimmery black riverine swath triggered images of what awaited me at the morgue. Setting my tiny cup on its tiny saucer, I told Ryan about the body parts we'd found at Bickerdike Basin.

"You'll head to the port again tomorrow?" he asked.

"I don't think so. The team leader is a guy named Pen Olsen. Do you know him?"

"Olsen and I worked a few cases back in the day. He seemed like a bright guy."

"That was my impression. Before leaving, Olsen and I devised a plan. If a diver finds anything that looks even remotely human, he'll shoot me video and pics. Should I be unable to make a call from the images, he'll send the remains to the morgue."

"They'll love you at intake. Nothing says pungent like a decomposing squid."

"*That* I could probably spot, squids being invertebrates and having their arms attached to their heads and all. Anyway, I'll leave diving to the team and get started on what we've already recovered. How about you? Are you still working the great electronics heist?"

"Wrapped up today."

"That was fast. Did the store owner get her property back?"

"She did."

"Did the cops make an arrest?"

"They did."

"The night guard was assaulted. Is he all right?"

"Interesting question."

When Ryan didn't elaborate, I poked: "Are you trying to annoy me?"

"The security guard said the intruders entered through a basement window, beat the crap out of him, and tied him to a chair. When he managed to escape, he dimed nine-one-one."

"Poor guy."

"Since the total loss was less than a thousand bucks, the cops told the unhappy proprietor to basically kiss it off. At least that was her version."

"Seriously?"

"That's what she said."

"Is that likely true?"

Ryan waggled a hand. Maybe yes, maybe no.

"That's why she called you."

"It is. Turned out my *grand-mère* could have cracked this case."

"Your grandmother was a PI?"

Ryan ignored that. "These guys weren't exactly geniuses when it came to a redistribution plan. Took me less than two days to locate the stolen goods."

"Let me guess. A pawn shop?"

Ryan nodded. "The brain trust was composed of the security guard, his cousin, and a fence in Longueuil. Another cousin."

"All off to the slammer."

"Probably not for long."

"What's up for you tomorrow?" I asked.

"I've been meaning to talk to you about that."

I raised my brows in question.

Leaning forward, Ryan took both my hands in his.

His next statement shocked me.

5

"Tomorrow morning, I'll be ten floors below you at Wilfrid-Derome."

"I don't understand."

"I've been asked to rejoin my old squad."

"Crimes Contre la Personne?" Crimes against persons. Assaults. Murders. The rough stuff.

"Yes," Ryan said.

"You're returning to the SQ?" I was so stunned I was babbling. We'd discussed Ryan's retirement *ad nauseam* before he'd finally decided to pull the plug.

"Yes."

"But you just left."

"They've cajoled me back for a special assignment."

"What's so 'special'"—pulling my hands free to hook air quotes—"that suddenly they can't manage without you?"

"I think they miss my boyish charm and cutting wit."

"And your humility."

"And that."

I said nothing. Though amused by Ryan's comments, I was not amused by the idea that, once again, he'd be in harm's way. Crimes against persons cops face bad people. All those years that he was on the street I'd learned to keep my fear in check. To ban thoughts of the dreaded phone call or knock on my door. That anxiety was supposed to be behind me now.

"There's a problem with the OCGs." Ryan used the acronym for outlaw criminal gangs.

"Montreal has always had a gang problem. I thought the violence had been toned down."

I was referring to a particularly bloody period when the Hells Angels were fighting a local group called the Rock Machine over control of the drug trade in the province. Roughly one hundred and fifty died during the biker war, each gang slaughtering its rivals with creative abandon.

Many victims were found shot and torched in burning vehicles, or floating headless and handless in the Lachine Canal. No faces, no dentals, no prints. You get the picture. Many of those corpses ended up in my lab.

Joe Q. Public was largely detached from it until a child got caught in the cross fire, blown to bits in a car bomb explosion. Finally, an outcry arose, and a multiagency task force was created. Arrests followed, trials, convictions. In the end, those still breathing and not behind bars decided it was better for business to rein in the bloodshed.

But that wild ride was long past. I'd heard little about the Angels or the Mafia for many years.

"Dozens of bikers went to jail," I said. "I thought that pretty much shut things down."

"You think being in the slammer stops these thugs? Besides, many of the old geezers are out now. And, more important, a new generation is trying to make its mark."

Ryan shook his head in disgust. I waited for him to continue.

"In my first briefing I learned that the island of Montreal is now divvied up between gangs associated with the Crips and gangs associated with the Bloods. Both gangs with Los Angeles origins. The

Crips are mostly northside, the Bloods mostly southside. Mostly. The situation is complex as hell."

"Don't the younger guys grasp the fact that joining forces is better than slaughtering each other?"

"Historically, Crips gangs have been more willing to collaborate with the Mafia and the bikers," Ryan said. "The Bloods prefer to maintain their independence. Not all, but most of the current bloodshed is due to conflict within the Bloods."

I said nothing.

"For example, there's ongoing hostility between the Profit Boys from Rivière-des-Prairies and Zone 43 from Montréal-Nord. That conflict accounts for a lot of the recent shootings and firebombings."

"What's at issue?"

"Same as always. Drugs, territory, unpaid debts, personal vendettas. And, believe me, those topping the food chain don't appreciate the media attention being drawn by the new spike in violence."

"Who's running the show these days?"

"For now, the Angels."

Several moments passed. Outside, a siren wailed, barely audible fifteen floors up. At my feet, Birdie purred softly. As opposing emotions struggled to gain control of my tongue, I chose my words carefully.

"I understand why the SQ might want your expertise, but—"

"I won't be working gangs directly. There's a unit in place for that."

That surprised me. I waited.

"These little pricks have invented a blood sport they call scoring. You were in Charlotte at the time, but last year a sixteen-year-old kid was shot to death on the street not far from his home."

"Jesus. Why?"

Ryan drew a deep breath, let it out slowly. When he spoke again, the anger in his voice was palpable.

"The game involves choosing random victims based on nothing more than their schools or neighborhoods."

"How *many* victims?"

"In the past year three more kids have been shot. One died."

The thought of children being targeted knotted my gut. Why wasn't I aware of these attacks? The cases weren't mine, so I hadn't paid attention?

"I'm amazed I haven't heard about this. Why isn't the press making a meal of it?"

"The media blackout has been intentional. And a bitch to maintain. But a decision was made to discourage any coverage that might in some twisted way raise the street creds of those involved."

"You're trying to avoid more scoring?"

Ryan nodded. "These shootings are being presented as routine gang squabbling."

"So not breaking news."

"It won't last. Any day now some eager-beaver journalist will catch on. Kids shooting kids for sport? Pulitzer stuff!"

"The SQ wants you to net the bad guys before that happens."

Ryan nodded. "I'll be working with an SQ cop named Roland Daigneault and an SPVM guy named Marty Sarazin. I know Daigneault. He's solid. Not sure about Sarazin. He seems pretty intense."

I thought for a moment, then asked, "Don't the cops know who all the gang members are?"

"Some. But our job is to ID and nail the particular mutants involved in scoring."

"Do you think this will interfere with our vacation?"

"Not a chance."

I reached sideways to take Ryan's hand. "I'm glad you're helping out." Honestly, was I? "If anyone can shut this down, it's you." I had zero doubt there.

Off to the east, perhaps over the McGill Ghetto, a lone peony exploded and swelled into a tiny pink orb, a silent bouquet against the dark summer sky.

"Happy July Fourth," Ryan said.

I'd completely forgotten.

FRIDAY, JULY 5

The temperature was well past eighty when I left home the next morning. In the underground garage, the air felt like a damp sweater wrapping my skin. Quebec would be enjoying another hot sticky one.

Ryan's Jeep was already gone. I'd been vaguely aware of him moving around the bedroom at dawn.

L'heure de pointe. Rush hour. Well, not exactly. Traffic was brutal and no one was going anywhere fast. The constant braking and accelerating was beginning to rattle my dental work.

Nibbling my way east through Centreville, bored and annoyed, I considered the faces behind the windows in the cars around me. A workman in a painters cap. A woman wearing pink Styrofoam curlers. A kid with Airpods poking from his ears. Their expressions were variations on the same theme: irritation.

For distraction, I turned on the radio. Garou was crooning a seventies tune about being alone. *Seul.*

Not now, Pierre. I killed the music and listened to the white monotone of the AC blowers. Drummed the wheel. Formulated a plan of attack.

First, I'd order X-rays of the remains already logged in at the morgue. Though I had only a foot and some portions of an arm and a leg, I wanted no surprises when I went digging into the flesh. No surgical plates or screws, needles, wires, nails, barbed wire, or shards of glass. I also wanted a peek at the bones to get a jump start on establishing that the remains all came from one person.

Next, I'd collect tissue samples for possible genetic sequencing. Hopefully, the DNA section would be able to amplify enough to allow a cop to run a profile through the NDDB, the National DNA Data Base. The NDDB is the Canadian equivalent of the NDIS in the US, the National DNA Index System. Both the NDDB and the NDIS use an FBI software program called CODIS, the Combined DNA Index System, for comparing profiles.

Maybe we'd get lucky and score a hit close to home. If not, the cops could shoot the profile south of the border. Or wherever seemed appropriate.

Then, I'd examine every millimeter of flesh and bone grossly and microscopically. I'd attempt to construct a bio-profile, including age, sex, ancestry, and height. I'd consider cause of death, being particularly alert to evidence of lightning trauma. Given that I'd have so little to eyeball and measure, I suspected that part of my analysis wouldn't take long.

Finally, satisfied that the remains could provide no further detail while fleshed, I'd request that a tech begin the maceration process.

That's how I thought my day would go.

I was wrong.

The only thing that went well was parking. Miraculously, I scored a spot just a block from Wilfred-Derome. An easy downhill walk on rue Parthenais. Still, by the time I reached the building, my shirt was damp and pasted to my back.

I rode an elevator packed with sweaty cops, clerical staff, technicians, and scientists, all complaining about the heat. *La vague de chaleur. La canicule.*

Funny. Les Québécois have many slang expressions for extreme cold weather, but none for hot. Perhaps that says something about the fleeting nature of summer.

Exiting on twelve, I stowed my purse, then logged into my computer. The Bickerdike remains had been assigned the case number LML 37911-24.

After calling downstairs to have LML 37911-24 transferred from a cooler to an autopsy room, I skimmed the scant data already in the file: the date and location at which the remains were collected; the time of their arrival at the morgue; a brief description of what was logged in.

Pierre LaManche was listed as *pathologiste*, I was *anthropolgue judiciaire*.

The fields for the decedent's name, address, and date of birth remained blank.

The police agency handling the case was the SPVM. The city police.

When I came to the line labeled *Nom enquêteur* my heart sank.

The detective in charge was Luc Claudel.

Claudel and I had collaborated on many investigations over the years. Though a good detective, the man had the personality of an un-lanced boil, and was unabashedly misogynistic. In other words, my time with Claudel had never been pleasant.

I wondered briefly why a homicide detective was assigned to a lightning death. Figured it was probably due to cutbacks in personnel at the SPVM.

After collecting my old-school clipboard and case forms, I walked the length of the corridor to an elevator whose buttons offered only three choices: Coroner. LSJML. Morgue.

In the basement, I changed into scrubs, then proceeded to *salle quatre*, an autopsy room outfitted with special ventilation. The stinky room. The room in which I perform many of my examinations.

Lisa, one of the techs, met me at the door and offered to assist. Delighted, I accepted. Lisa was the best of the lot. We entered together.

A gumbo of smells already packed the small room. Refrigerated flesh. Salt water. Dead vegetation.

"Eww." As was her habit, Lisa would speak English to me. I guess that qualified.

Either way, I agreed. The special fans would earn their keep with this one.

On the table lay a body bag—one that showed very small bulges. A foot and some partial limbs.

While Lisa collected a Nikon and Sony Handycam, I filled out my case form. It's a Luddite approach, granted. But putting my observations on paper helps me to organize my thoughts. And I like having a hard copy to cover the whole process.

Wordlessly, Lisa and I donned gloves, aprons, and goggles. Then, as she shot video, I unzipped the bag. The odor level jumped to Defcon 1.

The remains were as I recalled—a jumble of putrefying flesh wrapped in rotting seaweed. One by one I removed, cleaned, and arranged the body parts in their anatomical position on a stainless-steel gurney.

When I'd finished, Lisa and I studied my handiwork. The body I'd assembled consisted of an almost complete right foot, a segment of right lower leg, a segment of right thigh, and a segment of right upper arm. A person composed of more gaps than flesh.

"Radiographs?" Lisa asked.

"Please," I said.

She stepped close to roll the gurney to the X-ray unit. Stopped. Leaned in and pointed one gloved finger at the upper arm.

"What's that?"

I joined her.

We both stared.

Baffled.

6

"Is it a bruise?" Lisa asked.

"I don't think so," I said.

Lisa crossed to a drawer, withdrew a magnifier, and handed it to me. I raised and lowered the lens until the dark smudge came into focus on the pale flesh. Though blurred by decomp and days of immersion, a pattern was evident.

"What do you see?" I asked, handing Lisa the magnifier.

"Looks like a wheel with a digit in the middle." After peering through the glass for another thirty seconds. "Maybe a five?"

"What's the bump on top?"

"Right. Maybe it's a spider with legs curling down around the number?"

"Could it be an octopus?"

"Maybe."

"Have you ever seen this tattoo before?" I asked, knowing Lisa had attended hundreds, maybe thousands of conventional autopsies and had seen far more fleshed bodies than I.

"No."

"Let's get some photos. I don't want the detail compromised by dehydration."

She shot pics with both cameras, then wheeled the remains off for X-rays. By the time I'd filled out my forms, she was back and the films were ready for viewing.

Parking the gurney beside the autopsy table, Lisa keyed in the case number and brought up the first plate. The tattooed upper arm.

The limb had been severed—I suspected by a powerful boat propeller—below the shoulder and above the elbow. The truncated humerus glowed white within the mottled grays of the surrounding tissue. Lacking both ends, it yielded little info on the age of the decedent. The bone quality was good, the muscle attachments robust, which suggested a young adult male. I made notes, and we moved on.

The segment of thigh was equally uninformative. No femoral joints, so no age markers. Ditto the lower leg. The propeller had left only the mid-shaft portions of the tibia and fibula.

The foot was more promising. The propeller had struck high enough and hard enough to jam part of the lower tip of the fibula into the flesh of the foot.

"Yes!" I said out loud.

Lisa looked at me, eyes questioning above her mask.

"See that triangular fragment?" I pointed.

Lisa nodded.

"See that squiggly white line running across it?" I pointed again.

"I do."

"You know what epiphyses are, right?"

"Little caps that fuse onto bones at certain ages in kids."

"That"—tapping the white line on the screen—"is the ankle end of the fibula caught in the act of wrapping things up. Which puts this guy's age somewhere between sixteen and nineteen."

"So young," Lisa said sadly.

"Yes," I agreed.

"How did he die?"

"If this is the Jacques Cartier Bridge victim, he was struck by lightning."

"You don't sound convinced."

Lisa was right. I was seeing none of the typical signs of lightning trauma on the skin. But I had little to observe. And no organs.

"If I cut a bone sample, how soon could a histo tech have thin sections ready?"

She checked her watch. "With a little persuading, perhaps a bribe, I'm sure Marcel could produce some by this afternoon?"

"Perfect." If anyone could sweet-talk my case to the front of the line, it was Lisa. Maybe it was her aquamarine eyes and sunny smile. Everyone loved Lisa, especially the male cops and techs. Maybe that was her 42 double D's working.

I used a scalpel to strip putrefying tissue from the uppermost portion of the thigh, being careful to introduce no new nicks or scratches. Then Lisa revved up a Stryker saw and cut a three-inch plug from the newly exposed femur. After marking a plastic vial, I sealed the specimen inside and handed it to her.

"I can manage here," I said. "Let me know as soon as the slides are ready."

Giving a snappy salute, Lisa hurried upstairs to the histology lab.

Once I'd collected samples for DNA testing, I focused on phase three of my plan: observation of the body parts constituting LML 37911-24. Halfway through my exam, the anteroom desk phone rang. Suspecting who the caller was, I braced myself, stripped off a glove, lowered my mask, and answered.

"*Bonjour*. Dr. Brennan."

Without greeting or preamble, Claudel launched in.

"As you must know, I will be reviewing the incident that occurred on the Jacques Cartier Bridge last Saturday night. Since the death was accidental, the only outstanding question is the man's ID."

"Monsieur Claudel, I haven't yet determ—"

"I will be in your office at noon." Not a request, a directive. Typical Claudel.

I started to reply. Heard only dead air.

Easy, Brennan. The man is a boor.

After two hours' work, my notes were sparse, my conclusions sparser.

I could state that all the body parts came from the same individual. That the individual was a male in his late teens with a tattoo on his upper right arm. That the degree of decomposition was consistent with immersion in the river for a period of five days. That the trauma was consistent with dismemberment by a powerful propeller. That cause and manner of death were undetermined.

Claudel would be thrilled.

At 11:40, I wheeled the remains to the cooler and headed to the locker room.

Claudel was true to his word. Approaching my office, I could see the profile of his perfectly razor-cut hair through the open door. I hadn't yet arrived and already he was checking his Rolex.

Claudel looked my way when I entered but said nothing.

"*Bonjour, Monsieur Claudel. Comment ça va?*"

"*Bonjour.*"

I settled in my chair, placed my file on the blotter, folded my hands, and smiled across the desk.

Claudel studied me coolly. His face brought to mind a parrot, the features angling from his ears toward the center to culminate in a beak-like nose. Along the midline, his chin, mouth, and the tip of the beak cascaded downward in a stack of *V*s. When he smiled, which was rare, the *V* of his mouth widened and his lips drew in, rather than back.

He was not smiling now.

Fine. Through much practice, I'd learned to resist the man's charm.

Claudel drew a small notebook from his crisply ironed linen shirt and clicked a Mont Blanc ballpoint into readiness.

I briefed him on what I'd learned about LML 37911-24.

"That's all you can tell me?"

"Once the foot bones are cleaned, I may be able to provide a height estimate."

"Racial background?"

"No can do. I have no head and the skin is bleached due to exposure." I wasn't about to launch into an explanation of race as a social construct.

"Manner of death was accidental?" Claudel referred to one of five categories recognized by coroners and medical examiners: suicide, homicide, accident, natural, or undetermined.

"Undetermined," I said.

Claudel sighed. He was being exceedingly patient with me.

"Surely there must be something to indicate that this man was struck by lightning."

"If this *is* the man from the bridge, and so far I have no proof of that, I may find some microscopic evidence in the bone."

"And when might that be?"

"By end of day."

Claudel returned the notebook and Mont Blanc to his pocket. "I am a homicide detective. This should not be my problem."

Not asking why it was, I pulled a page from my file and slid it across the blotter, an image I'd printed before coming upstairs. The pic showed the inked spider/octopus encircling a number five.

"Perhaps you can run the tattoo?"

Claudel glanced at, then pocketed the printout.

"I will put someone on this." Clearly, Claudel thought himself too valuable for such a mundane task. "I will return at five."

When Detective Delightful had gone, I grabbed a quick lunch of peach yogurt and a banana, then spent several hours in my lab with the infant remains from Sainte-Agathe. I saw nothing to alter my impression that the babies had perished at intervals over a long period of time, and that none had died recently.

Marcel phoned at 3:40 to say that the thin sections were ready. After repackaging the baby bones, I hurried next door to the histo lab.

A thin section is a slice of bone mounted on a glass slide. Typically, the specimen has been impregnated with resin and ground to somewhere between sixty and seventy microns. In other words, damn thin.

Individual bone cells are called osteons. When viewed under magnification, osteons can be observed in a thin section.

Marcel had left a box holding twenty-four slides beside one of the microscopes. Removing its protective hood, I turned the scope on, set the level of magnification, and positioned a glass rectangle below the lens.

Peering through the eyepiece, I did some fine-tuning. The osteons snapped into focus. I studied them. Saw nothing of note. Increased the magnification. Still nothing. I took a pic and moved on to the next specimen.

Two dozen thin sections later, I turned off and covered the scope.

What the hell?

Confused, I collected the slides and photos and returned to my office, dreading my upcoming rendezvous.

Claudel arrived on the dot. He did not greet me. I did not greet him back.

As before, I slid a printout across the desktop. Claudel picked up and glanced at the image. His eyes rolled up in question.

"Bone cells are called osteons. Each osteon looks like a tiny volcano with a crater in the center. The crater is a canal that carries a blood vessel and a nerve fiber. Do you see them?"

"I have not come for an anatomy lesson."

Easy.

"You are viewing a photomicrograph, an image taken through a microscope. It shows magnified bone cells in what's called a thin section."

Though Claudel thought himself an exceptionally intelligent man, I shifted to the KISS principle. Keep. It. Simple. Stupid.

"In lightning deaths, it is common to see micro-fracturing within the bone caused by the passage of current."

Claudel raised his chin and canted his eyebrows. The move created another *V*, this one inverted. I took this as encouragement to elaborate.

"Micro-fracturing will appear as cracks radiating out from the centers of bone cells. Or jumping irregularly between clusters of cells."

"I see nothing like that."

"Exactly. Because it's not there."

"Perhaps this one thin whatever you call it didn't catch—"

I laid twenty-three additional pages on the blotter. Claudel snatched up and whipped through the first dozen images.

"What does this mean?" he asked, not bothering to hide his annoyance.

"I don't know," I said.

After a full minute had passed, Claudel reached into the pocket of his navy blazer and withdrew a printout of his own. Winging the page sideways onto my desk, he leaned back in his chair. Fingers steepled below his chin, he observed my reaction.

I picked up the paper. A blue header identified it as an FBI report. Printed below the header were the words: FBI Records: The Vault. Tattoo Recognition Database.

An image appeared halfway down the page. It showed the octopus/spider with its appendages encircling the number 5.

I read the accompanying text.

And looked at Claudel for explanation.

7

"TCI?"

Claudel nodded. "The Turks and Caicos Islands. As the report states."

"That's a long way from here."

"One can travel many places by air these days."

I ignored that. "The Cay Boys. Is that a gang of some sort?" I was plucking info from the report.

"When I ran the name, a descriptor came back stating that it is a group associated with the town of Five Cays on the island of Providenciales."

"That's the main island, right?"

"I am not an expert on Caribbean geography."

But you *are* an expert at being a dick. I didn't say it.

"If the victim isn't a Canadian citizen, that complicates things."

Claudel said nothing.

"He could be a tourist," I suggested. "Or a dual national."

"Or an illegal."

At that moment, Claudel's mobile buzzed. He dug the device from his pocket and answered, turning a shoulder to me.

"*Claudel.*"

He listened, face carefully blank. I heard a buzzy voice but could make out no words.

"*Oui.*"

I waited. The speaker took longer this time.

"*Oui.*"

I pulled a Claudel and looked at my watch. He ignored or failed to recognize my impatience.

"*D'accord.*"

After agreeing with the new round of buzzing, Claudel disconnected.

"I must go." He stood.

"Shouldn't someone call the TCI authorities?"

"Yes. But I am needed elsewhere. A man has stabbed two people at a gym in Saint-Leonard."

With that, he was gone.

I was googling "TCI police" when my desk phone rang. Recognizing LaManche's extension, I answered.

"I just received a call from the *bureau du coroner*. A cyclist biking the Chemin du Tour de L'Île spotted human remains washed ashore by a ferry ramp."

"On Île Sainte-Hélène?" I named a recreational island in the river, not far from Bickerdike Basin.

"*Oui.* Given the site's proximity to the Jacques Cartier Bridge, the remains are suspected to be those of Saturday's lightning victim."

"Are they complete?"

"The death investigator spoke of a partial body."

I knew what was coming.

"The remains will arrive at the morgue in the next few hours. I am hoping you can view them with me first thing tomorrow."

"Of course," I said, surprised he'd perform an autopsy on a Saturday. "And I may have something that will help put a name on the victim." I told him about the tattoo and its link to the Turks and Caicos Islands.

"*Bon.* Have you contacted the authorities down there?"

"Not yet."

"Perhaps you could handle that? I must meet with the next of kin in a house fire death shortly."

"I was thinking—"

"Hopefully we will be able to lift prints tomorrow. But in the meantime, the TCI police could begin searching their missing person files."

"Of course."

"Until tomorrow. *Bonsoir*."

"*Bonsoir*."

After we disconnected, I logged back into Google and found a nonemergency number for the Royal Turks and Caicos Islands Police Force. Activating the speakerphone function, I punched in the digits.

My call was answered after two rings.

"Police. How may I help you?" The voice was female. Melodic and businesslike at the same time.

I explained who I was and my reason for calling.

"Hold please."

I held, mercifully subjected to no tinny instrumentals.

Minutes passed. I drummed my fingers on the blotter. Straightened a stack of reports. Picked up and knuckle-wove a pen.

More minutes passed.

I wondered what time zone I was calling. What the TCI station looked like. What qualified the island force as "royal."

Across the way, the last of the pathologists locked his office and strode up the corridor, briefcase in hand. Closed doors told me the others had already left.

I glanced at the wall clock. Five-forty. Save for me, the floor was empty and filled with that hush that makes large buildings feel so abandoned after hours.

"Detective Musgrove." The voice snapped me out of my reverie.

"Dr. Temperance Brennan," I said. "I'm calling from the Laboratoire de sciences judiciaires et de médecine légale in Montreal."

"So I've been told." This voice was also female. And so British it might have been wearing wellies. "I understand one of our citizens has gotten himself killed in your town."

"That may be the case, although it's very early in the investigation. ID has yet to be established."

I repeated what I'd told the operator about the lightning, the bridge, the severed limbs, and the tattoo.

"The Cay Boys. Yes, that's one of our"—Musgrove hesitated, perhaps searching for the proper phrase—"local groups."

I briefed her on the body washed ashore on L'Île Sainte-Hélène.

"Right."

"We'll be performing an autopsy on those remains early tomorrow."

"Right," she repeated. I got the sense she'd made a decision and just wanted me to finish.

"So that's it for now. Shall I send you pics?"

"Yes. That would be good." She provided her email address.

"I'll keep you in the loop with any—"

"It's best that I come there."

"To Montreal?" Her choice surprised me.

"Yes."

"That's really not necessary."

"I believe it is."

"Perhaps you should wait for the results of the morning's post-mortem."

"I'll book a weekend flight. If you'll provide me with your contact information, I'll send my itinerary."

I did.

"Perhaps you could suggest a hotel?" she said.

"Colleagues have stayed at the Residence Inn on rue Peel. But I really don't—"

"I shall see you on Monday."

Great.

Hosting an out-of-town visitor wasn't topping my bucket list for the upcoming week.

SATURDAY, JULY 6

To use the word "partial" was being generous. Half the cranium, the right limbs, and a good chunk of the thorax were missing.

The good news. The arm, leg, and foot recovered from Bickerdike Basin filled the gaps nicely. There were no duplications between LML 37911-24 and this body, designated LML 37917-24. Everything was consistent between the two cases regarding decomp and anatomical detail.

At 8:40, LaManche and I were suited up in room four beginning the autopsy. Lisa, graciously sacrificing her Saturday off, was assisting. Her presence would speed the process.

Also assisting, though not sufficiently, was the ventilation system. Today's odor level was making yesterday's seem like a visit to a florist.

LML 37917-24 had arrived at the morgue wearing shredded and soggy jeans, jockeys, and remnants of a white tee. No jewelry. The one remaining foot was bare.

The man's pockets were empty save for two very waterlogged bills, a five and a twenty. He carried no wallet or any form of ID. Or none that had survived his time in the river. Or the lightning strike and fall if this *was* the man from the bridge. The clothing now hung from a drying rack at the side of the room.

The victim's genitalia declared that he was clearly male. His body bore no other scars or tattoos. His teeth suggested a young adult age range. And a disregard for dental hygiene or regular check-ups. An odontology work-up would not prove useful. No dental records would exist.

The man's nose, lips, and eyelids had disappeared into the bellies of scavenging sea creatures. What remained of his one orbit was so distorted that eye color was anyone's guess. His scalp retained a few strands of medium-length dark hair. His left cheek and jaw bore a scraggly stubble aspiring to status as a mustache and beard.

Before sending the man for X-rays, LaManche inspected the digits on his left hand.

"The fingertips are quite shrunken and wrinkled, but I think with some rejuvenation we can lift partials," he said to Lisa. "Let's try xylene."

Lisa disappeared to gather the necessary materials. While awaiting her return, I informed LaManche of Detective Musgrove's plan to travel to Montreal.

"That really isn't necessary," he said.

"Exactly what I told her. She insisted."

The mask hid LaManche's mouth. But the creases cornering his eyes crimped ever so slightly. "I'm sure Detective Claudel will enjoy the comradery afforded by the visit of a fellow officer from afar."

"That's an excellent thought," I said.

LaManche had no sooner made his excellent observation than the phone in the anteroom sounded.

"I'll get it," I said, again suspecting who the caller would be.

Again, I was right.

"*Bonjour*, Monsieur Claudel."

"*Bonjour*. Have you news for me?"

"Dr. LaManche and I are performing the autopsy now. It's early, but—"

"Have you made progress toward a positive ID?"

"We're hoping—"

"Ms. Brennan. An accidental death should not be requiring so much of my time. You have the man's profile and his country of origin."

Claudel had cut me off one time too many. It was petty, but I couldn't resist.

"Dr. LaManche and I are about to lift prints. Fortunate that you're working the weekend. We feel it would be best if you joined us here."

Not true. But I knew Claudel's reputation for avoiding autopsies. I wanted to discomfort the jerk. To see him sweat.

"I doubt—"

"We're in room four."

I disconnected and hurried to rejoin LaManche.

Shrinkage on the bulb portion of the fingers is common with immersion and decomposition. Sometimes it can be corrected by injecting a mixture of glycerin and gelatin between the nail and the skin. LaManche, Lisa, and I agreed. This man's digits were too far gone for that.

As we watched, Lisa applied a xylene solution to each fingertip. Repeated the process again and again. While we waited, LaManche began his preliminary exam, methodically inspecting the body, starting at the head and moving toward the feet.

"I think they're ready now," Lisa said, meaning the skin was sufficiently pliable.

LaManche nodded but didn't respond. He was staring at the man's chest. I noted tension in his neck and shoulders that hadn't been there before.

I was about to ask what he'd spotted but was distracted by a noise behind me. I turned.

Claudel stood framed in the open doorway, looking like a man trapped in a cage with venomous snakes. He didn't enter the room, but stood frozen, one hand on the knob. Present just enough to say that he'd been there.

I watched Claudel's gaze take in the glass-fronted cabinets with their stock of clear plastic containers, the steel countertops, the hanging scale, the tile floor. Everything but the man lying at center stage.

I'd seen seasoned cops react the same way. Crime scene photos were no threat. The blood and gore were elsewhere. Distant. The murder scene was a clinical exercise. A puzzle to be solved. No problem. But cut a *Y* incision in flesh and it was sayonara.

Claudel put his face into neutral, striving for cool.

"Thank you for coming. We're lifting prints now."

Claude said nothing.

LaManche remained riveted on whatever had caught his attention.

"Perhaps you could steady the wrist?" Lisa was requesting my help.

"Of course."

Puzzled by LaManche's fascination with the man's upper thorax, I grasped the lifeless arm and lifted the shriveled hand from the table.

Using a pair of curved rib shears, Lisa severed the digits at their bases. Each *crunch* mimicked the sound of a chicken bone breaking.

I glanced over my shoulder. Claudel's color had gone from pasty to ash.

Knowing the next steps, I said, "Perhaps you'd prefer to wait in the corridor?"

Swallowing, Claudel retreated.

Lisa teased the skin from each fingertip and placed it in a beaker containing a formaldehyde solution. The specimens sank, limp and translucent into the clear liquid.

A few minutes of soaking, then Lisa removed the first limp rectangle, wrapped it around her own gloved finger and gently dried its surface. A roll on the ink pad, then she pressed an oval of fuzzy loops and swirls onto the proper square on an old-fashioned print collection card.

It took several minutes to repeat the process with the other four digits. When she'd finished, we both looked at the results.

"Not great," she said. "But they're worth a try."

"Definitely," I said.

I crossed to the door and stepped into the hall. Claudel was pacing, hands clasped behind his pricey Italian knit blazer. Today's was a shade of tan probably called flax.

I held up the card.

He hurried over and took it from me. Frowned. Maybe nodded. Beelined to the elevator.

Resisting the urge to offer a one finger salute to his retreating back, I returned to room four.

LaManche was now studying the man's chest through a magnifier. He was bent close, unfazed by the noxious smell of putrefaction.

"Temperance. Please look at this."

"What is it?" I asked hurrying to his side.

Taking the lens, I adjusted the focus as I'd done when viewing the spider/octopus tattoo.

The object of LaManche's interest crystallized into sharp detail.

I studied it.

Raised my gaze to his.

The hound-dog eyes mirrored my own dismay.

8

Centered under the glass was a round black defect. A hole.

The hole lay at the level of the sternum, slightly to the left of the midline. I estimated its diameter at roughly ten millimeters.

"Is that what I think it is?" I asked, barely above a whisper.

"I don't want to probe until we obtain photos and X-rays. But yes. I am certain it is a gunshot wound."

"Have you observed any evidence of a lightning strike? Any Lichtenberg figures?"

I was asking about tattoo-like marks caused by electric current forcing blood cells out of the capillaries into the epidermis, turning the skin vivid red in the pattern of the underlying vessels.

"No," LaManche said.

I'd seen none, either.

Sonofabitch.

"Shall we have a quick look at his back?"

At LaManche's subtle request, Lisa stepped to the table. Tucking the man's left arm tight to his side, she grasped his left shoulder and rolled him gently.

Approximately four centimeters to the left of the midline, at the level of the ninth intercostal space, was a hole like the one on the man's chest. This one looked slightly larger, maybe twelve millimeters in diameter.

LaManche nodded glumly.

Lisa allowed the man to settle back into his original supine position. As we all stood mute, I reviewed what I knew about gunshot wounds.

A GSW can be either penetrating or perforating. In a penetrating wound, the bullet enters the victim and stays inside. In a perforating wound, the bullet passes completely through.

In a perforating GSW, the bullet creates an exit wound as it leaves the body. An exit wound differs from an entrance wound in several ways.

An entrance wound may be surrounded by a discolored area of abraded skin, known as an abrasion ring. In this case, had one existed around either the chest or vertebral hole, time and the river had obliterated all signs.

An exit wound is typically larger and more irregular than an entrance wound and may show extruded tissue drawn outward along the bullet's escape path. Usually, more blood is lost at an exit wound.

The blood, like the abrasion ring had there been one, was long gone. But the edges of the hole in the man's back were more ragged than those of the wound in his chest. On close inspection, I'd noted small tendrils drooping from its borders.

"Unless deflected by bone, a bullet will travel in a straight line." LaManche broke the silence. "That appears to be the situation here. I will, of course, do a full dissection, but I am certain I will find that the projectile passed through the lungs and heart causing a fatal hemothorax and hemopericardium."

"The guy was shot in the chest." I was doing the same as LaManche, voicing the thoughts spinning in my head.

"Yes."

"Not struck by lightning."

"No."

"He was murdered."

"Yes."

"Any guess what type of firearm?"

"No."

"Claudel is not going to be happy," I said.

"The gentleman is rarely happy."

Good point, boss.

"I will explain to Monsieur Claudel that after a bullet enters a body, elasticity causes the skin to retract," LaManche said. "Thus, a wound can appear smaller than the projectile that has passed through. To guess gun caliber would be folly."

I thought a moment, anxious for some morsel to offer Claudel.

"Can we get a height estimate?" I asked Lisa.

She collected a portable stadiometer, positioned one end of the long rod at the man's foot, slid the other to the top of his head.

"Sixty-five inches," she said.

I turned to LaManche. "The bullet trajectory is posterior and downward?"

He nodded.

"I can tell Claudel that the victim was short, the shooter probably taller."

"Possibly taller," LaManche cautioned.

"Possibly taller," I agreed.

We finished just before noon.

A full autopsy produced no more surprises. As LaManche had predicted, the gunshot wound to the man's chest had been fatal. The absence of water in his lungs and trachea suggested that he was dead before entering the river.

Back in my office, I emailed pictures of the man's face to Detective Musgrove. Not wanting to upstage LaManche, I said nothing to her about the new findings concerning cause and manner of death.

Next, I called Claudel. Got his voice mail. Left a message.

I was eating a soggy egg salad sandwich when my phone rang.

"Dr. Brennan," I answered.

"Deniz Been." Claudel bulled right in.

"Sorry?" I said, confused.

"The man's name is Deniz Been. I got a hit when I ran the prints."

"What database—"

"Been is nineteen years old, a citizen of the Turks and Caicos Islands."

"Why was he in the system?"

"The young man has a sheet, though it appears that most are juvenile offenses."

"Why—"

"Do you want to hear this?"

I held my tongue, inwardly counted to ten. The exercise slowed my pulse but did little to soothe my annoyance.

"On September tenth of last year Been reached Montreal aboard Delta flight #2907, having connected through Atlanta. Upon entry, he presented a British passport issued to citizens of the Turks and Caicos Islands. It is unknown where he resided for the seven months after his arrival. I am following up on that."

I let him go on.

"At the time of his accidental death, Been had significantly out-stayed the allotted time on his visa."

"It wasn't accidental."

My declaration was met with a series of irritated nasal breaths.

"Been was murdered," I added, picturing Claudel's indrawn lips and clenched nostrils.

After several more raspy inhalations, he said, "Go on."

I explained the entrance and exit holes. The absence of water in the lungs and trachea that would have indicated drowning.

"Bullet trajectory suggests Been was shot in the chest. And that his assailant might have been taller than he was. I'm guessing Been's sheet lists him at five-five to five-seven."

Claudel made a sound in his throat. I took it as confirmation. Perhaps encouragement to continue.

"Been's killer probably planned to use the fireworks to cover the sound of the gunfire. The storm and lightning were a bonus."

Claudel said nothing

Recalling the spider/octopus tattoo, I asked, "Did Been have gang connections?"

"Here? Or in the islands?"

Perfect opening.

I told Claudel about Musgrove's imminent arrival. Promised that, should the TCI detective contact me first, I would provide her with Claudel's mobile number.

Then, quickly, "Have a nice weekend, detective."

I disconnected, knowing Claudel might object to meeting with Musgrove. And that he'd have zero interest in the quality of my Saturday and Sunday.

MONDAY, JULY 8

Ryan and I stayed home Saturday night and ate a *toute garnie* Angela pizza while watching *True Grit*. He and Birdie are classic movies fans. The cat likes comedies. Ryan prefers westerns. Not sure how they made their choice.

The weather stayed warm and sunny. On Sunday, we took a hike up Mont Royal, the small hillock les Montrealais call "the mountain." Along with every other ambulatory resident of the city.

That evening, Ryan and I blew a chunk of our budget on dinner at Le Club Chasse et Pêche on rue Saint-Claude. The setting was elegant, the food exquisite. The only drawback was the restaurant's location. Being in the old port triggered flashbacks of Deniz Been's body parts rising from the river.

Monday morning, I found a woman awaiting my arrival in the lobby of the SQ building. Her hair was glossy black and cropped to jaw length. Thick bangs covered her forehead. Her eyes were hazel, her pale skin tanned and creased by too much time in the sun or too little blocker. I guessed her age at a bump north of forty.

The woman rose upon seeing me. I knew who she was before her self-introduction.

"Dr. Brennan?" Musgrove extended a hand in my direction. "Detective Tiersa Musgrove. I go by Ti."

We shook. Musgrove's grip was somewhere in the bench vise range.

"Temperance Brennan," I said, smiling. "Call me Tempe." Then for lack of a better opener, "Your flight was okay? Your hotel?"

"Yes, brilliant. I took your suggestion and am staying on rue Peel." Musgrove's English was, well, English. However, face-to-face, I detected something more exotic in her cadence.

"Shall we get you signed in?" I asked.

Stepping to the window, I explained to the officer on duty that Musgrove was a visiting member of law enforcement. She presented ID and was given a temporary pass. Together we rode to the twelfth floor and walked to my office.

"Please." I gestured to the chair facing my desk.

Musgrove sat, crossed her legs, and folded her hands in her lap. In the light of my office window, I noticed that a crescent moon darkened her right lower lid, either a birthmark or a bruise. She'd made an effort with concealer, but the blemish still peeked through.

"Would you like coffee?"

"Oh, heavens no. It's provided free in the hotel lobby. I've probably overdone my intake."

Though seriously in need of my morning jolt, I sacrificed the caffeine and settled in my chair.

"There have been some developments," I began. "The man who fell from the bridge has been identified as Deniz Been."

"Yes. I could see that from the autopsy photos you sent. The poor boy."

Not the response I'd expected. Recognizing Been, but unaware that he'd been murdered, why had Musgrove made such a long trip?

"At autopsy, we observed no evidence of lightning trauma or drowning."

Now Musgrove was the one to look surprised.

"The pathologist, Dr. Pierre LaManche, determined that Mr. Been had been fatally shot."

I described the entrance and exit wounds and handed Musgrove a set of images I'd had printed. Her chin dipped to study the photos.

Time passed. I pondered the part running the top of Musgrove's scalp. Wondered how she'd managed to get it so straight. Tucked my own hair behind my ears. Several offices down, a phone rang. A woman's heels clicked past in the hall.

Finally, Musgrove looked up.

"The detective handling this case, Detective Claudel, is with the city police," I said. "It was he who told me that the tattoo on Mr. Been's shoulder was associated with a crew calling themselves the Cay Boys. In our first conversation you said that they were one of your local groups. May I ask, are they a gang?"

"Eh."

I raised my brows in question.

Musgrove couldn't keep the sarcasm out of her voice: "In the words of the assistant police commissioner, young men on Providenciales who form into violent groups to inflict injuries on each other cannot be classified as gangs."

"Why not?" I asked.

"They do not meet the established criteria."

"Which are?"

"Gangs must have leaders and proper networking."

"That's not the case in the Turks and Caicos?"

"Of course, it is. Young men form groups, defend turfs, engage in a type of revenge killing called beefing."

"Sounds like gangs to me."

"Indeed."

"The Cay Boys is one of these groups?"

Musgrove nodded.

"I don't understand your deputy commissioner's thinking."

"According to him, these groups are merely copycats parading as gangs. If that's true, they're doing a cracking fine job of it. Not long ago a video made the rounds showing a kid kneeling over a gunshot victim as gangster rap plays in the background and the message *R.i.hell* appears over the body. Language such as 'shoot to kill,' 'devil want soul,' and the names of rival gang members are also featured in this cinematic gem."

"That sounds pretty hard core."

"According to the deputy commissioner, and I quote, 'There will be no gangs in the Turks and Caicos Islands. Plain and simple.'"

Musgrove read my confusion.

"Can you guess TCI's largest source of revenue?"

"Tourism," I said.

"Bingo."

"Might Mr. Been's murder be gang related?" I asked.

"Doubtful these punks have that kind of reach."

Musgrove flicked nonexistent lint from the knee of her pants. Her next words were unexpected.

"Deniz Been's murder is not the reason I've come."

9

"No sense arsing around. I'll come straight out with it."

Now I was the one to sit silent and listen.

"I feel sad for Deniz Been. Sad, but not surprised. The kid was a violent little wanker and finally crossed the wrong person."

That was cold. I didn't say it.

"Nevertheless, he should not be dead. He deserves justice and I intend to do all I can to help your local authorities find his killer. But Been is not the sole reason I'm here."

Musgrove paused, organizing her thoughts. Perhaps reviewing a speech she'd practiced in her head.

"There are others who also deserve justice. For seven years I've been busting my bum trying to solve the murder of an American tourist in Providenciales."

"Detective Musgrove, I'm—"

"Ti."

"Ti. I'm an anthropologist, not a detective."

"Hear me out. Please."

I nodded.

Musgrove drew a large envelope from a brown satchel slung over her shoulder, slid a photo from it, and laid it on the blotter. I leaned forward to study the image.

The subject was a young man with blond hair, green eyes, and teeth showing not a single irregularity. He was standing on the deck of a sailboat, arms crossed, feet spread, smiling straight into the lens.

"You're looking at Robert Galloway," Musgrove said. "Bobby to his friends."

Bobby Galloway's skin was tanned, his body toned. With his all-American good looks and bring-it-on confidence, he might have scored a leading role on *The Bachelor*.

Musgrove placed a second photo beside the first.

"Galloway was killed when he and three friends came to TCI to celebrate their upcoming high school graduation. He was eighteen years old."

The second shot was better focused than the first. Yellow police tape surrounded a long gully holding a cement culvert. Tiny colored markers indicated the location of individual pieces of evidence.

Wrapping one end of the culvert was what remained of Bobby Galloway. Though mud-caked and ghostly pale, the handsome face was clearly recognizable.

Galloway died wearing REI running shorts and a green tee that said *I Got This*, the inscription barely legible through the blossom of blood staining his chest. One foot wore an Adidas running shoe, the other was bare.

Only one of Galloway's arms was visible, thrown out at an unnatural angle, like one of those plastic dolls whose limbs can be twisted into odd positions. The arm ended at a truncated wrist, which gave way to flesh the color of uncooked hamburger. Maggots feasted on it. The severed hand was nowhere to be seen.

"Early one morning, Galloway left his mates at their rented condo at the Sunset Beach Villas to drive to Taylor Bay Beach for a run. He didn't return and his friends reported him missing that night. His body was found two days later in the Frenchman's Creek Nature Reserve."

"Is that by Taylor Bay."

"Nowhere near."

"An autopsy showed that Galloway died of a gunshot wound to the thorax. There were no drugs or alcohol in his system."

"What was the story on the friends?"

"All cleared. They stayed on the island as long as required, then flew back to Omaha."

"Any suspects?"

"None serious. And everyone who was questioned alibied out."

"What about the rental car?"

"It was found a week later parked at the airport."

"Did the car have built-in navigation?"

"It did. The history had been erased."

"You say this murder took place seven years ago," I said, unsure where this was going. "Why come to me now?"

"Since Galloway's murder, two more tourists have vanished."

Another photo hit the blotter.

"Ryder Palke disappeared four years back. He was twenty-two, an apprentice pipe fitter from Chicago. Palke was vacationing in TCI with his girlfriend, Sylvia Shorter. Their third day on the island, Palke went out on a SCUBA charter while Shorter stayed behind at the Royal West Indies Resort. Palke disembarked the boat at four that afternoon, was never seen again. Shorter gave it twenty-four hours, then filed an MP report."

The image showed a tall young man in a blazer and sharply creased pants casually shoulder-leaning on an ornamental lamppost. He had heavy straight brows, a David Beckham prickled updo, and a fashionably stubbled, very square chin. The shot looked professional, maybe taken for a composite, the type submitted when applying for work as an actor or model.

Before I could comment, Musgrove produced another image.

"Quentin Bonner was a twenty-year-old British freelance photographer traveling solo. Two years ago, he set off to film sea birds at Parrot Cay. Five days later, the manager of the Sibonné Beach Hotel reported that Bonner had skipped without paying his bill. When police opened the door to his room, Bonner's belongings were still there, including a collection of pricey camera equipment. His rental car was never returned."

Bonner had one thing in common with Galloway and Palke. He, too, was Hollywood leading-man handsome—hooded brown eyes only hinting at a smile, intriguingly crooked nose, dark hair doing that bad boy dip thing over one brow.

The shot, taken candid from a lower elevation, showed Bonner outdoors, hiking stick in one hand, glancing downhill over his left shoulder.

Again, I started to protest.

"Until last Friday, Palke and Bonner remained MPs."

Two more pics joined the lineup.

I looked down.

At last I understood.

The new shots resembled the crime scene photo of Bobby Galloway. Same evidence markers. Same yellow tape. What differed was the condition of the remains.

Both Palke and Bonner were skeletonized, their bones stained tea-brown by contact with the earth and with liquids of decomposition. Both were partially buried by soil and vegetation, some dead, some alive and growing intermingled with the bones. It appeared that both had been freshly exposed by tentative stripping and digging.

One skeleton was photographed from closer in. It appeared to be largely articulated, with the skull still topping the vertebrae, the rest of the bones curled in a semi-fetal position. I spotted immediately that one of the hands was missing.

The other picture was taken with a wide-angle lens to accommodate the fact that the remains were scattered, probably by scavenging animals. Plastic markers indicated the location of individual bones or bone clusters.

Centered in the scene were a pelvis, femora, tibiae, and fibulae. Wrapping them were faded denim and what appeared to be the waistband of a pair of tighty-whities.

Moving toward the periphery, I recognized vertebrae, ribs, and arm bones, one set straggling out to the right, the other to the left. I saw no skull, hands, or feet. No shirt or other clothing.

"Who found these?" I asked.

"A fisherman out walking his dog."

"Cause of death?"

"A gunshot wound that penetrated all the way through the chest."

"For both?"

"Yes."

"Like Galloway."

"Yes."

"Did you recover any bullet casings?"

"No."

"You think these are Palke and Bonner?" I tapped one of the last two prints.

Musgrove shrugged. Who knows? "No cell phone, wallet, or any form of ID was found with either body."

"Did you request dental records?"

"We did. Palke's dentist died three years ago. The gentleman who purchased his practice destroyed or deleted all files older than five years."

"Palke hadn't had a check-up in that time?"

"Apparently not."

"Great. And Bonner?"

"His dentist's office was destroyed in a fire."

"You've got to be kidding."

"Would that I were."

"DNA?"

"That will take eons. We lack the ability to do our own sequencing and must send specimens to a lab in Miami."

I refocused on the photos. Then,

"You said these bones were found last Friday?"

"Yes. Ironically, when you phoned about Deniz Been I was researching how to handle their recovery. Everything I read emphasized the importance of leaving skeletonized remains *in situ* until a forensic anthropologist could process the scene."

"Mm. Where were the bodies discovered?" The question was pointless. While I'd been to TCI, I didn't know the islands all that well.

"That's one of the strange things about these murders. The victims were all found in odd places. Locations that should be of no interest to a tourist."

"Body dumps?"

"At first we thought so, but now we're not sure."

"How did the men get to these *odd* locations?" Emphasizing her choice of adjective.

"All three had rental cars."

"From the same vendor?"

"Three different companies. Avis, Budget, and an outfit called Ecar Tci. Except for Galloway's, none of the vehicles has ever been found."

"Did any of the vics have a presence on social media?"

"Galloway died seven years ago, so not so much. The others, yes. My people have spent hours on Instagram, Facebook, Twitter—you know the players. So far, they've found nothing informative."

"Was any victim's credit or bank card used after his disappearance?"

"No. Neither their cards nor their mobile phones."

Despite myself, I was intrigued.

"All three had a severed hand?" I asked.

"Yes. Hacked off by machete, we believe. The hands were never retrieved."

"You think the three murders are linked?"

"I do," she said, gesticulating slightly as she ticked off her points. "Three young men, all tourists. All shot in the chest. All with a hand removed. All found in remote locations. All lacking phones, wallets, and IDs."

"You're thinking serial killer?" I asked.

"Yes. And the powers that be aren't eager to see word spread about tourists being picked off in TCI."

"They're hoping it all takes care of itself? Rather callous to the victims and their families." It came out curter than I intended.

"I actually agree," said Musgrove, nodding. "That's why I'm here. I've poured my soul into finding whatever sicko killed Galloway, and what happened to the other two." She swept a hand over the photos spread across my desk. "Now this."

"What would you like me to do?" Already knowing the answer.

"As you are aware, the first steps in solving any murder are to properly recover and identify the victim. These two bodies have been reduced to bone. That's a job for an anthropologist. There's no one in my country with your expertise."

Musgrove squared her shoulders. Lithely. The woman's every move seemed to flow with a dancer's grace.

"I invite you, respectfully, to come to the beautiful Turks and Caicos Islands. I am authorized to tell you that your travel will be covered, accommodations provided, every need met. And your normal fee will be paid, of course."

"I can't just drop everything here and take off."

"A killer is still out there, Dr. Brennan. Unless stopped, he or she will strike again, I fear. Is anything so pressing now that you can't help me prevent more deaths?"

Musgrove's tone was filled with new urgency. And she had a point. I'd finished with the Sainte-Agathe babies and had only to compose a report on Deniz Been.

"There are direct flights daily," Musgrove continued. "Should something imperative arise, you can be back in Montreal in a matter of hours."

I can't say the prospect of a brief sojourn in the islands

wasn't appealing. I'm from the Carolinas, a sand-and-surf girl at heart.

I glanced at the photo array on my desktop.

And felt a heaviness begin to build in my chest. I'd never met Bobby Galloway, Ryder Palke, or Quentin Bonner. Knew almost nothing about them. Still, the pics hit me hard. They'd been so buoyantly youthful, so full of life. A life denied them by a cold-blooded killer.

I was hit with an uninvited barrage of images. Severed limbs. A spider/octopus tattoo. A gunshot wound to the chest. A mangled and decomposing corpse.

"Could the Deniz Been shooting be connected to these deaths?" I asked.

"Unlikely." Musgrove executed another graceful shrug. "But, again, anything's possible."

"Could the TCI shootings be gang related?"

"Galloway, Palke, and Bonner were tourists. Murdering tourists would be atypical of the gang violence we see in Provo."

"When do you plan to return home?"

"When I've completed what I must do here with regard to Deniz Been."

"In the meantime, these remains are still lying outside exposed to the elements?"

Musgrove nodded. "Every article I read advised against rushing in without proper training and thus destroying possible evidence. If the bodies have been at the site long enough to skeletonize, the experts cautioned, a few days delay won't hurt."

What the hell.

I made a decision.

"Fine. I'll go with you. Please make travel arrangements and let me know."

"Thank you so much."

Musgrove leapt to her feet. For a moment I feared she intended to hug me.

"In the meantime, you should meet with the detective handling Mr. Been's case," I said.

"My very next stop." Looping the strap of her satchel back over her shoulder. "Does the bloke speak English?"

"Oh, yeah."

I scribbled Claudel's contact info and extended the Post-it to her.

10

Our 9:15 a.m. Air Canada flight took off at 10:06. The plane was full, and Musgrove and I were crammed into row twenty-three with a gray-haired woman of substantial girth. I was in the middle seat. The price one pays for last-minute booking.

I'm not one for chatty exchanges at thirty thousand feet. Call me callous, but I've no interest in the life stories of people I'll never see again. Just leave me alone with my book. At the moment, I was enjoying Niall Williams's *This Is Happiness*. Getting a feel for me grannies and grampies on the old sod.

Musgrove, who'd forfeited her aisle seat up front to sit to my left, must have shared my thinking. She spent most of the flight flipping through magazines she'd purchased at an airport kiosk. An eclectic collection. *Vanity Fair. Saltwater Sportsman. Simply Knitting.*

The woman on my right was hopeless at reading nonverbal clues. Within an hour, I'd learned that her name was Giselle, she was from Boucherville, had six grandchildren, was traveling to TCI to visit two of them—Marlene and Teddy—and that her daughter's divorce had not gone well.

To avoid a full dissertation on Giselle's entire family tree, at the first break in the flow, I turned to ask Musgrove about her meeting with Claudel.

"He's a lovely chap." Dropping the fishing journal to her lap.

"Luc Claudel? At the SPVM?"

"Yes. He was brilliant."

"Mmm."

"I told Luc what I knew about Deniz Been's background, his family, his juvie record, his wannabe status with the Cay Boys. Luc said he'd discovered that Been had a Quebecoise girlfriend."

Luc?

Musgrove dug an iPhone from her satchel and scrolled to the Notes app. "In a place called Terrebonne?"

I nodded. "Terrebonne is a town northwest of the island of Montreal."

"The girlfriend's name is Émilie Gaudreau. She's a receptionist at a nail salon. They met when Gaudreau was vacationing in TCI. While in Canada, Been crashed at Gaudreau's flat."

"Does Claudel have a theory on who shot Been?"

"He's thinking the kid may have gone freelance and begun selling drugs in a hood where he shouldn't have. That one of your local lads took exception and popped him."

"Did Claudel interview Gaudreau?"

"He did. Gaudreau said Been knew almost no one in Quebec. That he had no ties to any gang, at least none of which she was aware. She claimed they mostly hung out at her flat watching TV. She denied knowing anything about illegal drugs."

"No surprise there."

Changing course, Musgrove asked if I was married, had kids, the usual polite inquiries of a new acquaintance. I replied in the negative concerning marriage, asked the same of her. She said she had an ex, added that she usually referred to him as "shithead."

I was about to follow up on that intriguing declaration when a voice came over the intercom instructing us on the positioning of our seat backs and tray tables. As everyone prepared for landing, a thought occurred to me.

"Did Claudel ask why Been was alone on that bridge the night of the fireworks?"

"Gaudreau said that they'd quarreled the day before. That they'd sort of broken up."

"Sort of?"

Musgrove smiled. "Our minds work alike. I posed that very question. Luc said those were Gaudreau's exact words."

"What do *you* think?" I asked after a pause.

Musgrove's signature "who knows?" shrug was somewhat constrained by her seat belt and the tight space. "Been was a bit of a cockup back home. But as far as I know, he never dealt drugs."

The plane began its final descent. Giselle reached over to clutch my wrist. I patted her hand.

The wheels had barely kissed the tarmac when Musgrove's mobile pinged a series of incoming texts. A lot of them. She hit the icon and glanced at the screen.

Her brows dipped and her lips tightened. "Bloody hell."

"Bad news?" I asked.

The hazel eyes rolled up to mine below the dark bangs. She nodded, once, quick. Drew a breath.

"Yesterday at dawn, fishermen spotted a small boat drifting about a mile off the far western tip of Provo." Musgrove spoke so softly I had to strain to hear her. "The fishermen notified the marine branch of the RTCIPF."

"Royal Turks and Caicos Islands Police Force?"

"Yes. Sorry. Several people were on board, including at least one child. All are dead and have been for some time."

"Jesus." I couldn't keep the shock from my voice.

"My IO had no further information. Investigating officer," she added when I looked perplexed.

The plane stopped taxiing. A bong sounded. Around us, passengers began gathering their belongings.

Musgrove looked at me, earnest as a preacher on Sunday morning. "I hate to ask. I imagine it will be grim. But since you're here, we could really use your help on this."

"Of course."

As Musgrove dialed and spoke to someone, probably the IO who'd texted, I helped Giselle dig an enormous faux-leopard handbag from under the seat in front of her, and a battered red rollaboard from the compartment overhead.

Making my way up the aisle, I wondered, *Did Musgrove actually just learn of that drifting boat? Or did she know all along?*

Had I been double-ambushed?

The possibility didn't make me happy.

The Turks and Caicos lie southeast of the Bahamas and are situated on a plateau rising about ten thousand feet from the Atlantic Ocean floor. The plateau is split by the six-thousand-foot-deep, twenty-mile-wide Turks Island Passage, which separates the smaller islands—Grand Turk and Salt Cay—from the Caicos Islands archipelago and the extensive Caicos Banks.

The TCI land mass is limited and for the most part coastal. In fact, the farthest inland one can be from the ocean or a tidal wetland is about two miles. That's at a place called Kew on North Caicos. Elevations are low, with the highest points in the country being Blue Mountain on Providenciales and Flamingo Hill on East Caicos, each managing to reach a majestic 155 feet.

Except for a few tiny sandbar cays, the islands have a soft limestone foundation. The beaches, however, are composed primarily of crushed shells and coral. This composition, along with the fact that very little hard stone exists in the country to form gravel, results in the almost blindingly white brilliance of TCI's beaches.

I'd learned these nuggets from the tourism magazine tucked into the seat-back pocket in front of me. There was more, but my new BFF had allowed little time for reading.

At her request, I exited the plane ahead of Giselle. She followed, one arthritic hand braced on my back, the other death-gripping the rail. I carried my shoulder bag, and her red rollaboard and feral-looking purse.

The air felt like melted butter, warm and moist and smooth on my skin. A warm breeze carried a bouquet of jet fuel and flowers. I guessed oleander, lantana, maybe bougainvillea. But what do I know about tropical flora?

Descending the wobbly portable stairs, I noted two figures inside a white Jeep Wrangler. At the wheel was a man. Riding shotgun was a woman. On the door, looking very royal, was the TCI police force logo.

Upon seeing Musgrove, just behind Giselle, the pair alighted, squaring red-banded peaked caps onto their heads. Adjusting the shiny brims with identical moves.

The man was pear-shaped, of medium stature, fair and freckled. His nose was bullet straight, his eyes hidden by Maui Jim shades.

The woman made Giselle seem dainty in comparison. I guessed her height at six feet, her weight at two hundred pounds minimum. Her skin was the color of coffee, her dreads gathered into an enormous blond knot at the base of her cap.

Both the driver and his passenger were dressed in navy pants with red stripes running the legs. Their blue-and-white-pin-striped shirts had shoulder patches identifying the wearers as members of the RTCIPF. Silver epaulette pins provided additional messaging, lost on me.

The pair watched Musgrove approach, feet spread, arms at their sides. They didn't quite salute but straightened visibly when she drew near. The man's face was already going blotchy from the heat.

Words were exchanged, then Musgrove signaled me into the

Jeep. Apologizing to Giselle for leaving her on her own, I positioned the rollaboard so she could easily grasp the handle. Hoping she'd survive the long hot trek to the terminal, I hurried across the tarmac and climbed into the blessedly air-conditioned vehicle.

A few moments of conversation, then the others joined me. Musgrove introduced Pear-shape as Constable Gardiner, Blonde-bun as Constable Rigby. Both nodded. Neither turned to face us.

"If you're amenable, the officers will take us directly to the boat. I believe it's been brought to shore. I'm sorry I don't know more. I understand a crime scene unit is there, as well as members of our marine branch. I'm told that nothing has been touched. The coroner's representative has come and gone. She's ordered body bags and a refrigerated transport vehicle to accommodate multiple dead. Is there anything else you anticipate needing?"

I glanced down at my chambray blouse, white jeans, and sandals.

"The CSU truck will have boots, gloves, masks, and Tyvek suits for us," Musgrove said.

"I checked a suitcase."

"If you give Constable Rigby your claim ticket, she'll have the bag collected and delivered."

"Shouldn't I clear customs?" I asked as I detached the slip from my ticket and handed it forward to Rigby's upraised palm.

"All sorted," Musgrove said.

I leaned back, resigned. At least the skipping customs part was nice.

Gardiner put the Jeep into gear. As we set off, I took note of our route. No reason. It gave me something to do.

Gardiner left the airport on, not surprisingly, Airport Road, then turned onto Old Airport Road. Even in the islands, progress!

We traversed several densely populated residential areas. Lots of small stucco houses, mostly one-story, a few rising to a second level, sometimes finished, sometimes not—probably multifamily setups. Some homes were on stilts, some built at ground level. Many were or had at one time been painted bright pink, lavender, or green. Others featured more subtle shades of pastel. Or maybe they were just sun bleached.

Quite a few properties showed loving hands at work. Crisp white trim and a matching picket fence. A well-tended garden or window box. A mailbox decorated with dancing fish or crabs. An equal number hadn't seen a hammer or paintbrush in years.

Bikes lay abandoned on tiny green patches struggling to be lawns. Here and there a dog dozed on a concrete stoop or surveyed its world from an oyster shell drive. A brown one with a scabby nose and unbalanced ears lifted its head from its paws to object halfheartedly to our intrusion. Most didn't bother.

A short jog right, then Gardiner turned left onto a larger two-lane. A big loop, then we picked up speed.

Until that moment, Musgrove had concentrated on texting.

"Shit. Shit. Shit." Exasperated, she looked up from her mobile.

I cocked a quizzical brow.

"My bloody battery just died."

"Sorry." Wondering how a cop could allow that to happen.

Rigby's palm again came our way and Musgrove placed her phone on it. Rigby leaned toward the dash and, I assumed, attached the device to a charger cord.

Musgrove thanked the constable, then said to me, "We're on the Millennium Highway." Musgrove gestured toward my side of the Jeep. "The ocean is off that way. Blue Hills Road parallels the water and is much more scenic. But the route we're taking is faster."

"Where is Grace Bay?" One of the few features on the island I knew to name.

"Behind us, down the shore." Giving another, more backward flick of her wrist. "You'll see it later. That's where you're staying."

Musgrove fell silent again, her inner tension evidenced by the interlaced knuckles bulging white in her lap.

I refocused on the scene sliding by my window. Businesses straggled both sides of the road. At intervals, streets led off into neighborhoods, seemingly more upmarket than those closer to the airport.

We passed what appeared to be a warehouse. An outfit called Ecar Tci.

I felt a slight uptick in my pulse.

"Is that the company where one of your vics rented his car?" I asked Musgrove.

"Ryder Palke," she said.

"Why would he come way out here?"

"They deliver to the airport and to resorts."

"Did you find any link at *all* between the vics?"

"Both Bonner and Palke had visited a bar called Polly's Tiki Shack. We interviewed everyone from the owner down to the night cleaning crew. One bartender, a guy named Glen Wall got extra scrutiny."

"Why?"

"Aside from making my skin crawl, the guy had an impressive rap sheet. String of arrests, mostly for drunk and disorderly, but a few for assault. Wall did one short stretch for busting a guy's jaw and right arm."

"Sounds like a bad actor."

Musgrove nodded. "But Wall alibied out. Two cousins and a brother swore he was on a fishing boat with them the whole week Palke disappeared."

Again, silence filled the car.

I noticed a small stucco church. Read the sign identifying it as the New Birth Agape Fellowship.

I thought about that. Pictured a saint from the holy cards of my childhood, halo looping his head, mouth wide in surprise. Figured the word must have an alternate meaning unknown to me.

Miles ticked by. Then Musgrove spoke again. "We're skirting the community of Wheeland Settlement." She pronounced it Veeland. "Before that it was Blue Hills. Nothing much left between here and Northwest Point. Some small farm fields."

"Growing what?" I didn't much care, but Musgrove now seemed to want conversation. Or maybe she felt she should entertain me.

"Okra, maize, pigeon peas, squash. There are a couple of resorts over on the water, but there's very little up this way."

She went still again. I returned to my window gazing.

Grants Wheeland Gas Station. TCI Best Deal Pawn Shop. Tropical Aquariums pet store.

One last development, then, as Musgrove predicted, the homes and businesses yielded to open scrub interspersed with farm fields and small stretches of mangrove wetland.

Gardiner hooked a left, then made a right at Davie Bight Road. It was then I understood why we were in a four-wheel-drive vehicle.

Shortly, the pavement ended at a dirt road. Then the dirt gave way to sand, a trail so narrow two cars could never have passed.

The Jeep rocked gently. The sand *shushed* under our tires. Suddenly, we were at the ocean.

The beach was bone white and scattered with boulders of varying sizes and shades of gray. The ocean was vividly turquoise, the surreal blue broken only by froth geysering skyward where waves collided with rocks.

The sweeping grandeur was so unexpected it took my breath away.

"Wow," I said.

"Yeah," Musgrove agreed. "It never gets old."

After several more minutes of lurching and rolling, Gardiner braked to a stop and nodded to Rigby. Rigby rotated to face Musgrove. I figured the handoff between the two must involve rank.

"We in the park, ma'am. The boat be just yonder, over that ridge." Thumb-jabbing the window by her right shoulder. "It's best we walk from here."

The four of us got out and snaked along single file. Gardiner took the lead, then me, then Musgrove. Rigby brought up the rear. No one spoke.

Gulls circled and screeched overhead, reminding me of the day I'd pulled Deniz Been from Bickerdike Basin, and of my unresolved vacation plans with Ryan. I could easily imagine us in this place, me

enjoying the sand and surf, him coated with Hawaiian Tropic SPF
2000.

The sun was hot and still high in the sky. Halfway to the ridge, I
stopped to remove my sandals. To wipe sweat from my face. To take
in the view.

I wanted to forget my reason for being here. To savor the natural
beauty surrounding me. The bluer than blue sky with its billowy
white clouds. The coconut palms throwing razor straight shadows
across the beach. The sunlight sparking the ocean and foamy spray.

But frolicking and beachcombing were for another day.

Gardiner climbed the small knoll first, sending a cascade of sand
trickling down toward me. I followed.

Seconds later, Musgrove joined us.

"Binos?" she asked, reaching a hand toward Gardiner.

Gardiner produced a pair of binoculars. Musgrove raised them
to her eyes and adjusted focus.

"Well, bugger me."

Musgrove's mouth went agape, mimicking my imagined vision of
the holy card saint.

11

Musgrove was peering up the shoreline toward a narrow tongue of land jutting into the sea. Thirty yards off the tongue, two vessels bobbed side by side, anchored and going nowhere.

Wordlessly, she handed me the binoculars. I pointed them at the boats.

The first was clearly marked as belonging to the marine branch of the RTCIPF. The second was a sleek high-velocity number powered by inboard motors. Vinyl cushions spanned its rail-enclosed stern. Similar seating wrapped its mongo, kick-ass bow, which angled high above the water. At midship, an enormous boom awning shaded the helm and its controls. Gray tarps haphazardly covered the cockpit, their appearance jarringly at odds with the boat's swanky, hellcat style.

"Not what you were expecting?" I asked.

"Not at all."

I cocked a brow. Lost on Musgrove, as she wasn't looking at me.

"That, however"—she pointed up the beach—"I *was* expecting."

Musgrove was indicating a CSU truck, a coroner's van, and a

Jeep—this one much larger than the Wrangler that had brought us. Its broad flatbed and roomy crew cab suggested a model name like, say, the Shazam or the Godzilla. I later learned it was a Gladiator Sport.

A rubber Zodiac lay beached on the sand directly opposite the two boats. A black-and-white pop-up tent had been erected at the same spot.

Three men and one woman stood beside the tent. The men smoked. The woman just stood.

"What surprises you?" I asked, handing back the binoculars.

"I was anticipating migrants."

"Illegals?"

She nodded. "Human trafficking is a problem throughout the Caribbean. And things often go awry. A few years back, fourteen bodies were found on a sloop adrift off Tobago, another seven on a vessel off Grenada."

I didn't interrupt.

"In 2021, twenty corpses turned up in an open boat a mile off Grand Turk Island."

"Where do they come from?"

"The Turks and Caicos are a magnet for Haitians desperate to flee the gangs and the poverty in their homeland. The day following the recovery of the twenty dead, marine branch agents intercepted another vessel carrying forty-three Haitians." Her eyes met mine. "A forty-foot open boat driven by a single engine. Think about that."

We both fell silent, imagining the horror of such journeys.

"But TCI isn't usually the intended destination," Musgrove continued. "Human traffickers from everywhere use this region as a trans-shipment point. For example, the Tobago authorities determined that the vessel they towed ashore had been stolen in Mauritania."

"In northwest Africa."

She nodded.

I thought of the many articles I'd read about bodies discovered locked in the backs of vans and trucks. Men, women, and children dead of heat stroke, dehydration, and starvation, abandoned by the *coyotes* they'd paid to smuggle them north.

"And these bastards get away with it." I struggled to keep the loathing from my voice.

"Not always."

Musgrove raised the binoculars and returned her gaze to the boats. "If I'm not mistaken, that's a twenty-seven-foot Sea Ray SDX 270, probably a 2019 model." She could have told me it was *The Oracle* and I would have believed her. "Inboard Mercs, fiberglass hull, retractable swim platform. That baby cost at least a hundred grand."

"Not your typical human trafficker rig."

"Definitely not. I expected an open craft of some kind, a dinghy, maybe a small sloop." When I said nothing, she added, "A sloop is a single-masted boat, usually with a fore and aft mainsail and jib. Never mind."

"So why the dead bodies?"

"Let's find out."

Returning the binoculars to Gardiner, Musgrove headed down the dune, cut toward the ocean, and strode up the beach, keeping to the hard-packed crescent left beside the water at low tide. I rolled the cuffs of my jeans, tucked my sandals into my shoulder bag, and followed. Rigby chugged along at my back, Gardiner behind her, breathing hard.

Musgrove introduced the man and woman by the tent as Constables Stubbs and Kemp, the CSU team. Both wore navy polos tucked into cargo pants. The polos had the now familiar RTCIPF patch.

Stubbs was the shorter and darker of the two, her long black hair secured by a coral barrette almost as large as her head. Fleetingly, I considered the logistics of wearing a hat.

With his butterscotch complexion and sunny, eager-to-please demeanor—lots of smiling and nodding—Kemp brought to mind a golden retriever. All but the panting and dangling tongue.

The other member of the trio was the coroner's investigator, Iggie Bernadin. Bernadin had very dark skin and very bad teeth.

"Brief me." Musgrove directed her command to no one in particular.

Eager to comply, Kemp explained what we already knew. Fishermen stumbled across a boat drifting a mile offshore, pulled alongside, saw corpses, called the cops. Members of the marine branch boarded the vessel and covered the bodies. Finding the engine dead and the fuel gauge on empty, they ordered a tow.

"How many individuals?" I asked.

Kemp didn't know.

"Men? Women? Kids?" Musgrove asked.

Kemp didn't know.

"Other than placing the tarps, has anything out there been touched?"

"Not since Stubbs and I took over watch. But we haven't left the beach."

"And before the hand-off?"

Kemp didn't know.

Musgrove turned to me. "Ready?"

I nodded.

"Gear is in the truck." Kemp displayed more teeth than keys on a piano. "You can suit up in the tent. Shall I show you?"

"We can manage. Be ready to ferry us over."

"Yes, ma'am." Kemp nodded so hard I feared a vertebral dislocation.

We skipped the tent, choosing instead to slip into our Tyvek coveralls alfresco. The rest of the PPE—personal protective equipment—we secured in plastic sacks and carried with us.

When we returned to the shoreline, Kemp and Bernadin were similarly garbed. Stubbs had not suited up.

Bernadin was seated in the Zodiac's bow. Kemp was thigh deep in the surf, steadying the small inflatable with both hands. Stubbs, obviously the skipper, was in the stern, ready to start the outboard and work the tiller.

Musgrove and I waded out, holding our bagged gloves, masks,

and shoe covers at shoulder height, boots looping our necks by their tied laces. Musgrove sloshed to port, I to starboard. We tossed our bags onto a pile made up of the men's boots and two similar bags and, at a signal from Stubbs, climbed over the pontoons running along each side. Stubbs cranked the engine, Kemp hopped in, and we were off.

The crossing took less than ten minutes. As we drew close, I could see that the Sea Ray had been Christened the *Cod Bless Us*.

Stubbs maneuvered to the stern where a stainless-steel ladder ran from the swim platform into the water. Kemp grabbed hold of the lowest rung and clambered up. Bernadin went next, looking a bit like a spider stick-walking its web.

After tossing my boots and bagged PPE to Kemp, I followed. Musgrove came close on my heels. Stubbs remained at the tiller.

Even outdoors with a salty breeze caressing our faces and heavy laminated polyethylene covering the source, the odor was unambiguous. I knew whatever lay beneath the tarps had been dead for a while.

We all raised our hoods, booted, added shoe covers, gloves, and masks. As Kemp shot videos and stills, Musgrove and I captured our own images and recorded notes on our phones. The usual opening act, but this time performed on a rolling deck offshore.

Prelims finished, Musgrove said, "Let's see what we have."

Our foursome stepped down onto the wrap-around seating, down again onto the cockpit floor. Positioning ourselves in the narrow space between the bench and the tarp, we each grasped an edge of the polyethylene sheeting.

"Ready?" Musgrove asked.

Three nods.

"Lift."

We did.

The stench roared up like heat from a blast furnace, rank and foul as rotten meat. I sensed a waver in Kemp's smile, hidden by his mask.

Below the uppermost was another tarp of equal size and weight. Unlike its counterpart, this one lay off-kilter and rumpled, as though hurriedly tossed by those tasked with its placement.

Poking from one edge, extending almost to Kemp's right foot, was a putrefying forearm. The hand lay palm up with fingers splayed, as though reaching for help, even in death.

Kemp flinched and took an involuntary step backward. A small one, since little room remained between the bench at our backs and the grim cargo at our feet.

No reaction from Bernadin.

"Record this before proceeding," Musgrove said to Kemp.

As Musgrove and Bernadin held the tarp in its raised position, the CSU tech shot videos and stills. I let go long enough to snap a few photos with my phone, feet braced to counterbalance the boat's gentle rocking, hands sweaty inside my latex gloves.

Enough flesh had slithered free or been scavenged by seabirds to expose the bones of the lower arm and hand. While zooming in and framing, my brain logged details.

A few maggots were present on the rotting flesh. Not many. Recently hatched, I presumed they were the offspring of pilgrim females who'd ventured seaward once the boat was towed closer to shore. Or the ladies may have been stowaways on the marine agents who'd delivered the tarps. Perhaps passengers on the tarps themselves.

Despite the day's warmth, one observation sent an icy pang into my heart.

The human hand is a complex affair, composed of twenty-seven bones of differing forms and functions. The eight carpals, arranged in two rows of four, articulate with the lower arm bones—the radius and ulna—at the wrist. They are a very mixed lot, one shaped like a boat, others like a crescent, a pyramid, a pea.

The five metacarpals run across the back of the palm. Their round, bulging heads form the knuckles.

The fourteen phalanges are the slender, sometimes arrow-shaped bones that form the fingers. Three for each digit, two for the thumb.

As elsewhere in the skeleton, each hand bone develops following a predictable schedule. The carpals aren't present at birth, and there are multiple growth caps that fuse onto the metacarpals and phalanges.

I'd need X-rays for absolute medical certainty, the phrase a lawyer would use in court. But the pattern I saw was enough.

The distal epiphyses of the radius and ulna remained separate, held in place only by threads of ligamentous tissue. Though many of the epiphyses had been lost from the hand, the wavy joint surfaces left behind indicated that they, too, had not yet fused.

The outflung arm belonged to a kid of no more than sixteen years old.

"Ready?"

Musgrove's voice snapped me back to the present.

Pocketing my mobile, I regripped my edge. Careful not to disturb what lay below, we maneuvered the sheeting up and aft onto the swim platform.

Deep breath.

A meeting of eyes above surgical masks.

Musgrove nodded.

We lifted the lower tarp.

1 2

The ghastly sight was in stark contrast to the surreal beauty surrounding us.

"Bloody freakin' hell," Musgrove said on an indrawn breath.

I couldn't disagree.

The dead lay in a muddle of withered limbs and rotting apparel. A head count showed the muddle contained five people.

The teen lay closest to the starboard side. He or she had died wearing a neon green Under Armour tee and matching shorts. Thick carroty curls still clung to the child's skull. Neither the hair nor the outfit was informative as to sex.

Based on clothing, two of the other four victims appeared to be male. Like the teen, each wore shorts and a tee. Though the fabric was badly degraded, the messages on their chests were still legible. One said: *I Love My Wife, I Worship My Car*; the other said: *Real Men Don't Need Instructions*. The irony of the latter was lost on no one.

The pair lay supine, one between the helm and the captain's chair, the other parallel to the cockpit seating bordering the stern. The flesh was largely gone from their faces, the exposed teeth and facial bones bleached white as the sand at our backs.

Both men had been tall and, I suspected, fully adult. Both were emaciated, their limbs ropey and thin, making their clothing appear too large for their frames.

An off-kilter visor held some of the helm corpse's hair tight to his skull. The strands were long and gray. A faded elastic binder suggested they'd once formed a scraggly ponytail.

The remaining two victims lay facedown, the legs of one overlapping the shoulders of the other. Abundant body hair suggested they, too, were adult males.

The upper member of the pair had on Champion shorts and a UV sun protection shirt. The lower member had chosen to go bare chested his last day on earth. His board shorts were lavender and blue, his head bandanna striped yellow and black.

I turned to Musgrove. Her expression was a mix of surprise and dismay. I guessed she'd been anticipating skeletons, not fleshed corpses. Another dashed expectation.

"Think we can collect the remains undamaged?" Musgrove asked Bernadin.

"I surely try my best, ma'am. I unzip the bags and, wit' some help, together we tease one underneat' each body." His words rode melodious but melancholic on the soft sea air. "And we pray dese poor souls keeps demselves in one piece."

That's what we did.

The poor souls did their part.

The Zodiac made three round trips. Two hours later, the five corpses were strapped into the coroner's van and Musgrove and I were back on shore. Hungry, tired, and desperate to shower.

As its ill-fated passengers took their final journey, Kemp and Stubbs began processing the *Cod Bless Us*. Despite the boat's apparently long time adrift, they would attempt to collect biologicals—blood, body fluids, hair, and tissue. As well, they'd search for trace evidence—fibers, soil, vegetation, glass fragments—especially at logical entry points. They'd dust for latent prints from fingers, palms, or feet. They'd record footwear patterns or tool mark impressions. They'd confiscate any drugs, firearms, or cell phones found on board. Using every trick in their CSU arsenal, they'd do their best to help answer the myriad questions on everyone's mind.

Constable Rigby drove us back to civilization in the same Jeep Wrangler that had brought us to the scene. Constable Gardiner stayed behind to guard the beach while Stubbs and Kemp were out tossing the *Cod Bless Us*.

I asked Musgrove about the need for such tight security. She said that Northwest Point was a high crime area. Taking in the uninhabited landscape and the endless, empty sea, I wondered how that could possibly be, but I didn't question her statement.

During the early part of the ride, Musgrove and I compiled a list of troubling issues. A long one. That done, we considered the logical next steps in the investigation.

Once her signal kicked in, Musgrove's phone exploded with a series of pings. She abandoned the conversation to focus on reading and sending texts. I went back to my tried and true. Window gazing.

We were rolling along the Leeward Highway, passing the Graceway IGA, when Musgrove spoke again.

"Brilliant news. Unless someone throws a spanner in the works, I have the boat inspection and autopsy sorted."

I said nothing, awaiting further explanation.

"When Kemp and Stubbs finish with the *Cod Bless Us*—" She broke off to shake her head, turn to me, and ask, "Really. What is it with these boaters and their silly names?"

I had no answer for her.

"Anyway, when the CSU team finishes and releases the scene, a marine agent will board the vessel, refuel her, and attempt to crank up the Mercs."

"The inboard motors."

"Yes. If her engines work, the *Cod* will be piloted to one of our docks. If they don't, she'll be towed."

Musgrove glanced down at the sound of yet another incoming text. Scanned the message. Resumed speaking.

"Either way, in the next few days, a forensic engineer will fly here from Miami. He'll dissect every bloody inch of her. Stem to stern, as they say."

"To determine why she ended up dead in the water."

Tight nod. "A forensic patho will accompany the engineer."

That I understood. The pathologist would analyze the five DOAs now rolling toward the TCI mortuary with the same diligence the engineer would apply to the boat. Stem to stern. Head to toe.

"Is the patho with the Miami-Dade ME?" The Miami-Dade County Medical Examiner Department is one of the largest in the country. I queried a name, figuring the person coming to TCI might be someone I knew.

"Sort of."

"Meaning?"

"His name is Harvey Lindstrom. He's a freelancer, but cuts *Y*s for Dade County when they need extra hands."

"Is he good?" I'd never heard of Harvey Lindstrom.

"He's a bit of a tosser but seems to know his stuff."

I chose not to follow up on Musgrove's character assessment. "And the engineer?"

"No idea. Lindstrom said the fellow was crackerjack and offered to make a call. The chap was available and willing to travel."

"When do they arrive?"

"By Friday." Musgrove's lips tightened into a wry smile. "Hope-fully."

"Unless someone throws a spanner in the works," I said.

"Unless that."

Unsmiling, Musgrove refocused on her phone.

A few miles later, she offered to treat me to dinner once I'd had the opportunity to shower and change.

I expressed a preference for takeout and early bed.

Looking relieved, Musgrove told Gardiner to swing by a place called Cocovan. In due course we pulled up beside an airstream trailer surrounded by outdoor tables.

"What do you like?" Musgrove asked.

"Anything that isn't puffy."

"Seriously?"

I nodded. Irrational, I know. But unless it crunches, I dislike airy food. Cheetos, okay. Chilean sea bass and omelets, not my thing.

Musgrove disappeared, returned shortly with a grease-stained paper sack, which she handed to me. Then we were rolling again.

The sack's contents smelled like something that might have earned Gordon Ramsey another star. Or maybe it was simply that I was starving. I couldn't wait to arrive at wherever I was being taken.

Still, I felt a hint of unease.

Musgrove had never described my housing.

The Cocovan sack held duck tacos and gorgonzola fries. Paired with a can of Goombay Punch that I found in the fridge—think bananas and pineapples—the meal was a Caribbean delight.

I needn't have worried about the accommodations.

Parked smack in the middle of Grace Bay beach, the Villa Renaissance describes itself as a boutique resort featuring elegantly styled one-to-seven-bedroom condos. Niceties include daily maid service, a pool with a waterside bar, tennis courts, a fitness center, and a spa.

I learned all of this by flipping through the management's propaganda materials while enjoying my island repast. But I was already aware of the amenities. I'd stayed at the complex before. In a rented condo two stories up.

My sister, Harriet Brennan Jeter Howard Daewood Crone, currently single and living in Houston, has been married four times. Thus, the impressively long list of names.

Harry wed her teen sweetheart, Brad Jeter, before the ink had dried on their high school diplomas. Brad aspired to ride the rodeo circuit but developed a severe allergy to horses. You can imagine how that worked out.

Husband number two, Howard Howard, was a west Texas oilman who lasted a few heartbeats longer than Brad. When Howard moved on, he left baby sister and their son, Kit, with very deep pockets. Estaban Daewood came and went so quickly I can't recall his face.

Harry's fourth nuptials were with Striker Crone. Their short-lived vows were exchanged under a floral trellis spanning the beach access path over which my windows now looked. The wedding party and most of the guests stayed at the Villa Renaissance.

Entering my unit felt like walking back a decade in time. Same Italian marble floor. Same granite countertops. Same fans rotating slowly overhead. Same sliding glass doors opening onto a balcony view of the spectacularly turquoise water and white sand of Grace Bay.

The Villa Renaissance was as distant from the scene at Northwest Point as Hollywood is from Appalachia. After my dinner and a very long shower I should have felt satiated and cleansed.

I felt agitated as hell.

Moved by nostalgia, I tried calling Harry. Got voice mail.

Ryan. Voice mail.

Katy. Voice mail.

Didn't anyone answer their goddam phones anymore?

But the arduous day had left me exhausted. And Musgrove would be picking me up at seven a.m. I wasn't clear why she wanted me to view the dead boaters at the morgue. But her reasoning had been persuasive. I suspected her arguments always were.

Maybe it was fatigue. Maybe Musgrove was right. Whatever. I'd agreed.

After rinsing my utensils and discarding my empty soda can and trash, I headed to the bedroom. Screw unpacking. Leaving the drapes wide, the sliding door open, I killed the light and dropped into bed.

Beyond the balcony, the pool, the dunes, and the beach, the ocean throbbed its steady rhythm. A sound that should have lulled me to sleep.

It didn't.

Like the waves, flashback visions rolled in my head. A propeller-slashed body on stainless steel. Bones in a culvert. Desiccated corpses on the deck of a boat.

Questions pounded.

Who were the "poor souls" on the *Cod Bless Us*? From what port had they sailed? When? For what purpose?

Why had they died on a vessel equipped with powerful engines? Had the system failed? Had the boat run out of gas? If so, why hadn't the skipper radioed or called for assistance?

Were the deaths accidental, a cruel but all-too-common toll extracted by the briny deep? Had the *Cod* encountered a violent storm? A rogue wave?

Or was foul play involved? Had the *Cod Bless Us* crossed paths with a malevolent human force? Had hostiles boarded the vessel and murdered everyone on it? If so, why kill the passengers and leave behind the hundred grand Sea Ray?

I'd spotted no evidence of physical trauma while bagging the bodies. No slashes or stab marks, no gunshot wounds, no blunt-instrument fractures.

I'd noted only one commonality among the dead. Every corpse looked appallingly wasted and gaunt. Was the shrinkage relevant to cause of death? A postmortem alteration caused by prolonged exposure?

Who killed Deniz Been? Was his death gang related? Was it connected to the murders here in TCI?

What had happened to Bobby Galloway, Ryder Palke, and Quentin Bonner? Were they specifically targeted? If so, why them? By whom?

At some point exhaustion won out.

I fell into a troubled sleep peopled by shadowy phantoms. Some I knew. Most I didn't.

None I would remember.

13

Musgrove arrived bearing cellophane-wrapped muffins and lidded Styrofoam cups containing good island coffee. By seven-ten we were motoring along the Leeward Highway, following the same route we'd taken with Gardiner and Rigby.

Though still post-dawn groggy, I was determined to make this outing quick. I hadn't come to TCI to inspect dead boaters. I was anxious to begin my analysis of the remains that might be Ryder Palke and Quentin Bonner. Remains that had been lying out in the elements for far too long.

Musgrove was driving a fire engine red VW Taos displaying no police logo. An air freshener in the shape of a potted plant projected from an AC vent. I suspected the small SUV was her personal vehicle.

"How's the flat?" she asked.

"Far beyond expectations." It was true. I'd anticipated an unmemorable but adequate hotel room. "Thank you so much."

"It's no biggie. The place belongs to a cousin who spends most of his time in London."

"It's very generous of him to allow a stranger into his home."

"Let's just say the bloke owes me." Delivered in a tone suggesting the topic was closed.

Today Musgrove wore jeans and a khaki shirt with the sleeves rolled to the elbows. Her hair was pulled into a spiky pony at the back of her head. Military shades and concealer failed to hide a bruise on her right cheek.

Sudden flashback image. Musgrove in my office on our first meeting. Monday's crescent-shaped discoloration was now largely gone.

This time I asked.

"Have a run-in with a door handle?" I said lightly while gesturing at her face.

Musgrove snorted a laugh. "That nails it, no pun intended. Have I told you I'm a bloody klutz? Recently I had a wall cabinet installed in my loo, and I keep forgetting the thing is there. *And* I keep leaving the door wide open. Not a good combo."

"You look good in black and blue," I joked, a bit uneasy.

Musgrove nodded but said nothing. Had the mood in the car suddenly changed? Or was I imagining it.

When I'd finished my muffin, which contained unidentifiable gummy masses but tasted pretty good, I asked about policing in TCI, mainly wanting to relieve the tension. Imagined tension?

Some of what Musgrove told me I already knew. Some I didn't.

"Only Provo and Grand Turk have detectives," she began.

"What happens on the other islands?"

"We use police boats. Or planes."

"Explain rank."

"I'm a superintendent. Below me are ASPs, assistant superintendents, and SIOs, senior investigating officers. These are the folks in charge of murder investigations. Below that level are the IOs, investigating officers, mostly detective constables or detective sergeants who deal operationally with the murder, complete the file, and attend court."

"What about forensics?" I asked, feeling this was much more detail than I needed.

"Officers in the FSU, the forensics support unit, are well trained in the collection of evidence. But the only analysis they can perform start to finish is for prints. All evidential comparisons must be sent away."

"To Miami."

"Usually."

"Tell me about the coroner."

"The coroner operates as you'd expect, in terms of notification of next of kin, death certificates, authority for autopsies, et cetera. That's how cause of death will be determined for the boaters."

"By the pathologist from Miami."

"Yes. Harvey Lindstrom."

"Where were the bodies taken?" I asked.

"To the morgue by the Cheshire Hall Medical Centre. Lindstrom prefers to do his cutting at the hospital. But the free-standing morgue isn't bad."

When I said nothing in response to that ringing endorsement, she expanded.

"The Provo mortuary isn't as big as the one on Grand Turk. That facility can store up to twenty cadavers. Ours can take six. It lacks a few things, radiology, a decent microscope, but still beats the snot out of the local funeral homes," Musgrove went on. "They have no refrigeration at all."

"Must be a motivator for quick turnarounds."

Musgrove chuckled softly at my lame joke. "The Cheshire Hall Medical Centre houses a pathology department. The catch is, as you already know, there's no resident pathologist on the island."

"So Lindstrom commutes as needed."

"He, or some other patho, is supposed to come weekly. But that doesn't always happen."

"Must be frustrating for families."

"Indeed. After an autopsy, getting the registered death certificate signed might take up to three weeks. Waiting that long can be torture for those wanting to bury a loved one."

"No death certificate, no repatriation of remains back to home soil."

"Exactly."

Musgrove made a left.

"The good news is that our mortuary has a trained technician. You met him."

I must have looked blank.

"Iggie Bernadin. The chap knows nix about bones, but he's affable and a quick learner. You'll like working with him."

Musgrove made another turn, this time onto Hospital Road. Again, I admired the straightforward approach Provo took toward naming its streets.

The Cheshire Hall Medical Centre lay straight ahead, beyond moderately well-populated parking lots, given the early hour. The lots were separated by a triangular expanse of very green, very well-manicured grass.

The hospital was larger and more modern than I expected. The front-facing portion was two-tone white and yellow stucco, long and low, with narrow white columns supporting a central overhang shading double glass doors.

Blue hurricane shutters jutted out over windows running both levels of the building. A hedge, flowering shrubs, and precisely positioned palms graced its front.

An elderly man waited in a wheelchair outside the main entrance, gnarled hands resting on the curved handle of his cane, legs covered with a homemade multicolored wool blanket. The patchwork pattern made me think of the many afghans Gran had crocheted. Or maybe it was the old gent's knobby fingers.

I flicked a wave at Gramps as we rolled by. He didn't respond. Perhaps didn't see. Maybe didn't care.

Musgrove continued past the hospital to a small building of similar design but significantly less elegant landscaping. She parked on the strip of asphalt abutting the structure and we both got out.

An unmarked glass door gave onto a no-nonsense lobby. Mint green cinder block walls. Gray tile floor. Wooden chairs lining two sides. Unmanned desk straight ahead.

Our entrance must have triggered an alarm in back. Almost immediately, a man appeared through a door to the left of the desk.

I hadn't taken much note of Iggie Bernadin the previous day. Now I couldn't imagine how that had happened.

Bernadin was thin—very thin—with purple-black skin that gleamed like a well-polished eggplant. His hair, fast retreating from his forehead, was gray and buzzed close to his scalp. A raised scar squiggled like a night crawler beside his left eye.

"Iggie, this is Dr. Brennan." Musgrove made introductions. "You two met yesterday."

"Yes, ma'am," Iggie said, smiling with rows of teeth that testified to years of smoking.

"You did a terrific job with the body bags," I said, extending a hand.

When we shook, Iggie's palm felt rough as steel wool.

"Thank you, ma'am. I does my best."

Musgrove got straight to the point. "Since Dr. Lindstrom won't arrive until tomorrow, I'd like to get on with prelims. Take photos. Search for IDs. You know the drill. If we pull any names, my investigators can begin making inquiries."

"Yes, ma'am. I roll them out to you one by one?"

"That would be good."

As Bernadin disappeared down the short hall, Musgrove turned to me. "In the meantime, hopefully I'll get word regarding the boat's registration. You ready?"

"Always."

Musgrove led me to a bank of lockers where we suited up over our civvies. Paper caps, gowns, and shoe covers. Masks. Gloves.

From the dressing area we crossed to an unremarkable autopsy room outfitted with the usual paraphernalia.

Bernadin joined us shortly, similarly garbed. The gurney he was pushing held a black body bag.

Following a nod from Musgrove, Bernadin prepared a handwritten ID card and shot several pics. Then he unzipped the bag.

The teen lay inside, his skin more shriveled, his orange hair damp with refrigeration. Otherwise, he looked as I remembered him.

"Check his labels, his pockets," Musgrove directed.

The neon green shirt yielded nothing. A quick two-handed pat down, then Iggie pulled a plastic rectangle from a side pocket of the shorts. Gingerly laying his find on the counter, he stepped aside so Musgrove and I could see.

"Kyle Samuel Overby." Musgrove read the name from a driver's license issued by the state of Florida. "Lived in Vero Beach. Born in 2008."

"Sixteen years old," I said, feeling the same gut twist I'd felt at first seeing the kid on the boat.

"Note the expiration date."

"Jesus. He'd had his license less than a year."

The twist tightened as I imagined the boy's joy at having successfully navigated that adolescent rite of passage.

We moved on.

I observed each victim, vigilant for the subtlest hint of trauma. Iggie searched for personal items and took photos. Musgrove dictated notes into her phone.

By ten we'd collected four licenses, one Mastercard, one Visa, one comb, a set of keys, and five hundred and eighty-nine dollars in badly weathered cash. The licenses and credit cards provided three additional names. In all, we had four presumptive IDs:

Kyle Samuel Overby, sixteen, a resident of Vero Beach, Florida.

Samuel Joseph Overby, forty-nine, a resident of Vero Beach, Florida.

Conrad Paul Malvino, forty-six, a resident of Fort Pierce, Florida.

Martin Patrick Doyle, thirty-two, a resident of Grand Harbor, Grand Cayman.

The bare-chested passenger had opted to carry nothing on his person.

I spotted zilch to indicate why these people were dead. But the state of their bodies was suggesting a gruesome possibility.

"What do you think?" Musgrove asked at one point.

"I hate to speculate before Lindstrom has a look at the internal organs."

"Do it anyway."

"It appears there's been a lot of postmortem shrinkage. Still."

"Still?"

"Did your investigators find fresh water on the boat?"

"I'll have to ask them. Why?"

I hesitated. Reluctant. Recalling a similar case from Montreal years back.

"My impression is that these people died from lack of nourishment."

"They starved to death?"

"Or died of dehydration."

Musgrove curled her fingers in a "give me more" gesture.

"A person can survive weeks without access to food."

"Seriously? Weeks?"

"The body breaks down tissue and stored fat, releasing fuel that allows the organs to continue to function. But there's no way to replace fluids."

"Meaning?"

"Water is critical. Most people can survive only two to four days without drinking."

"Didn't Gandhi go three weeks without food?"

"Perfect example. Gandhi stopped eating but allowed himself sips of water."

Musgrove studied the final body lying on its gurney.

"Do you recall the case of Nancy Cruzan?" I asked.

Musgrove shook her head without raising her eyes to me.

"She was at the center of a famous Supreme Court decision. Long story short, Cruzan was in a persistent vegetative state for many years until she died twelve days after sustenance was discontinued. Since that time, there have been many other reports on terminated feeding in PVS patients. Death typically occurs after ten to fourteen days."

"You think that's what happened here?"

"I'm only speculating. Lindstrom will determine cause of death when he does the autopsies."

Musgrove's mobile buzzed. Sliding the device from under her gown, she glanced at the screen. Clicked on.

"Musgrove."

A buzzy voice sounded. I could make out no words.

"Hold on." Musgrove was also having difficulty hearing. "You're breaking up."

Tipping her head to indicate that she'd take the call in the hall, she elbowed open the door, phone to one ear, free finger pressed to the other.

I looked at Bernadin. He gave me a smile, toothy and yellow as a New York taxi.

"I be wit' you again shortly," he said.

"Thanks. I'm fine by myself."

Bernadin withdrew, grinning the whole way out.

The second hand made its rounds of an old-fashioned analog clock on one wall.

Tic. Tic. Tic.

Eight ticky circuits, then Musgrove was back.

"The *Cod Bless Us* belongs to Martin Patrick Doyle and is registered out of the Bahamas. The boat left Nassau twelve days ago, never returned to the marina."

"Did she not have radar? A navigation system? A radio?" I asked, perplexed.

"The engineer will determine all that."

"Did no one notice that the *Cod* was gone a long time?"

Musgrove gave one of her lilting shrugs.

"Was Doyle reported missing?"

Another shrug.

"How far is Nassau from Provo?" I asked.

"Roughly six hundred miles."

I said nothing. Pictured all that open sea.

Musgrove was about to comment further when her mobile rang again. She answered with a not so gracious, "Musgrove."

The caller launched in, galloped forward, not pausing for breath. This time the voice was male. And the reception was good.

Apparently, the news was not.

Musgrove's cheeks flushed as she reacted with fervor.

"Sonofafreakingzombiebitchanditsspawn!"

I had to respect that.

"Keep me looped in. I mean everything. Every. Bloody. Thing."

Not waiting for a response, Musgrove clicked off and pressed the phone to her chest. She stared at me, face pinched and anxious.

1 4

waited, alarmed but not wishing to elevate Musgrove's distress.

Tic.

Tic.

Tic.

Then, "There may be another."

I cocked a brow.

"Another MP."

"Shit," I said.

"High and deep on this one. The man's name is Calvin Cloke. Goes by CC."

Of course, he does. I didn't say it.

"Cloke's an FBI special agent. He arrived in Provo six days ago."

"On assignment?"

"Unclear."

"Wouldn't a special agent here on official business announce himself to your office? As a courtesy?"

"I would assume so."

"What's his—"

"All I know is Cloke landed on the island, rented a car, then slipped off the radar. Now the folks back home have started making inquiries."

"Sounds a bit like Quentin Bonner and the others."

"Yes." Terse. "Though most tourists rent vehicles when they arrive. Hopefully, Cloke's just having himself a bender. Or he's off shagging the love of his life."

There seemed little chance of that.

"My investigators are on it. When they know more, we'll know more. In the meantime, let's focus on the remains for which I brought you from Montreal."

That's what we did.

By eleven a.m., Musgrove and I were turning from the Millennium Highway onto a narrow sand road in the Wheeland Settlement. A sign identified a complex to our left as the TCI waste disposal facility. Musgrove drove past it until the road dead-ended at the edge of a woodland. I guessed the distance at roughly two hundred yards.

Ahead, an unoccupied Jeep sat just before the trees, the usual decal declaring it the property of the RTCIPF. The CSU van waited at its front bumper.

The same pair of techs occupied the van's front seat, Stubbs at the wheel, Kemp riding shotgun. Both sat silent.

As we drew closer, I could see that the empty Jeep straddled an opening in the trees. The path, if it could be called that, was little more than a thinning of the trunks and the ground cover spreading across the sand between them.

When Musgrove rolled to a stop, Kemp and Stubbs alighted. So did we.

The sun was mid-morning high, struggling to bump the sky from a dirt gray to a lighter dirt gray. The air was already muggy and warm.

Musgrove spoke as we walked toward the two constables.

"The site's been guarded twenty-four/seven since the bones were reported last Friday. My people came, strung tape, shot pics. I can't vouch for what went on before we took over."

Though I agreed in principle with Musgrove's plan, I felt sympathy for those tasked with round-the-clock surveillance for six days. Said nothing.

Musgrove slapped at a mosquito lunching on her cheek, flicked the corpse, unrolled her sleeves down to wrist level. Drawing a can of Cutter insect repellent from her shoulder-hanging satchel, she coated her exposed skin, and handed the can to me.

I sprayed with alacrity. Forget organics—eucalyptus and essential oils. When it comes to mosquitoes, fleas, ticks, black flies, whatever, I douse liberally with the chemicals that will get the job done.

Moving in a cloud of Cutter, Musgrove and I continued forward. When we'd joined Kemp and Stubbs, Musgrove spoke again, her comments directed to me but for her subordinates' benefit.

"My officers know their stuff. Direct them clearly, they'll do a crack-up job."

Kemp smiled and overnodded his willingness to help. Stubbs's expression remained impassive.

"Which set of remains is at this location?" I asked, thinking of the pics I'd viewed back in Montreal.

"Both," Musgrove said.

One part of the story bothered me.

"When we first met in my offices, you said a fisherman found the bones?" My tone implied a question.

"Achilles Slanter."

"What was Slanter doing in these woods?"

"Claimed he was hunting mushrooms. Said his mama's favorites grow here."

"What's his story?"

"Slanter says he was here with his dog, Thursday."

"Wait. A full week ago?"

"Thursday is the dog. As Slanter tells it, when Thursday took to yapping at a mound of sand, he poked with his 'shroom stick and hit something hard. He dug a bit, stripped away vines and creepers, spotted a human skull."

"That explains the first set of bones."

"Yes. Hoping to score easy money, who knows how the chap thought that would work, Slanter dragged Thursday and his son back out the next day for a wider look-see."

"They found the second set."

Musgrove nodded. "That pooch must have one helluva nose. Less entrepreneurial than his old man, the kid insisted they call the cops."

"Does his account sound reasonable?"

"We ran the old geezer a million ways to Sunday. And the son. Both checked out clean." Musgrove arced an arm toward the van. "Shall we suit up?"

Wordlessly, the four of us donned the usual Tyvek zip-ups and booties. While doing so, we discussed strategy.

The sandy substrate made pushing a wheeled gurney or cart impossible. Since we were expecting only dry bones, we decided to keep our equipment to a minimum. Should we encounter the unexpected, someone could return to the van for whatever was needed. Or we could call for backup.

We entered the woods single file. Constable. Detective. Anthropologist. Constable.

Kemp lugged a wooden-framed screen and two collapsible sawhorses. Stubbs shouldered pruning shears and shovels, buckets swinging on their handles. Musgrove and I hauled recovery kits.

I'd viewed the scene photos in Montreal, studied them more closely while riding out from the morgue. Soon I began to recognize the terrain. A Jamaican caper tree here. A pair of wild tamarinds there.

Before long, a uniformed cop materialized within the fuzzy web of light seeping through the foliage overhead. Tall and needle-thin, the man's gray hair and furrowed skin—a shade somewhere between that of mud and dead leaves—made a postscript of his youth.

The man's body language radiated unhappiness as clearly as Plante's had at Bickerdike Basin. Or maybe the old guy was just tired. Shoulder-slumped, head turtling forward on a reedy neck, he turned at the sound of us rattling his way.

The man's name plaque said *Constable Love*. As Musgrove and I set down our cases, she requested a briefing.

Voice flatlined with displeasure, fatigue, or boredom, Love said he'd been in position since shift handoff at midnight. Save for two dogs, an armada of geckos, and one misguided bat, no one and nothing had come calling.

"Where's the first vic?" Musgrove asked.

"Just yonder." A skinny digit pointed downward over the right side of the path. "Ground slopes like a sonofabitch into a ravine. First DOA's at the bottom. The other's a slog into the woods." The digit veered left. "That away."

"Is this a good place to set up?" Musgrove asked, looking around.

"You won't get no further with all that truck." Love chin-cocked our collection of gear.

Musgrove circled a hand in the air, then pointed at the ground. Kemp found a level spot on the path and began assembling the screen. Stubbs dug out video and still cameras and started filming.

I opened my kit and ran through my somewhat OCD pre-op check. Evidence bags. Syringe tubes. Labels. Scale. Scalpels. Hammer. Trowel. Dental picks. Tweezers. Tape measure. Magnifier. Bone chart. You get the picture.

When Stubbs was satisfied with her footage, and I was satisfied with my inventory, we began picking our way downhill, zigzagging from tree to tree to keep from hurtling at the whim of gravity. Harder for me, still dragging my kit.

The photos I'd viewed had also been shot by Constable Stubbs. Her capture of the scene was spot on, the colors true, the distances and angles undistorted. The yellow tape. The tea-brown bones. The faded denim.

The first skeleton lay at the bottom of the incline. It had darkened considerably over time, rendering it almost invisible within the ground cover, both living and dead.

Musgrove, Stubbs, and Kemp watched as I squatted beside the bones. Listened as I dictated notes onto my iPhone.

"The skull is rotated in a way inconsistent with the orientation of the vertebrae. The mandible is detached from the skull, but with little displacement."

I paused, feeling that familiar kink in my gut. The victim's empty orbits seemed to stare up at the sky, as though startled to find themselves in this new situation.

My eyes roved the remains. Stem to stern.

"The decedent is lying on his or her left side. Most bones are present and in anatomical position."

My gaze spread outward, searching for elements that might be AWOL. Came up empty.

I rose, knees protesting the sudden shift in weight.

"The left hand is missing. Constable Kemp, please grid-walk the area." To Musgrove and Stubbs. "You two, please assist me."

I'm a skeptic of the "scene processing must follow strict archaeological protocol" school of thought. Yes, everything must be properly labeled and photographed *in situ*, cataloged, bagged, and sealed. Yes, contextual info is as important as physical evidence. Yes, all soil must be screened lest tiny items be missed. But I see no need for fancy grids, measurement to the millimeter, and excavation by minute stratigraphic levels.

The steep gradient rendered the archaeology versus practicality argument moot. While Kemp searched for the missing hand, Musgrove and I did our best to lay out a rough ten-by-ten-foot square using the old tried and true. Stakes and string. Then I dislodged, collected, and tagged evidence, while Musgrove hauled buckets of dirt to the screen and Stubbs sifted. Kemp joined us when he'd finished his search, which yielded nothing.

By six we'd collected every bone and associated fragment of clothing. Surprisingly, nothing else. None of the usual cigarette butts, candy wrappers, condoms, or aluminum cans.

Good news: the site truly was off the beaten path. Bad news: the killer had left nothing behind.

Stubbs and Kemp drove the boxed bones to the morgue in the CSU van.

Stripping off our PPE, Musgrove and I climbed into her Taos. Exhausted, filthy, and, despite drenching ourselves with Cutter, itchy with bites, we rode in silence, not in the mood for conversation.

Musgrove's mobile rang as soon as we reconnected with signal. She answered, listened. Asked a clipped question or two. I didn't bother to eavesdrop. Figured she'd share what was relevant.

She did.

"That was Delroy Monck, one of my SIOs." Musgrove tossed her phone onto the dash. "You'll meet him. Everyone refers to him as 'The Monk.'"

"He's okay with that?"

"Beats Delroy."

Del was another option. Or Roy. I didn't say it.

"The bloke's Irish-Jamaican and claims descent from royalty," Musgrove continued.

"There's a sizable Irish population in Jamaica?"

Musgrove viewed me as if I'd asked if cheese was edible.

"When Jamaica was captured from the Spanish in 1655, Oliver Cromwell ordered thousands of Irish transported to the island, primarily to work the plantations. Two years later, King James II appointed Christopher Monck, the Second Duke of Albemarle, as Lieutenant Governor."

"You know a lot about Jamaican history," I said.

"British history is my hobby. Jamaican history is The Monk's passion. If you ask him anything, be prepared for a long oration."

"Noted."

"Anyway, Monck pulled some intel on Doyle and the *Cod Bless Us*. Doyle's outing was to be a six-hour fishing charter."

"So Doyle would've provided food and water for a day."

"Presumably."

"No one reported him missing?"

"The bloke was a loner, lived by himself. Correction. A turtle named Irma inhabited a pen in his kitchen."

"What about Doyle's passengers? No one missed them?"

"Apparently their two-week trip to the Bahamas was to be a macho bonding thing. Overby and his son, Kyle, and Overby's two buddies made a big deal of allowing no female 'meddling,' as Malvino's wife put it. The men swore a pact agreeing to zero communication with those back home. Wanted to teach Kyle how real men operate."

"Sounds like a dick move to me."

"Ya *think*?" Musgrove's response oozed disdain.

"The group had been incommunicado since leaving home, so no one noticed when they went radio silent," I reasoned out loud.

"Yes."

"Who was the shirtless guy?"

"Barry Bernstein, age forty-three, also a resident of Vero Beach."

"The boat ran out of gas and ended up six hundred miles from home. Jesus. How does that happen?"

"Hopefully the engineer will find something to explain it. Lindstrom confirmed they'd both arrive in Provo early tomorrow. The guy's name is Flores, by the way. Lindstrom plans to complete all needed autopsies by the end of the weekend."

"Sounds ambitious."

"His call. Since we'll be out collecting the second set of bones tomorrow, I scheduled a meet for Saturday morning. Probably best you sit in."

Musgrove didn't make that meeting.

By Saturday, she was dead.

15

F riday was another day of bones and bugs. A more complicated one since the second skeleton was scattered over an area approximately forty meters square. Bone distribution suggested tag team scavengers. Gnaw mark patterning suggested dogs.

By seven p.m. we'd collected everything but three distal toe phalanges.

And the left hand. Search as we might, the hand was nowhere to be found.

Musgrove insisted on taking me to a place called Da Conch Shack before dropping me at my condo. When I mentioned our less than immaculate state, she handed me wet wipes and said we'd be sitting outside.

Hunger trumped hygiene. I didn't argue.

Ten minutes later we were barefooting down a sand trail bordered by sun-bleached conch shells. Hundreds of them. The path led to a cluster of tables that would have made Schiaparelli proud. The luminous paint looked joyful against the white sand.

We'd just slid onto benches when a pink-shirted waiter appeared at Musgrove's side, cocoa skin glistening with sweat, enormous teeth beaming. The two hugged like old friends. Which they probably were. The waiter's name was Arthur.

A moment of small talk, then Musgrove ordered a drink whose name implied an overly complicated relationship with rum. I craved the solace the magic brown liquid would bring, the fiery trip down my throat, the honeyed warmth in my gut. In deference to my history with booze, I asked for island punch, virgin style.

Arthur had barely gone when Musgrove's phone pinged an incoming text. Her brows rose as she read the message.

"I'll be damned." Murmured under her breath as she tossed the device onto the table.

"Good news?" I asked.

She waggled a hand, maybe yes, maybe no. "I sent out feelers and just got some preliminary feedback. Best I don't elaborate until I know more."

While awaiting our drinks, we eyed the rolling surf on Blue Hills Beach. At least I did. Musgrove seemed distracted. After what felt like a full minute of tense silence, I tried to reengage.

"Big weekend plans?" I asked.

"What? Oh, right. After the briefing tomorrow morning—" Her tired eyes met mine. "You are coming, right?"

"I'd like to get started on—"

"I think you should hear what Flores has to say. You know. To get the whole picture."

"Sure." Uneasy with the intensity in her voice. "I'll be there."

"Good. To answer your question, after Flores I'm going over to Grand Turk to see my sister. She lives in Cockburn Town." Sudden thought. "Unless you want me to stay here in Provo. I can—"

"No, not at all. I'll be diving into those bones right after the meeting. Hopefully with someone to assist?"

"Iggie will be at the morgue." Then, as though struck by a sudden gap in her planning, "I'll have an officer leave a vehicle at your condo tonight. Are you comfortable driving?"

"Of course." I wasn't. In TCI they drive on the left, love roundabouts, and haven't a single traffic light in the whole country. Not one. On any island.

Musgrove was already dialing when Arthur returned. Her beverage was tall and frosty and topped with enough fruit to supply a school lunch program. Mine had no garnish.

I took a sip. Despite the name, it had no punch, either.

Glancing at the menu Arthur set before me, I could see that Da Shack was true to its name. Conch fritters. Conch chowder. Conch salad. Conch stew. Conch curry. Beaucoup fish.

Musgrove went for the grilled snapper. I chose the cracked conch with peas and rice. We shared an order of Johnny fries.

Musgrove was right. The food was well worth the detour.

I was back at my condo by nine. As I showered, a text from Musgrove landed on my phone.

Vehicle parked in slot belonging to your unit. Honda Accord. Keys under the fender on the left front tire.

Crafty, I thought. That'll foil any thief.

After crawling into bed, I dialed Ryan. He answered before the end of the second ring. Buzz. Whatever.

"*Bonjour, ma chère. Comment ça va?*"

"I'm good," I said. "You sound tired."

"Long couple of days."

"Are the bangers still playing their sick little game? What's it called?"

"Scoring. An eighteen-year-old was shot yesterday on rue Ducas near Parc Angrignon. He's at LaSalle Hospital, may or may not make it."

"What's the story?"

"There isn't one. The kid was crossing a parking lot, and some-one capped him."

"Is he gang affiliated?"

"Apparently not. How about you? How goes your island quest?"

"It's not a quest. A dog named Thursday found the bones before I got here. We spent the past two days collecting them."

"You and Musgrove?"

"And her CSU team. They're quite good."

"Now what?"

"Today, an engineer from Miami inspected the boat carrying the five DOAs. Tomorrow, he briefs us on what he's learned."

"Have the vics been IDed?"

I listed the names and described their manly bonding scheme.

"Sounds like exceptionally dumbass thinking."

"The passengers are all from Florida."

"Makes sense now."

"That's not what I meant."

Ryan stifled a yawn.

"Am I keeping you up?" I asked.

"Not very well. Why are dead boaters your concern?"

I'd asked myself that same question.

"Musgrove can be very persuasive," I said. "How's Birdie?"

"Displeased with the canned food I bought."

"He only likes the pâté style."

"Now you tell me. When do you think you'll return to Montreal?"

"Soon," I said, not really believing it.

A little mushy stuff from Ryan, then we disconnected.

I was asleep by ten.

The Honda was there as promised, a boxy affair whose mustard yellow paint was losing its battle with rust. I guessed the thing had rolled off the assembly line back in the sixties. And had a hard life since. The windshield was cracked. The AC worked but had only a vague understanding of what it was supposed to do.

Fifteen minutes after setting out, I pulled into the lot at the RTCIPF Grace Bay Station. Inside, a uniformed officer inspected my ID, then led me down a short hall to a small back room. Offered coffee. Disappeared.

Luna Flores, the forensic engineer, was already there. And contrary to Musgrove's assumption, Flores *wasn't* a guy but a sister double X—I refer to chromosomes, of course.

Flores's hair was black and styled in a no-nonsense boy cut, her skin cinnamon, her eyes a heart-stopping blue. Based on a hint of jawline sag, crinkling at the eye corners, and the presence of a few renegade gray hairs, I guessed her age at mid-fifties minimum.

Flores wore cargo pants, probably size six extra-long, and a shirt several shades quieter than her eyes. Small gold hoops hung from both ears.

She was seated in one of four folding chairs at a government-issue gray metal table. She rose when I appeared. Following a handshake and self-intros, I took a place opposite her.

Like me, Flores didn't excel at casual banter. We exchanged a few comments about breakfast, the weather, her flight to Provo. The woman's accent and vocabulary suggested she'd probably grown up rough. Maybe Miami. Definitely south Florida.

When our awkward exchange petered out, I checked my surroundings. The room was cramped and stuffy and had no view to exploit. Photos of Queen Elizabeth II and the island's governor, Nigel John Dakin, hung on one wall. With the queen having passed not that long ago, I wondered vaguely if someone had dropped the ball by not putting the image of King Charles up there. Did British territory police departments get demerits for such things?

Minutes dragged by.

Five.

Ten.

Flores and I repeatedly checked our watches. Our phones. Neither of us commented on Musgrove's tardiness.

Perhaps uncomfortable with the silence, perhaps out of genuine curiosity, eventually Flores asked about my field. I explained forensic anthropology, then queried her training.

Flores held a doctorate in naval architecture and marine engineering from the University of Michigan and had interned with the US Department of Defense. She'd passed both the FE, Fundamentals of Engineering, and the NCEES, National Council of Examiners for Engineering and Surveying exams. She'd worked for ExxonMobil, MAERSK, the Virginia Department of Transportation. She was currently employed by the McKee Engineering Group, a private outfit headquartered in Miami.

No question the woman was qualified.

By eleven we'd both checked our mobiles a billion times. And we'd both run out of patience. I wanted to begin examining the two sets of bones. Flores undoubtedly had plans of her own.

"This is bullshit."

I looked up.

Flores eyes were on me, showing a ferocious and somewhat unnerving intensity.

"Let me phone her," I said.

"I did that."

"I'll try again."

I dialed. Got voice mail. Left a less than serene message.

"Shall I go out front to see if she's called the main line here?"

Flores nodded.

The cop at the desk was not the same one who'd parked me with Flores. This guy was short with well-muscled arms. Or maybe he carried his height in his legs. His name tag said *R. Chanson*. He was perusing a copy of *Popular Mechanics*.

R. Chanson was exceedingly uninformative. Or skillfully evasive. He knew nothing about Musgrove's nonappearance. Offered to phone her mobile. When I told him I'd done that, he shrugged.

I asked R. Chanson to contact Delroy Monck. Knowing who I meant, he punched a few keys. Listened.

Voice mail, he explained, cupping the receiver.

I requested that he leave my name and number. Provided both.

R. Chanson did as asked, disconnected, and picked up his magazine. I was being dismissed.

I rejoined Flores. A yellow legal pad now lay on the tabletop before her. A pen.

I shook my head to indicate that I'd learned nothing.

"Look, I can't fuck around here all day." The cant of her neck and shoulders told me she was pissed as hell. "I have things to do."

"As do I."

"Here's how it's going to play." Jabbing the pen toward my chair.

Irked at Flores's arrogant tone, I took my time sitting.

"You got pen and paper?"

"I prefer to record notes on my phone." I scrolled to the appropriate app.

"Suit yourself. I'm going to give you a quick verbal. If Musgrove has questions, she knows where to find me. Otherwise, everything will be in my report."

I gestured with a twirled finger that she should proceed.

"The boat was in perfect working order, but out of gas. The captain—"

"Martin Patrick Doyle," I supplied while trying to process what Flores had just said.

"Doyle had an onboard management system that connected to his mobile device. VesselView."

"VesselView is a program that transfers data to a phone." I wanted to be sure I understood.

"Yes. The captain uses Bluetooth to display gauge information on his or her iPhone or Android. The system allows him or her to monitor all engines and customize data points across screens. Got it?"

I nodded, not totally clear but figuring I could google a full explanation later.

"The captain receives alerts if something isn't right with the engine. The program assists with troubleshooting. I'm really abbreviating here."

"It would troubleshoot a problem like low fuel?"

"Yes."

"Doyle was an experienced captain."

"So I'm told."

"How could he have run out of gas?" I began spitting out issues as they came to me. "Wouldn't he have known the tank was low? Why didn't he radio for help or head back to the marina?"

"Excellent questions. Which I can't answer."

"And where the hell is Musgrove?"

"And another."

More tense silence.

As minutes ticked by, I felt my gut clench. Musgrove was anxious to clarify these boater deaths. She'd been planning to visit her sister after this meeting.

There are cells in my subconscious that nag when something smells off. I suspect everyone has them. But mine can be quite bullish. Right then they were clamorously sounding alarms.

"This isn't right," I said.

"What's not right is this bitch wasting my time."

"I've gotten to know Detective Musgrove over the past week. I'm certain she wouldn't just blow us off."

Flores studied me, blue eyes hard.

"She could be sick," I said. "We should check on her."

"Hell no. Colossal hell no."

"Let's swing by her home."

"Chica, my time here is limited. I—"

"So is mine, *chica*. And I have two DOAs waiting at the morgue."

Several seconds passed. Then Flores lips drew up on one side. "You know where she lives?"

"I do." Sort of. Musgrove had once mentioned the name of the complex.

"Okay." Flores stood. "The lady better have one righteous excuse."

16

"How did we ever find our own asses before these navigation apps?" Flores asked, not really wanting an answer.

"Rand McNally and gas station attendants," I said.

"What's a gas station attendant?"

In one thousand feet, turn right.

I did as the Google Maps lady instructed. Turned again when she directed me two minutes later.

You've arrived at your destination. Your destination is on the left.

She was correct. Lettering on a low stone wall said *Leeward Townhomes*, the info I'd entered into the program. We were on Walnut Road, a quiet, palm-shaded street unfashionably far from the ocean.

Leeward was technically a gated community. But the wrought-iron barrier stood wide and unlocked.

"Tight security," Flores snorted.

I entered the property and followed an oyster shell drive to the townhomes. There were eight in all, faded avocado stucco, strung together in a single row. The roof was blue metal, the hurricane shutters a dirty white.

"Which is her pad?" Flores asked, unbuckling her seat belt.

"I don't know the number."

"Are you shitting me?"

"Look for a bright red Taos." Already scanning for Musgrove's VW.

"That it?" Flores indicated a vehicle to our right.

"Good eye."

I drove to the end of the shells and parked beside Musgrove's SUV. We both got out.

Rain was falling now, a persistent drip that made me think of a leaky tap. A drip that looked like it might continue until someone called a plumber. Or got a wrench.

While passing the Taos, I peeked through the windshield. Saw the potted plant air freshener jutting from the AC vent.

Noticing Flores lay a hand on the hood, I raised both brows in question.

"Cold," she said. "This puppy hasn't gone anywhere for a while."

We walked a smaller oyster shell path bisecting a dolefully dry patch of grass. Stepped onto a low concrete stoop covered by the same blue material topping the complex.

The front door, a perkier green than the walls, had a brass knocker shaped like a conch. I lifted the corroded shell and tapped three times.

Nothing.

I tapped again. With more force.

More nothing.

I looked at Flores. She shrugged. Whatever.

The door's handle was an old-fashioned key-operated affair, with a long scrolly grip and square push button.

I grasped the pull and thumbed the button.

The latch disengaged and the door popped open a hair.

I looked at Flores.

"Now here's a bitch of a legal dilemma," she said.

Fleetingly, I thought of legal dilemmas.

"I say we dime the cops." Flores sounded adamant.

"How about we call out but don't enter the premises?" I countered.

The vivid blues rolled. The rain was picking up and Flores's enthusiasm, never monumental, was quickly fading.

Creating a six-inch gap, I shouted into the condo.

"Detective Musgrove?"

No response.

"Detective Musgrove." Louder. "Ti? It's Tempe Brennan."

Silence.

I was about to yield to Flores's undoubtedly wiser advice when the wind blew in a sudden hard gust, ripping the rain-slicked handle from my fingers. The door flew inward and smacked a wall.

Crack!

Sounds drifted out. A male voice, harsh with anger. A female reply, high and stretched and trembling with fear.

A scream.

I didn't think. I rushed in.

The small, tiled foyer had a mirrored wall on the left, a sideboard on the right. A rubber floor mat sat beside the door. An umbrella stand occupied one corner. Ahead, a staircase rose to a second floor.

Though my heart was racing, my id was logging minutiae like a court reporter on steroids. Later I'd recall details I didn't remember taking in.

The sideboard was a jarring electric blue. On it sat several framed photos: a dog on a bench; a horse in a paddock; a middle-aged woman in a sweater far too large for her frame.

The floor mat held sandals and boots, the latter the lace-up kind Musgrove and I had worn in the field. Cast-off sand surrounded the footwear.

The umbrella stand was ceramic and decorated with Chinese figures and symbols. The word *brollies* scrolled across the front.

The staircase had a polished wooden handrail and a faux-leopard runner. Parallel tracks in the nap indicated recent vacuuming. A framed poster for Prince's 2007 Earth tour at London's O2 arena decorated the wall beside the risers.

To the right of the stairs, across a narrow hall, an archway gave onto an expanded space. Through the opening I could see the arm of a sofa beside an overturned end table. Spilling from the table, a broken lamp, a shattered vase, scattered flowers.

The voices, much louder now, were coming from that room. Sounding affected? Melodramatic?

Barely breathing, I grabbed an umbrella and crept forward. Flores followed, not exactly on my heels, but close enough.

At the archway, we both froze.

Musgrove lay supine on a woven jute rug, face ashen, lips and eyelids violet-blue. From the angle of her head, the striated bruising stark against the softness of her throat, I suspected she'd been strangled, and her neck broken.

"Oh, Christ," Flores whispered.

Fingers shaky, I punched digits on my phone.

"Nine one one," a female voice came on. "How may I help you?"

"I want to report a homicide!" I barked.

"I'm having trouble understanding you, ma'am. Can you lower the volume on your television?" Barely interested. "And speak more clearly."

"Fuck, fuck, fuck." Flores crossed to a flat screen blaring at a decibel level equal to that on an airport runway. Using a shirt tail, she lifted a remote and hit a button. The actors' bickering voices went mute.

I kept talking. "Your SIO has been killed."

"Please repeat." No longer bored. "And provide your location."

Death is my business. I see it daily. Yet here I was, acting like a rookie cop at her first murder scene.

I tried again. Slower.

"Detective Tiersa Musgrove is dead. I am Dr. Temperance Brennan. I'm at her residence. Dr. Luna Flores is with me."

"The *superintendent?*" the dispatcher asked, leaning into Musgrove's title. She seemed shaken.

"Yes." I provided a more coherent synopsis.

"Do you need medical attention?"

"No." Jesus.

"Do you need me to stay on the line?"

"No."

"Help is on the way."

Dead air.

Phone pressed to my chest, I breathed deeply, and looked around.

The room was small and furnished very matchy-matchy. Sofa and side chair. Coffee and end tables. All probably ordered online.

My eyes drifted to the now silent TV.

Days of Our Lives. That accounted for the male and female voices we'd heard outside the door. This certainly was a day to remember. Funny where your brain goes in moments of stress.

My gaze returned to the battered body on the rug.

I almost wept at the irony of the dispatcher's words.

Tiersa Musgrove was beyond whatever help was barreling our way.

The rain had stopped, so Flores and I decided to wait outside. It wasn't long before we heard the distant whine of sirens, faint at first, earsplitting as cruisers flew around the corner and screamed up Walnut.

Soon vehicles crammed the street and the oyster shell drive, jammed at random angles, engines running, occupants warily scanning their surroundings. The strobing lights turned the path, the lawn, and the stucco at our backs into a pulsating red and blue tableau.

The armada included three prowlers, an unmarked Ford Explorer, the now familiar CSU truck, and an ambulance. Given the carnival-parade character of their arrival, I figured the media wouldn't be far behind.

I watched a man maneuver from behind the wheel of the Explorer, long, spindly legs preceding the rest of him by several seconds. His pants were orange, maybe meant for golf, his shoes pale suede loafers, minimally size thirteen. No socks.

When the man's upper body appeared, it was equally as gangly as his lower limbs. And missing its left arm. His shirt was an eye-blistering white, its long sleeves pressed into creases sharp enough to cut through cheddar. No tie. No blazer.

The man's prosthetic hand looked like something designed by the Star Wars special effects team. His hair, curly on top and scalp-buzzed on the sides, was shiny and black. I put his age at a bump south of forty.

On seeing Spindly Legs, the six cops exited their cruisers. Car doors winging, radios spitting static onto the moist morning air, they stood at relaxed attention, awaiting instruction.

Spindly Legs crossed to the nearest pair. The three conversed, then he turned and strode in our direction. Behind him, the duo split to talk to the other teams, presumably to share a plan of action.

Drawing near the stoop, Spindly Legs pulled a badge from his belt and extended it toward us with his prosthetic hand. His skin was caramel, his freckles so dark they stood out like chocolate sprinkles on coffee ice cream.

"Detective Delroy Monck," he said. "Division B, Grace Bay Station."

Flores and I nodded. The Monk, I thought.

"Which one's Brennan?"

"I am," I said.

"You called in the nine one one?" Monck's voice was that of a well-aged oboe, the shaping of his vowels suggestive of both London and the islands. And a high level of tightly wrapped anger.

"I did."

"What do we have here?" Drawing a pen and notepad from a pocket of the relentlessly crisp shirt.

"A homicide."

"I'll decide about that."

"I know a homicide when I see one."

"Do you." A pause, then, "Did either of you spot anyone else on the premises?"

I shook my head. So did Flores.

"Did you search the town house?"

"The moment we saw Musgrove we called it in."

"Did you touch anything?"

"At the request of the dispatcher, the TV remote. No naked fingers."

"Did you manipulate the body—"

"I know my way around a death scene," I said, a bit too sharply.

"Stay here." Barked with an intensity that startled us both.

Monck gestured two uniforms into the house. Shortly, they declared the scene clear. Monck gloved his right hand, slipped on shoe covers, and disappeared through the front door.

Twenty minutes later, Monck reappeared and told CSU to proceed. We all vacated the stoop so the team—neither Stubbs nor Kemp—could pass with their equipment.

Monck's next question was directed to me.

"You're the forensic anthropologist?"

"I am."

"And you are?" To Flores.

"Luna Flores."

"The forensic engineer?"

"Yes." Flores's icy tone told me she wasn't digging this guy.

Holding his cell phone in the prosthetic hand, Monck shifted back to me. "Describe what you saw, what you did. Succinctly. No speculation, just facts. I'm recording."

I did as asked. *Succinctly.* The meeting. Musgrove's unexplained absence. Flores and I performing a wellness check. The TV voices and the scream. The body on the rug.

A few beats. Then,

"You gals were working the dead boaters with Superintendent Musgrove?"

Gals?

"Among other things," I said.

"The missing tourists."

"Yes."

"How's that going?"

"Detective Monck," I said, now frosty as Flores. "Ti Musgrove was murdered, probably strangled, probably sometime last night. Your most urgent task right now is to find her killer."

Monck slipped his mobile into his pocket. Regarded me for a very long moment.

"Thank you for that." Monck swallowed, then his jaw muscles bunched, relaxed. "But I know exactly who killed her."

17

WTF?

Monck knew Musgrove's killer?!

As much as I grilled him, the arrogant prick refused to elaborate. While leaving, he actually hit Flores and me with the classic: Don't plan any trips.

Dead boaters I hadn't signed up for. Bug bites up my ying-yang. A murdered colleague. An asshole detective treating me like I wasn't quite bright.

And where the flip was Harvey Lindstrom? The elusive pathologist had yet to make an appearance. Not that Doyle and his passengers were my responsibility.

I'd had it.

Fearing a brain bleed if I stayed on the island much longer, I went directly from Musgrove's townhome to the morgue. Iggie was there. And not thrilled to see me.

"You be workin' today? In dis place?"

The craggy face went craggier when I responded in the affirmative. Ignoring the man's displeasure, I asked that he collect the bones from the cooler.

Iggie showed me to the sole autopsy room, trudged off with the enthusiasm of a eunuch at an orgy.

"Thank you," I said when he returned.

"I be genuine sorry, ma'am." As he set down the boxes. "I can't stay wit' you today."

"Oh?"

"I be powerful sad. Miz Musgrove, she one fine woman. My mind keep settlin' on thoughts of her."

"Of course," I said, not surprised that he already knew about the murder of his boss. Musgrove was a cop. All of law enforcement would be in an uproar, slathering to take down the thug who'd killed one of their own.

"You have all the tools you be wantin'?"

"Let's check."

The setup was basic but had what I'd need. Except for one thing.

"I may wish to view items under magnification. Does the morgue have a dissecting scope?"

"There be one over to the hospital. You want I should call and see if that's free?"

"Please," I said, recalling that Musgrove had told me that.

Turned out the microscope wouldn't be available until Lindstrom finished with the boaters. Maybe Monday.

Crap.

But the small room did have one perk: a television mounted high in a corner, an old thirteen-inch Sharp at least two feet thick.

"Does that work?" I asked, pointing at the TV.

"Yes, ma'am."

A random fact about me. I like inane dialogue or color commentary playing softly as I grind through butt-in-the-chair tedious tasks. Tax returns. Algebra homework. Ironing. Skull reconstruction. Mindless drivel in the background helps my concentration.

Devastated over Musgrove's death, I needed calming more than ever right then.

When Iggie had gone, I searched for a remote. I know. Call me an optimist.

Finding none, I dragged a chair close and went at the relic old style. By punching random buttons along the bottom front, I powered the TV on and determined that it received three channels: PTV8, Channel 4 News, and a very snowy station broadcasting a soccer game, probably from Mars.

Unenthused about local news, perhaps fearing coverage of Musgrove's death, I chose the sporting event. I'd be focused on the bones, so image clarity was irrelevant.

I spent the rest of that day and all of the following one—a goddam Sunday—analyzing the remains sniffed out by the olfactorily gifted canine, Thursday. And listening to the play-by-play of match after match.

For each individual, I determined sex, estimated age, ancestry, and height, and noted medical and dental peculiarities. I took measurements and collected bone and tooth samples for potential DNA testing. You know the drill.

By Sunday evening I'd determined the following:

The skeleton from the gully was consistent with the known profile of Ryder Palke.

The skeleton from the woods was consistent with the known profile of Quentin Bonner.

Both men had suffered through-and-through gunshot wounds to the chest.

Both men's left hands had been removed with a tool of indeterminate type.

Until I got access to the scope, that's all I could say.

MONDAY, JULY 15

"A detective be coming to see you," Iggie greeted me when I entered the morgue.

"Are you feeling better today?" I asked.

"I t'ink dis old fellow be blue a long, long time. The po-lice gonna catch the man what hurt Miz. Musgrove?"

"They will." Then, "What detective?"

"Folks calls him The Monk. I don't be doin' that."

"Thanks. Please bring Detective Monck to me when he arrives."

Reaching the autopsy room, I phoned the hospital pathology department. A woman answered and I made my request. She told me the scope was still unavailable.

Damn.

I'd barely disconnected when Monck appeared, a leather bag clutched in his prosthetic hand. Today the pants were ecru, the shirt coral. Same loafers.

"Doc," he said from the doorway. Dark bags scalloped his lower lids. Too little sleep? Too much booze? Torment over the loss of his boss?

"How may I help you, detective." Cool but polite.

"I thought you'd like an update."

That surprised me. "I would."

"Is there somewhere we can sit?"

I'd noticed an upholstered grouping in the room next door, a space probably used for notification of next of kin. I led him there.

I took the chair. Dropping onto the sofa, Monck propped his prosthetic hand on one knee and dug a legal pad from the bag with his other. The real hand was shaking, not a lot, but enough to notice. The skin behind his freckles looked pale as his pants.

"First off, I apologize for my manners on Saturday. Superintendent Musgrove was a hell of a woman. Her death is hitting me hard."

"You claimed to know the identity of her killer," I said, arrowing right in.

"I had to vet you before sharing confidential intel."

"Vet me?" Sharper than I intended.

"Nothing personal."

A brittle silence filled the small space. Iggie passed by in the hall pushing a gurney with one squeaky wheel.

Monck ran the shaky hand over his face. Breathed deeply. His next statement suggested I'd passed muster, whatever that involved.

"I believe the superintendent's ex finally killed her."

"He was violent?"

"The prick has a habit of getting tanked and tuning her up."

"You have a name?" All I knew was "shithead."

"Milo Willis."

"Have you proof Willis did it?"

"Not yet."

"Why didn't Musgrove get a restraining order?"

"She had one."

The anger was as intense as a physical blow.

"Have you arrested Willis?" Fighting to keep my voice neutral.

"He's in the wind. I have people doing door to doors, and I've issued a BOLO for all islands. Every cop on the force is busting ass on this. We'll get the sonofabitch."

I circled back to Monck's opener.

"And the updates?"

"Over the weekend I talked to the superintendent's sister, Raina Ewing. Ewing lives on Grand Turk."

"Musgrove planned to visit her after our meeting with Flores."

"Ewing says her sister confirmed Friday night that she planned to arrive by two the next day. She never showed up. The pathologist—I forget his name."

"Harvey Lindstrom."

"Yeah, that's it. Anyway, Lindstrom began cutting his *Y*s Saturday, took a break from the boaters to do the superintendent. You'd think he was the goddam pope, all the glad mouthing about being happy to work on Sunday." Monck swallowed, looking decidedly unwell. "Anyway, Lindstrom confirmed COD was by manual strangulation. He put TOD at sometime between ten p.m. Friday and four a.m Saturday."

"Musgrove and I had dinner at Da Conch Shack Friday night. She dropped me off around nine. Willis may have surprised her when she arrived home."

"That's our thinking."

"Any signs of forced entry at the town house?" I asked, cursing myself for not noticing.

"No. But there were indications she put up a good fight."

Flash image. An overturned table. A broken vase. Scattered flowers. I felt a tremor in my chest. By sheer willpower I flattened it.

"What now?" I asked.

"Now I do what Musgrove would have wanted."

"Drop a net on the hand-hacking predator taking out tourists?" I ventured.

Monck nodded. "And I start by tracking the new MP."

"Calvin Cloke?"

Monck nodded again.

"What have you learned so far?" I asked, unable to mask my intense curiosity.

"Cloke is a feeb."

"Yes, Detective Musgrove had mentioned it. An FBI agent."

"*Special* agent," Monck stressed, his voice oozing sarcasm.

"Doing what?"

"When I called headquarters in DC, the dude they bounced me to wasn't exactly forthcoming."

"Did Cloke travel to Provo on official business?"

"They wouldn't say."

"Why was he here?"

"Are you listening to me?"

"Fine. What *do* you have?"

I watched Monck debate. Discretion versus the possibility of getting my help in finishing what Musgrove had started. The latter won out. Or the anger-fueled grief. Or the hangover. If that's what it was.

"Upon landing in Provo, Cloke rented a car, then checked into a condo complex called The Ocean Paradise. Which is neither. The place is a dump and miles from the water."

"You've interviewed the staff?"

"The *staff* consists of the owner and his wife, each with the IQ of a potted fern. Both say they haven't laid eyes on Cloke since handing him a key."

Monck stopped. Again, weighing options?

"That's it?" I prompted.

"When we tossed the unit, I found a crumpled paper in a wastebasket containing a handwritten address and phone number."

"You ran them?"

Monck nodded.

"And?"

"They click." Monck slid the tablet back into his bag. Stood. "I'm heading there now."

What the hell? I couldn't use the microscope today, anyway.

I stood. "I'm going with you."

Monck started to protest.

"Does that *click* for you, detective?" I asked, still a bit snappish. "Like a Zippo lighter."

With no hint of a smile, Monck strode toward the door.

18

Unfamiliar with the hood, Monck programmed his GPS with Cloke's scribbled address. While driving, he briefed me on what he knew of the property. The briefing was brief.

"Title is in the name of Joe Benjamin. Benjamin has no record of arrests, convictions, or encounters with law enforcement."

"That's it?" When he said nothing further.

"That's it."

"Do you know anything at all about the guy?"

"No."

"You've never heard of him?"

Monck swiveled to face me. "TCI's population is close to forty thousand. If a citizen stays clean and keeps a low profile, it's possible he or she will never cross paths with the cops."

"I didn't mean to impl—"

"But we shall make Mr. Benjamin's acquaintance shortly."

"How do you know he's there?"

"Because I'm one lucky son of a gun."

Unimpressed, I suggested, "How about I phone him?"

Monck dug the crumpled scrap from his breast pocket and handed it to me. I tapped the digits on my phone.

Four rings, then my call was kicked to voice mail.

"You've reached Joe. I'm busy milking the yaks. Leave one."

"The guy's a comedian," I said as Monck rolled to a stop.

The GPS had directed us to a home on Karst Way, an unmarked stretch of blacktop snaking up a precipice whose exposed layers of limestone were now carved by eons of wind and water. I estimated it was a half mile inland from the beach to which the dead boaters had been brought.

A mailbox stood where the oyster shells of the driveway met the crumbling edge of the asphalt. The name *Benjamin* ran in black letters down both sides of the post.

Monck turned onto the drive, crunched forward, and shifted into park. I lowered my window.

Overhead, birds voiced their indignation at our intrusion. Inside the Explorer, silence as Monck and I scoped out the place.

The house was set back across a stretch of hard-packed mud hosting maybe twenty blades of grass. It was a buff stucco one-story affair with lattice-paned casement windows, all cranked wide. No screens. The roof hosted a gray dish with a small cylinder jutting from its base.

"What's that?"

Monck glanced up at the thing.

"Probably a WiFi signal booster."

A two-car garage sat just beyond the house. A battered black pickup, maybe a Toyota, was bumpered-up to one of its double doors. A motorcycle was parked outside the other.

Though vague on the truck, I knew the bike. A red and black Kawasaki Ninja 250. Harry had owned one during her brief brush with college.

Disorganized shrubs obscured the home's front facing, thriving despite—perhaps because of—a lack of pruning. The backyard, large and fenced, had a glass-windowed storage shed in one corner, a homemade doghouse in another.

Wordlessly, Monck elbow-popped his door handle, did the leg

pivot thing, and pulled himself from behind the wheel. I got out and followed him across the yard.

The home's main entrance had double doors, the inner one made of wood and painted a nauseous chartreuse, the outer one screened. Both were set at ground level, no porch or stoop, but below an overhang.

Blue ceramic planters flanked the double doors, each hosting a discouraged-looking philodendron. A Ring doorbell glowed on the frame beside them.

Monck hit the button with a bionic thumb. I had to admit: his dexterity with the prosthesis was remarkable.

A dog went wild.

No human answered.

We waited.

Reinforcements were adding their voices to the avian first responders. Dozens of birds, mostly crows, now looped in the sky and screamed from the sole palm shading the yard.

Monck pressed the glowing blue circle again.

The dog flew into a frenzy, yapping and clawing the inside of the door.

Monck was about to ring again when a tinny voice came through the speaker, backgrounded by a vaguely familiar tune.

"Yes?"

"Police!" Monck shouted over the cawing and yapping and scratching and crooning. "I need to talk to the property owner."

"I'm sorry. I can't hear ya."

Monck leaned closer to the device.

"Mr. Benjamin?"

"What's the problem, officer?"

"It's Detective, not officer. Detective Delroy Monck, Division B, Grace Bay Station. I must speak with you, sir."

"About what?" Not friendly, not hostile.

"I'd rather not have this conversation from out here."

"Hold on."

A pause as man negotiated with canine. Then locks snicked and the wooden door opened a foot.

"You got ID?"

Monck badged him through the screen.

The man studied the shield. Maybe Monck's hand. I estimated he topped out at about five foot six. Couldn't see enough of him to assess build.

When Monck finally dropped his arm, the man ordered the dog to sit, then opened both doors fully. Dylan was blasting away somewhere in the house.

"You are Joe Benjamin?" Monck repeated his question.

"That's me. Sorry 'bout that. Can't be too careful these days." With its drawn-out vowels and dropped r's, Benjamin's accent invoked images of Yankee Stadium and the Brooklyn Bridge.

"I'd like to ask you some questions, sir," Monck said.

"I'm pretty busy today."

"This should only take a minute."

"Of course."

Benjamin led us down a hall hung with framed black-and-white photos featuring planes, trains, and boats. Some were quite striking, given the shadow play captured by the photographer. The dog tagged along, nails clicking on the polished tile floor.

Turning right under a faux wood–trimmed arch, we entered a living room decorated with way too much orange. Glass doors gave onto a terrace overlooking the sea.

Monck and I sat on opposite ends of a tangerine couch hosting a mountain range of cushions. Benjamin settled on its twin, across a teak coffee table. Matching end tables flanked both sofas. Snatching a remote from one, he killed the music.

"Apologies," he said. "It calms the mutt."

The mutt slumped onto one haunch, back pressed to its owner's leg, eyeing us warily. Its coat was black, its muzzle tan, its tail recurved like the plume on a vintage lady's hat. Tan crescents above its eyes simulated questioning brows.

"Nice pooch," I said. "What's her name?"

"Betty. Her bein' a potcake."

"Potcake?"

"Ya know. Potcake. Cupcake. Betty Crocker."

"I'm sorry. I don't follow."

"Potcakes are feral dogs native to the Turks and Caicos. They got the handle 'cause the locals used to toss 'em caked remains from cooking pots."

"Like hushpuppies in the south."

Benjamin either failed to catch or chose to ignore my comment. "There's a center on the island that rescues and places pups. I figured what the heck? I have a big house, I live alone, I could use some company. So, I got me a potcake."

I reached a hand toward Betty. She bared her teeth and growled low in her throat.

All righty, then.

As we'd agreed, Monck took the lead. While he posed questions, I studied his interviewee.

Joe Benjamin wasn't the homeliest man I'd ever seen. But he was a contender. His eyes were close set and hooded, his goatee black and wispy, his brows bushy and reaching wide to hold hands with each other.

Benjamin was definitely not a sun lover. His skin was a sallow gray underlain with tones of yellow. Perhaps to compensate for the lack of melanin, he wore a long-sleeved tee with a dizzying graphic across the front—3D stripes in neon yellow and green.

"What's this about?" Smiling, Benjamin crossed his legs and dropped one hand onto Betty's head.

"Your name came up in an investigation," Monck said.

"No kidding?" Brows spiraling up like shaggy worms testing the breeze. "What investigation?"

"I'm afraid I can't share that information."

"Whoo-hoo. Very Sam Spade." Benjamin lifted and fondled Betty's left ear. The dog never took her eyes off Monck and me.

"May I ask what you do for a living, Mr. Benjamin?"

"Make magic with digital ecosystems." Waggling jazz hands beside his face.

Irritation tightened Monck's lips.

"I'm in cyber tech. Web design, mainly."

"You work from home."

"I do. Well, mostly. I have a night gig answering phones. Helps pay the bills."

As Benjamin spoke, my eyes roved the room.

The walls held standard poster art, probably purchased at Target or Walmart. Sunflowers, a dog on a bike, the left half of an owl.

In one corner, a tall, open-shelved cabinet displayed an eclectic collection of tchotchkes. A faux-marble glass Buddha. A long skinny sword with a curved blade and decorative handle positioned upright in a stand, another half its size beside it. A ceramic plate with a phosphorescent sunrise at its center.

"How long have you lived in Provo?" Monck asked.

"Ten years."

"May I ask why you moved here?"

"It was my father's idea. He'd heard about a new Chabad—"

"Chabad?" Monck interrupted.

"A Hasidic synagogue. The word itself is meant to evoke wisdom, understanding, and knowledge," Benjamin went on, not bothering to hide his disdain. "Don't get me wrong, I'm not judging. But heavy-duty orthodoxy has never been my jam. My father drank the Kool-Aid his entire life."

Benjamin's gaze drifted off into the distance. Perhaps into an earlier place or time. Then he snapped back.

"Life in New York was copacetic until my brother died. That slammed Dad hard. He'd barely finished sitting shivah when a cancer diagnosis sucker punched him again. After that all he talked about was 'big city tsuris.'" Hooking finger quotes. "That became his mantra."

"Tsuris?" Monck prompted.

"Troubles, worries, aggravation, woes. Yiddish ain't always precise. For Dad it meant snow, smog, taxes, lumpy sidewalks, hucksters, pretty boys, COVID, pollution, traffic, the closing of his favorite bagel shop. You name it. He grew to hate the place.

"Anyway, rumors were circulating about a new Chabad in Provo. The old man was circling the drain. I can work from anywhere in the world, so I figured why not the Caribbean for a few years?"

"Was a Chabad ever established here?" I couldn't help asking.

"Eventually." Pointedly, Benjamin checked his watch. "I don't want to be rude, but—"

"Please bear with me," Monck said.

Benjamin sighed.

Monck got to the point. "Are you acquainted with an FBI special agent named Calvin Cloke? Goes by CC?"

Benjamin thought. Or appeared to. Wagged his head no.

"Do you know why Special Agent Cloke might have flown to Provo last week?"

"No idea."

"Cloke had your contact information in his possession."

"That's impossib—" Benjamin snapped and pointed an index finger. "Wait a minute. Some time back I *did* have a call from an FBI agent. Now that I think of it, the guy's name could have been Cloke."

"What did he want?"

"Let me think." The fuzzy worms dipped. "Got it. He wanted to know about a man named Uri Stribbe."

"Who's Uri Stribbe?" Monck asked.

"Stribbe's family was part of the Chabad-Lubavitch group that migrated from Crown Heights to Provo." At Monck's blank look. "It's a Hasidic movement in Orthodox Judaism. Holier than thou."

"The jam you're not into."

"You got it."

"What's Stribbe's story?"

"He's a *shochet*. An animal slaughterer. Or at least he was back in the day."

The word sent a chill down my spine.

"Why was the FBI interested in Stribbe?"

"No flippin' clue."

"Weren't you curious?"

"Eh." Benjamin hiked then dropped a shoulder. "Me and Betty prefer to keep to ourselves."

Hearing her name, the dog lifted her chin and turned her head. Was rewarded with her master's renewed attention to her ears.

"Do you know where we can find Mr. Stribbe?"

"Not really. Since Dad died, may he rest, I have nothing to do with those folks."

Monck started to ask a follow-up. "Where—"

Benjamin did the finger-snap thing again. He seemed to like doing it. "Hold on."

Pushing to his feet, Benjamin hurried from the room.

Monck slid a sidelong glance my way. I knew what he was thinking. I was traveling the same path. Stribbe was a butcher. A person familiar with dismembering carcasses.

A full minute passed.

Annoyed at being displaced, Betty stood glaring at me. I may have glared back.

Five minutes of hostile canine scrutiny, then Benjamin returned and offered Monck a small scrap of paper.

"Not sure if that address is still good. As I said, it's been ages since I've seen any of those people."

Monck thanked him and stood.

I stood.

Benjamin walked us to the door.

"Sorry I had nothing more useful to offer," he said.

"You've been very helpful," Monck said.

"Life is what it is."

I watched Benjamin debate with himself. Discretion? Honesty? Honesty won.

"I know it's unkind to trash-talk others, but I gotta say it. I always had the impression something was off with Uri Stribbe."

"Off?" Monck asked.

"He's a *shochet*. A slaughterer. Fine. I get that some folks cling to tradition. But—"

Benjamin hosted another internal debate about principles.

"But?" Monck nudged.

"In my humble, Uri Stribbe enjoyed the bloodletting way too much."

19

Familiar with the address Benjamin had provided, Monck passed on navigational guidance and set out on his own. While driving, he contacted headquarters and asked for a run on the name Uri Stribbe.

While he did that, I made one more call to the hospital.

Nope. Scope still tied up. Maybe tomorrow.

Crapshitshittingcrapballs!

"So." Unvented frustration curdled my voice. "Is this dickhead in the system?"

Monck turned and raked me with his eyes. "Who bit you on the ass?"

"Is he?"

A beat, then, "No. Stribbe is not in the system."

After that surly exchange we opted for silence.

Traffic was light and, in minutes, we were idling outside a condo complex a short distance off Grace Bay Road, the island's main thoroughfare. A sign identified it as Villa Juba.

Would the place qualify as oceanfront? Technically, yes. Beachfront? Not without a long, hard scrabble down a whole lot of rock.

Villa Juba was built on a hilltop high above the Atlantic Ocean.

Composed of putty-colored cubes arranged in two levels, the place made me think of a child's blocks stacked haphazardly, then forgotten.

It also reminded me of Habitat 67, the architectural icon designed by Moshe Safdie for Expo 67. Which reminded me of Ryan, since he'd lived there for years. Which reminded me that I was homesick for Montreal.

Suck it up, Brennan. You owe it to Musgrove to see this through.

For a moment, we both assessed. Then Monck circled to the rear and parked.

"Where to?" I asked.

"Two-D."

We got out, found a not so obvious staircase, and climbed to the second level.

A stone walkway wound us to Stribbe's unit.

Monck pressed the Ring doorbell.

We waited.

Monck rang again.

We waited.

Stribbe's condo was at a point where the building's upper level made a right-angle turn. Craning around the corner wall, I could see that his, like those of his neighbors, had a shore-facing terrace and acres of glass.

Which brought to mind the home Ryan and I shared on rue Sherbrooke.

Jesus! Focus.

I could also see the roof and back patio of a single-story rectangular building spanning the hillside at a lower elevation. Similarities in color and design made me wonder if the two structures were somehow connected.

Monck's irritation was now at a level matching my own. Using the knuckles of his prosthetic hand, he hammered the door.

I looked a question at him.

"Titanium," he said.

The ploy worked.

"Go away. I don't want any."

"Police." Monck made zero attempt at masking his annoyance. "We need to speak to Uri Stribbe. Now."

"You cannot come to my door—"

"Open up or I'll break it down." A bluff. Apparently convincing.

Locks clicked. A lot of them. The door swung in.

Monck and I stared in surprise.

The woman wore an ankle-length black skirt, baggy green top, and long-sleeved red cardigan that hung to mid-thigh. Her papery skin was wrinkled and splotchy, her eyes the pale gray of a winter dawn.

White hairs wisped from a turquoise scarf wrapping the woman's head. Despite being elderly, her posture was that of a Buckingham Palace guard.

"I do not appreciate your *meshuggeneh* threats. Police or not, you are a very rude young man." Another Big Apple accent.

"Sorry if my manners are wanting." Monck's apology lacked even a hint of sincerity. "Uri Stribbe lives here?"

"Who wants to know?" the woman asked, warily eyeing the robotic arm.

Monck identified himself.

Like Benjamin, the woman requested ID.

Monck held out his shield.

"I need to speak with Mr. Stribbe."

"What do you want?"

"With all *courtesy*, ma'am, that's none of your business."

"Everything Uri does is my business." A finger came up and jabbed the air, long and bony as the rest of the woman. I guessed her height at six feet, her age at about two thousand.

"Why is that?" Monck demanded.

"Uri is my son."

"And you are?"

"Adeera Stribbe."

"I must talk to your son."

"Can't happen."

"Why not?"

"He isn't here."

"Where is he?"

"With all *courtesy*, that's none of your business."

Adeera was matching Monck's hostility with hostility. I stepped in.

"I understand Uri is a *shochet*?"

The nearly colorless eyes shifted to me. "Are you Jewish?"

"I'm not." I smiled humbly. "Did I pronounce that word correctly."

"No. Who are you?"

"Dr. Temperance Brennan." I left it at that. "Joe Benjamin mentioned Uri's profession."

Adeera sniffed and cocked her chin, a gesture identical to the combo Gran employed to indicate scorn.

"Young Benjamin is posing as a Judaic expert now, is he? Such chutzpah."

"Not at all. He was only being helpful."

"That *chazer* is only helpful when he wants something. Then he has no shame asking—"

"When will Uri be home?" Monck cut her off.

Adeera glanced at her watch, an ancient Timex with a man's wide leather band. "One hour. Every day, I make him lunch."

"We'll wait." Monck didn't frame it as a question.

"This nonsense is so urgent?"

"It is." Monck snapped.

"In the meantime, I'd love to know more about being a *shochet*." I said it mostly to appease Adeera, who was now regarding Monck with open contempt. "Perhaps you could explain the process for me?"

Adeera sighed, stepped back, and held the door wide. "Remove your shoes."

We did, students obeying a stern teacher.

The condo resembled many I'd seen in Provo. White tile floor.

White walls. Veranda overlooking surf pounding sand. The view from this one was a long way down.

There all similarity ended. Not in a good way.

Adeera's furnishings looked like they'd been purchased in the fifties, retained unaltered, then transferred and positioned as in their previous life. A life that had enjoyed significantly greater square footage.

Snaking between a purple velvet couch and a carved mahogany coffee table, I took a seat on one of two closely packed Queen Anne chairs. Monck took the other.

"I will get refreshments."

"Please don't trouble yourself," I said.

Adeera looked at me as though I'd suggested breathing was unnecessary. Disappeared.

Rattling noises drifted from a kitchen that must have been off to the left. A refrigerator door *whished* open, *thumped* shut.

I looked around.

Every inch of every wall was crammed with framed Judaic art and Hebrew prayers. The floor at our feet was covered with an antique area rug featuring a menorah flanked by what looked like feathers.

Across the hall, ice rattled. Glass clinked.

A sideboard stretched behind the sofa, somberly dark like the low table gouging my knees. On it, framed portraits sat to either side of an enormous menorah. Each showed a man, one tall and thin, one of medium height and bulkier.

This time I thought not of Ryan but of John Samuel Dobzhansky. J.S., currently a psychologist and profiler for the FBI, who was my boyfriend throughout my junior and senior years of high school. And, more relevant, Jewish. Or at least half Jewish. But that half was enough. I learned a lot of Yiddish during our time together.

The subject of each photo had a beard and *payot*, a long side curl. The taller man wore a *shtreimel*, a fur hat, on his head, and a tallit, a black-and-white-striped shawl, draped around his shoulders.

The shorter man was in a black suit wrapped with a tzitzit at the waist.

I wondered if one of the pair could be Uri Stribbe.

My speculation was cut short by Adeera's reappearance. Moving briskly, she placed a tray on the table. It held a pitcher of lemonade, four glasses, coasters, and a plate of homemade cookies.

Though curious, I didn't query the extra tumbler.

Without asking our wishes, Adeera poured and distributed drinks, carefully placing one on each of the tiny mats. Then she sat on the sofa, crossed her ankles, and tucked her skirt tight to her legs. Folding her hands in her lap, she did not lean back.

"So. You're curious about animal slaughter."

"I am."

"You know what *shechita* is?"

"The only method allowed by Jewish law for producing kosher meat and poultry."

"Not bad for a shiksa."

"I—"

"Eat." Adeera gestured at the tray.

I took a cookie. Monck did not.

I was dutifully nibbling one edge, thinking what I really needed was a jolt of caffeine, when a door slammed somewhere out of sight. In seconds, a man burst into the room, face red, breath coming fast. A quick scan of Monck, then the man's dark eyes locked onto me.

"How dare you harass my mother with—"

"Dovid!" The pointing finger now jabbed at a chair off to one side. "Sit down."

Dovid remained frozen in place.

"Sit!" As one might order a poodle.

Dovid started to object, decided against it. Sat.

"I am explaining the laws of *shechita* to this young lady."

"Why—"

Adeera hushed him with a blistering *ssshhh* that would have made Gran proud. To me, she said, "Dovid works down the hill at the chabat. He, too, occasionally forgets his manners."

Then why did you phone and ask him to join us? I didn't ask.

Dovid crossed his arms, thrust out his legs, and scowled. He was tall, much taller than the photo suggested, with a lot more hair on his chin than his head. No *shtreimel* or tallit, but he was clearly the man in portrait number one.

"The laws of *shechita* were divinely given to Moses at Mount Sinai," Adeera began. "The rules are clearly defined to ensure a swift and painless slaughter. The animal's welfare is of the utmost importance."

I didn't interrupt. The cookie was oatmeal raisin. And delicious.

"*Shechita* is performed by a trained *shochet*. Rather than the more common practice of first stunning an animal with a bolt to the head, the procedure consists of a single transverse cut to the throat. The animal must be alive and must die from loss of blood."

I noticed that Adeera's tone had become somewhat robotic, her accent less pronounced, as though she'd delivered this lecture many times. I wondered if the woman had done some teaching in her day.

Dovid's scowl never wavered.

"The cut is made with a *chalef*, a specially made knife honed to surgical sharpness. It severs the trachea, esophagus, carotid arteries, jugular veins, and vagus nerve. This causes an instant drop in blood pressure in the brain, which results in loss of consciousness, which renders the animal insensible to pain. The killing is done with both respect and compassion."

Or one could forgo meat, I thought. Hypocritical, I know. I'm hardly vegetarian.

"Is there a required course of education, a form of certification necessary to be a *shochet*?" I asked when Adeera settled back two millimeters, presumably done talking.

"Certification is not mandatory."

"Where did Uri train?"

"With a rabbi in New York."

In my peripheral vision, I noticed Dovid flick an annoyed wave.

"That's where you're from?" I inquired, now mainly to pass the time.

Adeera nodded.

"How long have you lived in Provo?"

"Why do you need to know these things?" Dovid snapped.

"Just curious," I said. "I'm sorry if that question was too personal."

"Where is Uri employed?" Monck asked, tone indicating he was *not* inquiring merely out of curiosity.

"Greenberg's Farm."

"Out near Pidgeon Pond?"

"Yes."

A few beats, then I asked Dovid, "Do you work in the building down the hill?"

Tight nod.

"What happens there?"

"Shabbat services and meals. Passover seders. It's the residence of the rabbi and his wife."

"You're a doctor of what?"

Adeera's abrupt segue threw me a bit. "Forensic anthropology."

"That involves bones."

"Yes."

"You're not local."

"I'm here on business. Billeted at the Villa Renaissance, so it's not tough duty." Flashing what I hoped was an endearing grin.

Adeera did not smile back. "What business?"

"I'm consulting on a police matter."

The squared shoulders went even more rigid. "Why are the police pestering my son?"

"Detective Monck simply wants to ask—"

"What are you accusing Uri of?"

"Mrs. Stribbe, we're not accusing—"

Footsteps sounded, this time behind us. Heavy boots.

The watery eyes lifted toward a spot over my head.

Monck and I swiveled.

Monck's good hand jumped toward the holster underhanging his arm.

20

My brain registered a single flashbulb image.

Bloody shirt. Wild hair. Terrified eyes.

Before I could process, the man whirled and fled.

Monck sprang from his chair and sprinted, legs pumping hard.

Dovid was right on his heels.

My gaze flicked to Adeera. The winter-dawn eyes met mine, level and stony.

Stay! A gaggle of neurons screamed.

Go! A more reckless cluster bellowed.

Without thinking, I flew into action.

Wending too fast through the mash-up of furniture, I cracked one knee on the hideous table.

Pain exploded in my proximal fibula.

Cursing, I hobble-ran out the front door. Caught only two words of the admonition shrieked at my back.

The men had already cleared the stone walkway. Boots pounded one floor below.

"Stop!" Monck yelled. "Police!"

The pounding continued, receding fast.

I double-stepped down the stairs as best I could. Reached ground level gasping and shaky.

Heard only the distant rhythm of surf.

Call out?

Press on?

Go back?

Dial 911?

Hell, yeah.

In my haste I hadn't brought my phone.

I held my breath, eyes and ears straining.

Why no birdsong? Why not a single hint of another presence?

The parking lot lay straight ahead, beyond it, a patch of fossiliferous limestone interspersed with stunted trees and tangled creepers. Past the vegetation, the hillside dropped off sharply.

Another moment of indecision.

What if Stribbe was armed?

Was it Stribbe?

What if Monck was hurt?

A quick scan of the area, I told myself. Then back to the Stribbes' unit, 2D. And 911.

Senses on high alert, I limped forward.

Ten yards, then I spotted a dark shape in the shadow of a craggy boulder.

I froze.

The shape didn't move.

Around me, nothing but wide, eerie silence.

A few more shambling steps.

My heart leapt into my throat.

Monck lay belly-up in the rock's shadow, looking like a roadkill squirrel.

I totter-raced to him. Was relieved to see no blood.

Squatting, I pressed two fingers to Monck's throat. Felt his carotid pulsing strong.

"Detective." I prodded him gently.

He didn't stir.

"Monck."

My breath began coming in short hitches.

Do not cry!

"Damn it, Monck! Wake up!"

That did it.

Monck's lids fluttered, opened. He appeared dazed but, after a moment, managed to focus.

"I'm good," he said, struggling to sit up.

"You're not good. You may have a concussion."

"I don't get concussions."

My eyes rolled. A response born of relief, not ridicule.

Monck's face was the same pale gray as the sedimentary extrusion behind him. Elbowing to his butt he drew in his knees. "Aren't you going to ask what happened?"

"What happened?"

"I was ambushed."

"One of them clocked you."

"In my defense, the asshole had home-court advantage." While gingerly exploring his scalp.

"Was the newcomer Uri Stribbe?"

Monck shrugged. Winced.

"What do you *think*?" I pushed.

"The guy's shirt was a blood-spatter analyst's wet dream. So, yeah. My money's on him being the *slochet*."

"*Shochet.*"

"Whatever."

"I should drive you to an ER."

"Not a chance."

Monck stood and brushed sand from his clothes.

"Now what?" I asked.

"Now I bag the sonofabitch."

We skipped lunch. A bad idea.

While driving, Monck called HQ to issue a second BOLO, this one for Uri Stribbe.

I phoned the hospital. Again. Was told by the same woman that the scope was unavailable. Again.

I asked the woman's name.

Della Pratt.

I asked Della Pratt when the scope would be free.

Answer: when Dr. Lindstrom has finished his analysis.

Della Pratt disconnected.

What's the definition of crazy?

By the time Monck dropped me at the morgue it was half past two.

Frustrated, and cranky due to my throbbing knee, I spent the rest of the afternoon eyeballing the cut ends of Palke's and Bonner's lower arm bones.

Without the benefit of magnification, I knew the exercise would produce little useful data. Still, I wanted to stay busy. To not think about Musgrove. To wrap up the freaking case so I could head north.

My stomach, less dedicated than my mind, registered almost nonstop complaint. Soft at first, the growls gradually attained an impressive volume.

A variety of tools can efficiently dismember a human corpse, machetes, cleavers, and axes being among the more popular. My goal was to determine what implement the killer had used to hack the hands from his vics.

Employing only a badly scratched handheld lens, I examined each cut's horizontal face and scanned for associated fracturing. I looked for kerfs—false starts—hoping to observe shape and estimate width and depth. Actual measurement would have to wait for amplification.

Every few minutes my gut grumbled its displeasure at being ignored. Each time, I glanced at my phone, hoping Monck's BOLO had worked and that a patrol unit had netted either Musgrove's abusive ex, Willis, or the animal slaughterer, Stribbe.

No word came. Both persons of interest remained in the wind.

At six, Iggie came by to tell me he was leaving for the day. I assured him I'd be close behind. And that I'd lock up.

The next time I glanced at the wall clock its hands were pointing to the seven and the two. Seven-ten.

In the islands, the sun arrives and departs with year-round predictability. Up by six, down by seven. Ish.

The small room had no window, but I knew that outside shadows were deepening as light faded from the day. That ole sol was probably setting the horizon on fire.

I'd been squinting through the scratched lens for five hours. A headache was knocking at my frontal lobe.

My insights were meager. Two, to be exact.

The cleanness of the cuts suggested an extremely sharp-edged tool.

The absence of false starts suggested a very skilled perp.

Brilliant. Now you're getting somewhere, Brennan.

My stomach growled with an intensity that probably registered on devices in the Yukon. Blood vessels hammered my brain. My knee demanded Advil.

Was that trifecta the reason for the self-flagellation?

My conclusions, though limited, were helpful.

Frighteningly helpful.

Monck didn't answer his phone.

It was less than twenty minutes from the morgue to Villa Renaissance. On the way, I stopped at Danny Buoy's.

Intrigued by its name, I ordered the Intoxicated Chicken. The contents of the takeout container filled the car's interior with the smell of exotic spices and mojo sauce.

Upon entering the condo, I left my food in the kitchen, dropped my clothes in a heap on the bathroom floor, and took a quick, hot shower. Big surprise.

After dressing in sweats, I towel dried my hair, and knocked back two Advil. Then I dived into the chow. The poultry, roast sweet potato, and corn on the cob were all that their enticing aromas had promised.

Belly full, knee and frontal lobe drugged into submission, I brushed my teeth, cracked the glass doors, drew the drapes, and crawled into bed. While plugging my iPhone into its charger, I noticed the date.

Only five days on the island—still, it felt like a lifetime. No Birdie. No Ryan. And now no Musgrove.

Suck it up, Brennan. Do your job. Do it for Musgrove.

Reinvigorated by my pithy self-help pitch, maybe by the pepper and garlic in the mojo sauce, I dialed Monck. This time he answered.

"Detective Monck."

"I called you earlier," I said in a rush. *Too accusatory?*

"We got a tip on Milo Willis."

"Go on."

"Caller said Mr. Elusive was at the Turtle Cove Marina."

"Was he?"

"No."

"Who phoned in the tip?"

"Whoever it was refused to provide a name," Monck said, sighing.

"Any joy with Uri Stribbe?"

"No."

"You'll get them," I said.

"We will." Monck's clipped answers hinted that he wished to keep the call short. Or end it.

I summarized my two findings.

"Anything else?"

"As I was leaving, Uri's mother yelled what I think was a warning." Monck waited.

"Something about a fiery cataclysm."

"The Old Testament is chockful of that end-of-times crap."

"You think Adeera was quoting the Bible?"

"Probably."

"Benjamin said the Stribbes belong to a faction that's holier than thou."

"His exact words."

A series of beeps indicated an incoming call. FaceTime.

"Keep me updated," I said, finger combing my wet hair back behind my ears.

"Right."

Clicking over to Ryan, I wondered if Monck would bother.

"*Bonsoir, me chère.*"

"*Bonsoir,*" I replied, feeling better just seeing his face. His beyond blue eyes. "What's up, ace?"

"The mercury. Nothing else. Except I ran into your boss in the lobby yesterday."

"Dr. LaManche."

"No, King Charles."

"Funny. What did he want?"

"He has a set of remains with your name on them. That didn't come out right."

"No. It didn't."

"He asked when you'd be back."

As if I wasn't feeling pressured enough.

"Any progress on Deniz Been?" I asked.

"The more I talk to the girlfriend, the shadier she looks."

"Émilie Gaudreau?"

"Yes." Ryan must have noticed the pillows I'd stacked behind me. "Are you in bed?"

"I am."

"What are you wearing?"

"Tell me about Birdie."

"He's got on red slippers and some sort of hat. Maybe a sombrero."

My eyes rolled. "How goes your assignment with the SQ?"

"We made an arrest and are working to flip the kid. Predictably, things have gone quiet on the scoring front."

"Good job."

"Is it that little black teddy with lace on the—"

"Monck thinks Musgrove was killed by her ex. A man named Milo Willis."

"Has he hauled in Willis?"

"Not yet, but he will. He seems gutted by her murder."

I told Ryan about Uri Stribbe. About my findings concerning the tool and the person that hacked off Palke's and Bonner's hands.

"So Stribbe is looking good for this serial?"

"Both vics were mutilated by a person skilled with a sharp instrument. Uri Stribbe is a *shochet*."

"A slaughterer."

"Yes."

"A butcher sure fits your profile."

"It does."

"Motive?"

"He's batshit crazy?"

"Always a decent theory. How much longer will you be there?"

"I'm not sure."

"LaManche misses you."

"Uh-huh."

"Birdie and I miss you."

"I miss you more."

Ryan's sign-off proposal could have melted the Greenland ice sheet.

I unstacked the pillows and pulled the covers to my chin.

In minutes I was dead to the world.

21

I felt weight on my chest.

Birdie? No. Too heavy.

I opened my eyes.

Total blackness.

Before I could orient, a hand mashed down on my mouth.

Then recall.

Turks and Caicos. Musgrove. Monck.

My memory cells flashed a terrifying image.

Bloody shirt. Wild eyes and hair.

Had Uri Stribbe found my condo?

Had he followed me to Villa Renaissance?

I tried to shrug my attacker off, but the pressure on my upper body was too great.

Panicked, I twisted my head to free my mouth. To breathe. To scream.

Fingers grabbed my hair and yanked me back faceup.

Click!

179

A pistol slide ratcheting home?

The sound sent high voltage fear surging through me.

My mind raced.

Was it Stribbe? Had he gotten in through the unsecured sliding door?

Was this how he'd overpowered his victims?

Was this how I'd die?

But Stribbe's victims had all been shot. Why risk physical contact if you're armed?

Calm down!

The hand on my face felt oddly smooth. My nose was taking in a familiar smell.

Think!

All the weight on me was from my waist up. My attacker was straddling my rib cage, using his legs to pin my arms to the mattress. But my lower body was unconstrained.

Rookie mistake.

What happened next seemed to go on forever. In truth, the action probably lasted less than a minute.

Marshaling the tsunami of adrenaline coursing through me, and all the strength I could muster, I flexed my knees fast, planted my feet, and thrust up with my hips. The unexpected move tilted my attacker forward. His head slammed the headboard with a brassy clunk.

The heaviness eased on my left side. My arm broke free.

With a one-handed shove, I pushed my assailant sideways. He resisted, arms flailing. Gravity won. He tumbled from the bed and hit the tile hard.

Disengaging from the blankets, I sat up and pivoted to see who he was.

The guy was nothing but a shadow moving in the darkness. He wasn't large, wasn't small. No details of his features or clothing were visible.

Righting himself, the man began crawling and running his hands over the floor. Searching for the gun?

In seconds he was back at the bed. Rising on his knees, he extended both arms in my direction.

To strangle me? Shoot me?

I didn't wait to find out.

Uttering a feral cry, I lunged forward, flexed my right arm, and drove my elbow into his throat.

The man fell back again, lungs in spasm. Hands clasping his neck, he fought for air.

911!

I groped for my phone. In my frenzy I knocked it from the bedside table.

Shit!

The man drew a single, ragged breath.

I swiveled back, coiled for another lunge.

Bracing with his free hand, the man struggled to his feet. Legs unsteady, he lurched across the room and disappeared through the sliding glass doors.

Eighteen minutes after I called, two cops showed up. Landers and Winston. Or Winters and Landston. Whatever. It was the middle of the night and I'd just been attacked.

I'd made myself tea, Ryan's antidote for any stressful situation. The herbal brew was calming me some. That and the fact that every light in the condo was now burning.

Landers/Landston was the taller and older of the pair, with a pencil-thin mustache riding an equally thin upper lip. Winston/Winters may have hit five feet six in his boots. A complicated tat wrapped his overly developed right bicep.

Landers/Landston took the lead, his interview style unflavored by warmth.

"Are you in need of medical attention?"

"No."

"Did the alleged attacker harm you?"

Alleged?

"No."

"State your name."

I did.

"Your business in Provo."

I kept my description to the bare minimum.

"You're involved in the probe into Superintendent Musgrove's death?" Tiniest hint of surprise.

"Peripherally."

"With Detective Monck?"

"Yes." It registered that the man's name tag said *Landers*.

That part of the questioning went well. From then on, my answers seemed to disappoint.

"What time did the attack begin?"

"I didn't check a clock. I'm guessing just past two."

Landers jotted in a small spiral tablet. Did every cop have one?

"How long was the intruder inside the condo?"

"Not long."

"Any thoughts on why he chose here?"

"It damn well wasn't to bring me fritters."

"Any idea how he gained entrance?"

"I'd left the terrace doors unlocked."

Landers sighed his disapproval. "Tourists are often targeted for just that reason. Folks are on vacation, having a good time, they throw caution to the wind. A woman was killed over by the Club Med a few years back. A New Yorker."

Face burning, I took a sip from my mug. The pompous jerk was right.

"Unsecured doors are a bad idea." Landers refocused on the intruder. "Can you describe the man?"

"It was dark. I never got a good look at his face."

"What was he wearing?"

"Pants. I know because he straddled my chest. Beyond that, no clue."

As Landers questioned me, Winston/Winters moved from room to room, taking pics with his phone, carefully touching nothing except with a pen.

"Was anything stolen?" Landers asked, not looking up.

I shrugged and raised my free palm. "It's not my condo."

"Describe the incident again."

My head and knee were clamoring with renewed vigor. My tea was gone. I wanted to down more Advil and return to bed. In the guest room. With the doors locked.

Knowing Landers was looking for inconsistencies in my story, I repeated my account. Exactly as I'd given it initially.

When I'd finished, Landers tucked his pen into the tablet's spiral binding. "I won't lie to you. We get quite a few B and E calls from these complexes. The stealy boys hit and split. Mostly we don't catch 'em. Mostly no one gets hurt."

"Don't thieves typically hit a place when the occupants are away?"

"That's true."

"Are they usually armed?"

"No. But it happens."

"My attacker may be the man I mentioned. Uri Stribbe."

"What makes you think that?"

I shared as much as I could without compromising Monck's investigation.

"You should speak to Detective Monck."

"Rest assured, I will." Landers knew I was withholding some info but didn't press.

"Thank you, officer."

"Anything else?" Slipping the tablet into a pants pocket, then signaling to his partner.

"No."

At the door, I was nudged by a stray thought.

"Wait," I said. "There is something else."

Both cops paused.

"I think my assailant was wearing gloves."

"What kind of gloves?" Landers asked.

"They felt smooth. And the smell made me think of a hospital."

The pair just looked at me.

"Some surgical gloves are designed to be cut resistant."

The looks held.

Jesus!

"They're the type of protection a butcher might wear."

"Or a burglar." Clearly, Landers was channeled on the B&E theory. "CSU will be by in the morning. In the meantime, touch nothing."

If given that order again, I'd scream.

When they'd gone, I hurried to the guest bedroom. Double-checked the glass doors and all the windows.

Too wired to sleep, I surfed a bit, looking for a new ringtone. Made a choice. *Law & Order.* Katy found my use of musical alerts beyond archaic, but the show's opener seemed appropriate. Loud and authoritative.

Popping two more Advil, I dropped into bed.

Sleep was still a long time coming.

Questions churned within a steady procession.

Was Landers right? Had I been the victim of a random B&E? The victim of my own stupidity?

Or was my attacker Uri Stribbe?

How would Stribbe have known where to find me? Easy one. I'd mentioned Villa Renaissance to his mother.

How would Stribbe have known my schedule? Might he have followed me?

Had Monck and I spooked Stribbe with our visit to his home?

Could Uri Stribbe be Provo's hand-hacking serial killer?

Whether Stribbe or some other psycho, why murder young male tourists? *Was* that the victim profile, or were there others that Musgrove had missed?

How did the killer overtake his victims? Where did the murders take place?

Why shoot a victim, then hack off his left hand? Using what tool?

How did Been's death on the Jacques Cartier Bridge in Montreal connect to the killings here in Provo? Or was there no connection at all?

Had Uri Stribbe killed Ti Musgrove? Was Musgrove getting too close?

Musgrove had received a text during our dinner at Da Conch Shack. What had she learned? Did the info implicate Uri Stribbe? Had he somehow learned of that?

Or had Milo Willis strangled his ex-wife? The inevitable outcome of an escalating pattern of drunken abuse?

Why had Cloke traveled to Provo? Why was Joe Benjamin's contact info at his condo? Why had Cloke phoned Benjamin about Stribbe?

Where was Cloke?

Where was Willis?

Where was Stribbe?

Round and round.

No answers.

Except one.

A big yes on the issue of my stupidity.

22

Dum! *Dum! Da da da da dum!*

I clawed my way to the surface from a deep sleep.

Opened my eyes.

The room was dim. The drapes were still tightly closed.

The *Law & Order* theme was blasting from the phone on my bedside table.

I reached over and checked the screen.

The time was 9:17. The caller was Monck.

"Hello! Hello!" I shouted to no one, hoping a warm-up might snap me alert.

I clicked on.

"Brennan."

"We got him." Monck sounded pumped.

Too much too quick. I struggled to comprehend.

"You—"

"Uri Stribbe." When I said nothing. "He's in a cage."

"Wow." Swinging my legs over the side of the bed. "Well done."

"We nailed him about an hour ago."

"Where?"

"Greenberg's Farm, out by Pidgeon Pond. I've had eyes on the place since yesterday. Stribbe showed up for work this morning right on time."

"There's something you might want to know."

I told Monck about the intruder.

"Sonofabitch. Are you okay?"

"Other than not sleeping half the night, fit as a fiddle."

"What did the responding officers think?"

"Probably stealy boys."

A moment as Monck thought about that. Then,

"I plan to let Stribbe sweat for an hour, then grill him. You want to observe? Watch for something that might ID him as your attacker?"

"Hell, yeah."

"He's at the Chalk Sound station. Do you know where that is?"

"I can find it."

"Take the Leeward Highway. Shouldn't be more than fifteen minutes. If you hit Taylor Beach, you've gone too far."

"Got it."

How hard could that be?

Harder than I thought. Even with GPS guiding my way.

From Grace Bay Road, I meandered a couple of smaller streets, then hit the first roundabout. I'm not great with roundabouts. My approach. Loop until you figure it out.

I did better at the second roundabout. South Dock Road, a right onto Chalk Sound Road, then I was there.

The station was a two-story white box with a concrete walkway and pillars running the first level, a roofed and iron-railed balcony skirting the second. Several cruisers sat parked in front.

The lobby resembled a thousand others in police stations around the globe. Small and dourly municipal, it had a few posters hanging on the walls, each promoting a benevolent but somewhat depressing enterprise. Other, smaller flyers showed the faces of those wanted for offenses ranging from public peeing to homicide. An equally disheartening display.

When I entered, a female in civvies looked up and scowled from the far side of a reception desk. I explained my purpose in being there. Rolling her shoulders, the woman scanned me from head to foot.

"You carrying?" she asked.

"No."

Appearing ready to pin me to a wall should I make a false move, the woman rose and led me down a short corridor to the first of two doors. Gestured me to go in.

I did. Considered my surroundings. There wasn't much to consider.

The room was small and furnished with two wooden chairs. A rectangular window took up most of one wall. I figured the window's far side was probably mirrored.

No terminals. No monitors. I'd be viewing Monck's interrogation old-school.

I crossed to the one-way window. Through the murky glass I could see a brightly lit cubicle similar to many I'd visited over the years. Fluorescents overhead. Battered table and chairs at the center. Phone high on one wall. I didn't see a mic, but a humming speaker at my back made it clear the interview room was wired for audio.

I noted two deficiencies. No duress alarm. No CCTV camera.

Three.

No Stribbe.

Five minutes passed. Ten.

I was getting antsy when the door opened, and Monck strode in. Dark circles rimmed his bloodshot eyes. Fatigue again? Drink? Or was that the guy's normal look in the morning?

"How you doing?" he asked, joining me at the observation window.

"Couldn't be better."

"I pulled Landers's report. Rough night."

"The highlight not being Officer Friendly and his sidekick."

"Landers could use some sensitivity training." Delivered so deadpan I couldn't tell if Monck was serious or joking.

"Where's Stribbe?" I asked.

"They're bringing him over. Weird dude. Hostile as hell. Could be anger, could be nerves."

"That should work in your favor. You go in, all Mr. Nice Detective, apologize for the big bad officers who busted him. That approach might help break him down."

"Good cop bad cop is such a cliché."

"There's a reason clichés exist."

"Stribbe ain't exactly John Wayne Gacy. Guess who he contacted with his one call?"

"Who?"

"His mother."

"In case you didn't notice, Adeera Stribbe is one controlling mama. She may be Uri's main authority figure. Use that, too."

"Male-child guilt, *Psycho* style?"

"Hopefully, not to that violent extreme. Anyway, Adeera's old. She's made so many sacrifices for him. He's all she has. He's letting her down. Blah, blah, blah."

"Good point. The mother-son tie could be a vulnerable area."

Sounds spit from the speaker behind us.

A door opening. Heels clicking.

Monck and I watched an officer lead a handcuffed Stribbe to the table.

Chair legs scraped.

Stribbe sat, shoulders hunched, head hanging so low I couldn't see his face.

The cop said something I didn't catch.

A beat, then Stribbe's manacled hands clinked onto the tabletop, fingers clenched into tight fists.

The cop retreated and stood with his back to one wall, hands clasped at crotch level. Stribbe rocked gently in his chair, lips moving but no sound coming from them. I wondered if he was praying.

"Showtime," Monck said.

"You'll know how to play him."

A quick thumbs-up, then Monck withdrew, seconds later appeared in the adjacent room. Dropping into the chair opposite Stribbe, he placed his phone on the table and began.

"This interview is being recorded. Do you have any objection, Mr. Stribbe?"

"What do you think?" Belligerent as hell.

"Sir?"

The drooping head wagged slowly.

Stribbe's hair, dark and coarse, was combed straight back from his face. A scraggly mustache and beard struggled for recognition on his chin and cheeks. He wore no glasses. Had no visible birthmarks, scars, or tattoos. He wasn't tall or short, bulky or slight.

Was this the jackass that attacked me last night?

"Present for this interview are Detective Delroy Monck and Officer Simon Toole. Interviewee is Uri Stribbe. Questioning concerns the murders of Bobby Galloway, Ryder Palke, Quentin Bonner, and Tiersa Musgrove. And any and all connected homicides, assaults, crimes, and events."

As Monck worked through the formalities, Stribbe alternated between undulating gently and licking his lips, his body tense as a house cat stalking a mouse.

"Officer Toole, have you read Mr. Stribbe his rights?"

"I have."

"Mr. Stribbe, do you understand your rights in regard to these matters?"

Stribbe glanced up. He had his mother's eyes, the irises such a pale gray they appeared almost transparent. He said nothing.

"Please answer, sir."

"I didn't do anything."

"Do you understand your rights?"

"I'm not stupid." Snarled. "Why am I here? Why?"

"Where were you on April 16, 2017?" The day Bobby Galloway disappeared.

"I don't know."

"Where were you on the night of August 5, 2020?" Ryder Palke.

"I don't know."

"February 25, 2022." Quentin Bonner.

"I don't know."

"Are you acquainted with a woman named Tiersa Musgrove?"

"I don't know." Squint-glaring and blinking as though blinded by bright lights.

"You don't know? Or you don't know her?"

"I don't know. Don't know."

"Where were you last Friday night?"

The blinking stopped and the pale grays widened slightly. As though Monck's question offered a glimmer of hope. "At Shabbat services. Then I went home."

"Can anyone verify that?"

"The rabbi and his wife. My mother."

"You got home from the synagogue at what time?"

"I don't know. Not late."

"And you never left your condo?"

"No. You can ask my mother. Where is she?"

"Do you know a man named Bobby Galloway?"

"No."

"Quentin Bonner?"

"No."

"Ryder Palke?"

"No. No." Raising his cuffed hands and slamming them onto the table so loud the sound made me jump.

"Calvin Cloke?"

"Why are you asking me about these people?"

"What do you do for a living, Uri?"

"I'm a *shochet*."

"A butcher."

Stribbe nodded.

"What do you butcher?"

"Poultry and beef."

"Do you enjoy killing animals?" To throw Stribbe off guard.

"What? No!" More blinking. "Kosher slaughter must be done properly. It's a commandment of the torah. The torah."

"Of course it is."

Monck rose and circled the table. Placed his prosthetic hand on Stribbe's shoulder.

Stribbe recoiled as though shocked with an electric prod. "I don't want to be here. I want to go home."

"The sooner you cooperate, the sooner that can happen."

"My mother knows I'm here. I spoke to her. Where is she?"

Monck leaned one hip onto the edge of the table. Looked deep into Stribbe's eyes.

"You'll feel better if you get it off your chest, Uri. We know you don't want to keep doing these things. To keep hurting your mother."

"Doing what things?"

Monck didn't reply.

"I have no idea what you're talking about."

"We think you're a good man, Uri. We know you studied with a rabbi. Tell us everything and we'll do all we can to help you."

"It's a trick. You're trying to trick me." Pale eyes now hard and cold as ice.

Stribbe resumed rocking and licking his lips, body language suggesting extreme agitation.

"Why would we trick you, Uri?"

"You want me to confess to something I didn't do."

Monck returned to his side of the table. Resumed his seat, leaned back, and said nothing.

Ten seconds passed. Thirty.

I recognized another interview tactic. Stop talking. Uncomfortable with silence, the subject may feel compelled to fill it. A variation on the old tried and true. Give a guy enough rope, he may hang himself.

A full minute of blinking and swaying, then Stribbe took the bait.

"You're trying to get me to say things that aren't true."

"What things?" Monck's gaze remained level on Stribbe.

"You're trying to get me to say I killed people. People I don't even know."

Monck's eyes floated up to the window. Met mine. The left one winked.

Bingo.

"One last question, Uri."

"What?" Spit with venom.

"Who said anything about people being killed?"

23

I emerged to an outside much drearier than the one I'd left. A wind had kicked up and rain was threatening. Overhead, palm fronds waved like pennants above a marching band.

I hardly noticed. Monck's questions and Stribbe's answers were cycling and recycling through my brain. Stribbe was a paradox, a seeming mama's boy one second, hostile and aggressive the next. Could such a flip-switch wimp be a hand-hacking serial killer? Last night's attacker at my condo?

Was Stribbe the nervous mess he appeared to be most of the time? A man simmering with repressed anger?

Or an Academy Award–level actor?

Either way, watching him stutter and squirm had left me troubled.

I was rolling east on the Leeward Highway when my phone let loose a round of *da da dums.*

Recognizing the incoming number, I answered.

"Tempe Brennan."

"Luna Flores. How's it going?"

"Good. What's up?"

"I'm about to pull the pin on this baby and head home."

"When?"

"Today." I heard traffic sounds in the background. A turn signal blinking. Figured Flores was also on the road.

"Lucky you," I said.

"God loves me. If you're interested, I've printed an extra copy of my report."

"I'm interested. Grab a bite?"

"A sound plan. Where?"

I had to think about that. "Do you know the Shay Café?"

"In La Vele Plaza, off Grace Bay Road?"

"That's the one."

"It may be the *only* joint in Provo I know."

"See you there in ten?"

"Roger that. Ciao."

The Shay Café and Lounge was a schizoid combo of restaurant by day, raucous saloon and dance hall by night. In its sunup manifestation, the place had a reputation for serving primo breakfasts.

When I arrived, Flores was already at the counter placing an order. While waiting my turn, I looked around.

Just inside the entrance, a refrigerated case offered gelato in a dozen rainbow flavors. Rows of burlap coffee bags undulated across the ceiling, with large paper snowflakes hanging between.

A blackboard high on one wall forecast island conditions. *Hot! Chance of beautiful people and stunning beaches. Rum punch and bikinis expected all day! Chance of fun 99%.*

Given my mood, I seemed destined to be part of the outlier one percent.

Circling a barrier composed of a bicycle welded to a metal base, Flores moved to the register to pay. I stepped up to order.

No need to check the menu. On my sole visit to the Shay, Musgrove had ordered eggs Benedict. Watching her eat the yolk and butter-rich concoction, I'd regretted my healthier choice of avocado toast.

Without hesitation, I went with Benedict and his muffins and artery-clogging hollandaise sauce. How could a zillion extra carbs hurt? Besides, I needed a lift.

Flores and I took our food to an outdoor table shaded by a big square umbrella. Not that protection was necessary. The late-morning sun wasn't making the slightest effort.

Flores's plate held two rolled pancakes drizzled with choco-late, sprinkled with powdered sugar, and topped with a mountain of whipped cream.

"What is that?" I asked.

"Nutella and banana crepes."

Her choice left mine in the food-guilt dust.

While eating, we rewound our movements since parting on Saturday. At first, Flores seemed to shy away from the topic of the boaters. We discussed nothing of import. A pod of dolphins she'd sighted at sunrise. Her upcoming flight. A potcake pup she was taking home to her nephew.

Then the discussion grew more serious. The hand-hacking serial killer. Musgrove's murder. I shared Monck's theory that the doer was Musgrove's ex.

I debated telling Flores about the previous night's attack. About Uri Stribbe. Decided against both. Why burden her with intel that might bring her down, too?

Finally, bellies overfull, we leaned back with our drinks, mine coffee, hers orange-mango juice, both claiming organic status. Flores's beverage came with a straw.

Slurping noisily, Flores set down her glass, reached behind her and drew a folded envelope from her purse. Extending it to me, she said, "The report's only virtue is its brevity."

"Oh?"

"This case has been one colossal pain in the buttocks. I spent days tearing that engine apart. Then I tore every friggin' one of its parts apart."

I waited as Flores took another loud sip.

"I found zilch," she said.

"Nothing?" A bit strident, but what she'd said seemed impossible.

"There wasn't a fucking thing wrong with that boat."

"What about the gas gauge? The radar? The navigation?"

"All in working order." Flores pointed to the envelope. "The specs are detailed in there."

I picked up my coffee. Put it back down. Over on Grace Bay Road, a siren screamed its resolve to arrive at a destination in the shortest time possible.

No matter how I toggled Flores's statement, it didn't make sense.

"Let me get this straight," I said. "The *Cod Bless Us*, with every system functioning, goes six hundred miles off course, runs out of gas, and drifts at sea until everyone on board is dead. Doyle, the captain, makes no attempt to contact anyone. None of the passengers radios or calls for help."

"I can't explain it."

"Crap, crap, crap!"

"You really should work to broaden your vocabulary."

"Sorry. But that just doesn't play. It's not my case, I know. Still, I was hoping for *some* explanation why those people are dead."

"Lindstrom's still cutting. Maybe he'll find drugs or something."

I willed my face to look hopeful. To believe the autopsies might yield answers.

For the next half minute we sat there, not drinking, not looking at each other. Not a word passed between us.

I broke the silence.

"Has something like this ever happened before?"

"Like what?"

"Sweet suffering Jesus! A boat that—"

"Will you calm down."

"Sorry. A boat, a plane, a helicopter, a rocket, a covered wagon, whatever, a vessel or vehicle going lethally off course with no explanation."

"It's rare. But it happens. Occasionally, all we can assume is pilot error."

"But why not call for help?" Again, too shrill.

Lips pursed, Flores bunched her napkin and began gathering her utensils.

"I'm not blaming you," I said, quickly.

"Sounds like you might be."

"Not at all. Sorry if it came across that way." I was apologizing a lot. "Am I correct that you can't rule out foul play?"

"You are correct. I cannot." Flores scooched her chair back. "Look, I get it. I'm frustrated, too. But sometimes, as we say in the biz, shit happens."

"You've had other incidents you couldn't explain?"

Flores paused, plate in one hand, purse strap in the other.

"A couple, three years back, off the coast of one of the TCI islands, as a matter of fact, a Piaggio P.180 nose-dived into the sea."

"What's that?"

"One kick-ass plane. The pilot and his passenger both died. I did the consult. Found absolutely nothing wrong with the aircraft."

"An aviation mystery." Light. Not wanting Flores to depart angry. "Like Malaysia Airlines Flight 370."

"Not exactly."

Flores stood.

"The Piaggio's crash had to do with why, not where."

Flores's report left me even more discouraged. Or perhaps it was knowing she was leaving and I was not.

I agree. That sounds whiny. I was stuck where? In paradise. *Chance of fun 99%.* But I missed Ryan and Birdie. I'd been in Provo almost a week. I wanted to go home.

Walking back to the Honda, the morality police in my conscience went straight for the heart.

Shake it off, Brennan! Be an adult. Get on with it.

Get on with it how? Without access to the scope, I was stalled.

My subconsciousness maintained a reproachful silence.

But it had made a valid point. Why *should* I be stalled? Did Harvey Lindstrom consider his work more important than mine? Had the asshole pathologist never heard of collegiality?

Anger elbowing the self-pity aside, I made a decision. Willing or not, Lindstrom was about to acquire a skill he should have learned in kindergarten. Sharing.

Whipping a U-turn of questionable legality, I drove to the morgue. Once inside, I arrowed to the cooler, packaged Palke's and Bonner's radii and ulnae, left a signed note in each Tupperware container, and hurried back to my car. Well, I guess it was mine. They still hadn't taken it back.

The plan. I'd make a face-to-face request for time with the scope. If Lindstrom refused, or delayed, I'd tell him that I was happy to wait. In the meantime, I'd X-ray the bones.

I was at the hospital in less than five minutes. Entering the lobby, which resembled hospital lobbies everywhere, I asked the first employee I encountered for directions to the pathology department. The young man, an orderly or nurse, looked confused. After consulting a coworker, he provided guidance.

The autopsy room was also standard issue. Glass-fronted cabinets, stainless-steel countertops, floor-bolted table, hanging scale.

Unexpected was the zoom stereo microscope holding a place of honor on one counter. It was a good one, 3.5 to 225 X, with a 1.3 MP integrated digital camera. Two gooseneck LED lights flanked the scope, and a USB cable connected it to a closed laptop.

The equipment was identical to the setup I used at the LSJML.

Its quality was a pleasant surprise.

The other surprise was Harvey Lindstrom.

The pathologist was bent over the autopsy table, his back to the door. Before him lay a corpse from the *Cod Bless Us*, thorax gaping like one of the Kesh caves leading to Middle Earth.

"Dr. Lindstrom," I said when he didn't turn around.

No response.

Noticing an Air Pod in each of Lindstrom's ears, I circled to enter his field of vision.

My sudden appearance seemed to startle him. Laying down his scalpel, he pulled two tissues from a box and used them to remove the earbuds. An unidentifiable tune sputtered from each.

"Yes?"

"I'm Dr. Temperance Brennan," I said, in a not particularly friendly voice. "I've been calling about the scope?"

Lindstrom looked as confused as he was wide. Though roughly my height, an adult hippo had nothing on him in weight.

"Scope?" Lindstrom's brows, blond and wiry, arced high above the upper border of his surgical mask.

"The microscope. I'm working cold case homicides and have specimens I need to examine under magnification."

Placing his earbuds on the counter, Lindstrom unhooked a loop and let the mask drop below his mouth. Which was smiling broadly.

"There's a scope right here." Jabbing a chubby thumb at the item in question. "What's the problem?"

I explained the problem.

"Well of course you can use the microscope. I usually take case samples with me and prepare slides in my lab in Miami. Who did you speak with?"

"Della Pratt."

"Oh, my. I'm afraid Ms. Pratt tends to be overly protective of my interests." Lindstrom's cheeks flamed pink. "Truth is, the woman is a bit sweet on me."

Hardly the hostile reception for which I'd prepared.

"Thank you," I said, not sheepish, but markedly less bristly.

"Of course. I apologize for the misunderstanding." Another sunny grin. The man excelled at it. "This has turned out to be an extremely hectic rotation for me. These boaters." Extending an arm toward the man lying open on the table. "Ms. Musgrove. A lady driving into the sea near Cockburn Town."

"A suicide?" Having no real interest but wanting to compensate for my initial hostility.

"Tough one. The deceased left no note and had no history of depression. But I'm told there may have been trouble on the home front. It's one for the cops to sort out." Then a not-so-subtle hint. "I'm hoping to complete this last autopsy today so I can fly north tomorrow."

"I won't take up any more of your time. I've brought bones I'd like X-rayed. Perhaps you can direct me to radiology?"

He did. Then, "May I ask? Are your cold cases the ones that troubled Ms. Musgrove?"

"Yes."

"Dear, dear Ms. Musgrove. Such a terrible loss. And these poor souls." Again indicating the poor soul he was about to eviscerate.

"Are you finding anything to explain what happened on that boat?"

"Not a thing."

To get those X-rays taken, a phone call had to be made to the Grace Bay station. An explanation provided. Authorization given.

Once my request was granted, paperwork had to be filled out. Then, my "patients" being dead and therefore low priority, I had to wait.

All in all, the process took more than two hours. A delay that did nothing to improve my disposition.

Though I had the copies of the films on a thumb drive, I wanted to view them in a larger format, on a hospital system monitor. Not feeling the love in radiology, I returned to the autopsy room.

Lindstrom was still there. The corpse was still on the table.

Organ samples now floated in labeled jars or lay in slices on a cork cutting board.

When I hesitated at the door, Lindstrom waved me in.

"You won't bother me," he said, jovial as Santa at the mall.

"Actually, I might need your access code to view my films." A problem I should have anticipated, but in my agitation did not.

"Absoluto."

I punched in the sequence Lindstrom provided. Then the file number grudgingly assigned by the radiology tech.

The first of a half dozen images appeared on the screen. It showed two young and healthy lower arm bones, one set neatly severed above the wrist. Ditto for the second and third images.

Curious, or wanting a break from his autopsy, Lindstrom joined me and peered over my shoulder.

"Only radii and ulnae?" he asked as I brought up the fourth plate.

"Yes."

"Someone cut off the left hand?"

"Yes." My focus on the screen, I didn't elaborate.

"My golly, those are clean cuts. Your doer used one whack-a-doodle sharp blade."

"Any suggestions as to tool type?"

"Machete? Cleaver?"

Fifth image.

"What the dingle-donkey is that?"

24

A vertebrate long bone is built along the same lines as a pipe. Hard on the outside, hollow in the center.

The outer compact bone, being dense and able to block most X-ray particles, appears white on a radiograph. The same is true for metals and the majority of contrast media. Structures containing air appear black. Fat, muscle, organs, and fluid appear as shades of gray.

Lindstrom's dingle-donkey surprise looked like a tiny comet blazing in Quentin Bonner's distal left ulna.

"What *is* that?" Lindstrom asked again.

"I don't know," I said. "But it doesn't belong there."

"Care to view the anomaly under magnification?"

"Oh, yeah," I said.

"Would you like an assist?"

"I don't want to delay—"

"That fellow isn't going anywhere." Lindstrom chin-cocked the man on the table.

"Thanks."

While the pathologist fired up the scope and monitor, I gloved and slipped on an apron. When properly garbed, I maneuvered the ulna under the lens.

"This is going to be tricky," I said. "I'll angle the distal end and rotate until I get the best view of whatever it is."

"Say the word and I'll hold her in place while you adjust focus," Lindstrom said.

The man's hands were as steady as a neurosurgeon's.

"Looks like a splinter of metal," I said when the image settled on the screen. "Probably forced into the shaft when the wrist was severed."

"Makes sense. My guess, the hand was removed with a single powerful blow delivered quick and hard." Lindstrom demonstrated with a vertical chop. "That's an extraordinarily smooth cut."

"May I use your saw?" I asked.

"Let me clean it."

As Lindstrom did that, I snapped pics. When the saw was ready, I buzzed through the bone as near the inclusion as I dared.

"May I borrow—?"

Having anticipated my need, Lindstrom handed me a pair of mosquito forceps.

Moving gingerly, I clamped the visible edge of the splinter between the delicate jaws of the tweezers. At first it wouldn't budge.

I tugged harder. No go.

Forcing the jaws further back onto the object, I squeezed the handles and yanked.

A slight shimmy, then the bone reluctantly yielded its booty. I pulled the thing free and held it aloft.

The sliver of metal was flat, roughly rectangular, and measured about one by two centimeters.

"Must be steel," Lindstrom said. "To be strong enough to penetrate without bending."

Wordlessly, I placed the fragment under the scope. Focused. We both studied the new image.

"Three of its borders are smooth, the fourth is rough. Looks like a flake broken from something larger."

I agreed.

"Flip her over," Lindstrom suggested.

Using the forceps, I did.

"Is that writing?" Apparently, the man's eyesight was better than mine.

"Those dots?"

"Increase the magnification," he said. "Please."

When I did, the dots crystallized into angles and lines.

"More."

I zoomed higher.

"Hey, Mem, the vowel O, Tsade," Lindstrom read aloud. "The rest is missing."

I just looked at him.

Lindstrom shrugged. "I'm blessed with extraordinary vision. Perhaps the reason they pay me the mediocre bucks."

"That and your M.D."

"And that."

"Okay, Hawkeye. Explain what you're seeing."

"Hebrew lettering."

A quick snap of excitement sent my heart racing.

Easy, Brennan!

"You can read Hebrew?"

"I can."

With a name like Lindstrom? My face must have revealed that unspoken thought.

"My father was Swedish, my mother Jewish. It's thanks to her I got saddled with the name Harvey. Pops didn't like it and called me Ace."

"What do the letters spell out?" I asked.

Rueful grin. "There's too much missing. Perhaps someone with greater knowledge of Hebrew can help."

I was torn.

Stay and examine the cut surfaces under magnification?

Set out in hopes of a full translation?

The scope was now available anytime.

Decision.

Identifying tool type could wait.

I thanked Lindstrom and wished him a safe trip home. Then I printed a hard copy of every image, hurriedly repackaged the arm bones, and raced out the door.

I had a sense of how to get to the synagogue. Still, I wanted guidance.

Thankful that Google Maps was working in Provo, I scrolled to the app on my iPhone. Not knowing the congregation's official name, I entered Villa Juba as my destination, figuring I could blunder downhill from the Stribbes' complex on my own.

The navigation came back all business, the lady again sounding more British than Musgrove. Wondering why I'd chosen the accent, I mentally dubbed the voice Camilla as I propped the phone upright in the cup holder in the center console.

The early-morning clouds were now darkening the sky from horizon to horizon, their colors the ugly purple, yellow, and green of an aging bruise. Winding toward the Leeward Highway, I caught glimpses of a violently wrinkled sea. Not far offshore, a dense shroud of rain was turning the water's surface the deep blue-green of dried sage.

Awnings snapped on many of the buildings I passed. Crank-up umbrellas were cranked down and secured. The locals sensed a big one coming.

They were right. Within minutes, drops began pattering the Honda's unfortunate saffron paint. A few at first, fat and listless.

I flicked on the wipers. They were as lazy as the vehicle's AC.

In one thousand feet, turn left.

Unexpected. But, trusting Camilla's knowledge of island geography over my own, I hung a left.

Lightning flashed.

Thunder boomed.

It was as though a switch had been thrown.

Rain began falling in torrents, overpowering the wipers, and blurring my view of the road. In a heartbeat, the world beyond my headlights ceased to exist. I slowed to a crawl and peered intently through the windshield, wary of driving off the road.

Ten minutes, later Camilla spoke again.

In one thous— feet, —rn right.

Damn. I was losing signal.

Death-gripping the wheel, I turned.

Outside my little bubble, the deluge *thrummed* and the wind *whoshed* the palms. Now and then a runaway frond cartwheeled across my headlights or careened full force into the glass.

Inside, the air smelled of water sucked from the ocean. Of salt and seaweed and fish eggs and shrimp.

In one thou—nd —eet, turn —eft.

Really?

I wanted to glance sideways at my phone. To check the map. To see where I was. Too risky.

Turn left.

Craning forward, heart thumping, I did as directed, eyes glued to the murky fan of windshield briefly cleared by the overwhelmed wipers.

—urn left.

I turned again. Felt the engine grind into a lower gear.

The Honda was now struggling up a long, steep grade. I didn't recall the ascent from my previous trips.

Something wasn't right.

Lightning sparked again.

In the flash I could see that I was on a one-lane track, muddy now and growing muddier by the second. Ditches brimmed with water along both edges. Beyond the ditches, a vast dark emptiness.

—ontinue for an—ther quarter —ile.

I did.

In —ifty feet, —urn left.

I slowed.

Turn —eft.

No! A lone cell in my hindbrain screamed.

I slammed on the brakes.

Nerves pulsing with adrenaline, I sat frozen, drops hammering the Honda's hood and roof and sluicing through the twin beams gamely trying their best.

My ragged breathing sounded loud in the car.

Where was I?

Wait!

More good advice from my id. Again, I listened.

Ten minutes. Fifteen. An eon.

Gradually, the downpour eased, and the cloud cover lightened.

Nerves quieting back down slightly, I opened the door and stepped out of the car.

The Turks and Caicos aren't known for their mountain peaks. No Pico Duarte or Montagne Pelée. Nevertheless, the place where I found myself turned my blood cold.

I'd hit the brakes on a serpentine track on the spine of a ridge. The drop-off to either side was rocky and deadly.

Sweet Jesus! Had I turned left, the plunge from this elevation would have been fatal.

How did this happen? Why had Google Maps led me astray? Had I programmed the system wrong? Had I driven into an area where the signal was not only broken but scrambled?

The more important question. What to do now? Soldier on, hoping for a place wide enough to make an about-face? Reverse back down the way I came up? Try another system. WAZE? What3Words? Call for help? Would my phone even work?

Distrustful of all navigation apps, I went with option one. If no reasonable possibility appeared within half a mile, I'd reverse course. Literally.

Sliding behind the wheel, I crawled forward at a blazing fifteen mph. A quarter mile along the ridge, the road expanded enough for me to make a shaky seven-point turn.

Go home? Continue to the synagogue as planned?

Deciding that translation could wait, I pointed the Honda down-hill. The first person I encountered gave me directions to Grace Bay.

I was watching a fat orange sun sink below a pearl horizon when the condo's landline rang. Casting a puzzled glance at my mobile, I got up to answer.

"Where the blazes have you been?" Harry sounded wired, even for Harry.

"I'm in the Turks and Caicos."

"I know your location. I *mean*, why does your phone keep rolling me to voice mail?"

"I must have switched it to silent mode." Had I?

"Well, turn the damn thing on."

"Okay." Then, "Ring me."

"Why?"

"To test it."

Seconds later the *Law & Order* theme blasted loud and clear.

"What goofy ring tone are you using these days?" Harry knew of my quirky habit, and never missed a chance to scoff at my choices.

I told her. Then added, "In the criminal justice system, the people are represented by two separate yet equally important groups: the—"

"Yeah, yeah. The police who investigate crimes, and the district attorneys who do something else. You watch too much television, big sister."

"Apparently, you do, too."

"Guilty as charged. It's my one vice," she said with not a hint of irony.

As if, I thought. "How did you know I was in the islands?"

"Called Ryan. That monsieur is definitely a keeper." Pronounced miss-your.

"Are you still dating, is it Benton?"

Harry's love life is like a revolving door. Fast in, tumultuous whirl, fast out. As a result, I commit no name to memory until the guy has lasted several months.

"Boston. Boston Trivino." Derisive snort. "If the boy had a single brain cell it'd die of loneliness."

"I take that as a no."

"Sent him packing a couple weeks back." Then one of Harry's head-spinning segues. "What are you doing down there?"

"Looking at cold cases."

I left it at that. But my sister has the instincts of a nuclear detector at code red.

"Don't dance me around, Tempe. You sound nervous as a horse in a dog-food factory. What's up?"

"I had a little incident while driving today." No way I'd mention the part about almost plummeting to my death.

"I'm going to send you a meditation link. I find the stuff useful when my nerves are jangled."

"I don't—"

"Damnation, Tempe. Just give it a spin."

"Fine. But not tonight. Right now, I just want to sleep."

"Whatever greases your wagon."

Lying in bed, I was struck by a realization.

I hadn't a clue as to Harry's real purpose in calling.

25

I was at the hospital by eight. The only sentient being in the pathology department.

At nine, I phoned Caribbean Chabad House of Provo. After sharing the bare minimum—a criminal investigation, a fragment of metal bearing Hebrew lettering—the rabbi's wife, Leah Abrams, said she felt it was inappropriate that she or her husband get involved in a police matter.

Disappointed, I pushed the translation to the back of my mind and spent the morning viewing and photographing the eight bones that had formed Quentin Bonner's and Ryder Palke's lower arms.

As time passed, people came and went. I hardly noticed.

What I was seeing supported my naked eyeball impression that the perp had not used an axe or a machete to sever his victims' hands.

Not a mindblower, still good to have confirmation.

But other details had me tingling with excitement.

Anticipating Monck's skepticism, I sought additional corroboration.

Vaguely recalling a publication from years back, I booted my laptop and ran a search using three keywords: axe, cuts, bone.

Bingo! P. McCardle, 2015, *Forensic Research & Criminology International Journal.* I read the article twice. Almost did an arm pump. Almost.

There was one more class of characteristics to check.

After printing hard copy, I returned to the scope. Was repositioning Palke's right radius when my iPhone sounded.

"Dr. Brennan."

"You were out of pocket yesterday." Delivered more as statement than question. Had Monck tried to contact me?

"Long story." Still unsure how I'd ended up on that ridge. "I'm analyzing the cut marks on Palke and Bonner."

"Any progress?"

"Yes."

"I want you to walk me through it."

The line muffled, as though Monck was shielding the mouthpiece. I heard a muted exchange of male voices, then he was back.

"Sorry." No explanation.

"Are you ready?" I slid my notes closer, wanting to get through this and back to my analysis. "The blade's entry site appears—"

"Not by phone. I want to see it."

"I should finish by mid-afternoon."

"Now."

"I'm at the hospital. The pathology departm—"

"No can do. You come here."

Seriously? I should drop what I'm doing and rush to him?

"While you're here I'll brief you on where we are with the case."

"Musgrove or the serial?"

"Both."

"Fine." Tone radiating that it wasn't. "I'll be there shortly."

Reluctantly, I packaged the bones and set out.

Unlike Chalk Sound, the Grace Bay station had no dragon guarding its gate. I'd barely cleared the door when Monck appeared in the lobby. Today's outfit involved a violet shirt and purple tie dotted with green and orange whirligigs. Bold choices. The bags under his eyes were smaller, but still the size of carry-ons.

Monck led me to his office. Offered coffee.

I accepted. Lack of sleep had me craving caffeine.

When Monck disappeared, I sat. After digging the microphotographs from my purse, I looked around.

The room was undersized given its file cabinets, pair of desks, and six chairs. The décor was standard cop shop. Phones. Keyboards and screens. Unwashed mugs. Overflowing in- and out-baskets.

A corkboard layered with flyers and posters hung on one wall. A portable whiteboard was pushed to another, remnant jottings from some previous investigation still smearing its surface.

I noted only two island touches. An oscillating fan standing tall in one corner. A conch shell paperweight atop one of the cabinets.

Minutes after leaving—disappointingly soon for him to have brewed a fresh pot—Monck returned with a pair of thick ceramic mugs. Handing one to me, he circled the desk and dropped into its chair.

"Okay. Lay it down." Cupping his chin with his good hand and angling the prothesis across the blotter.

I reached out and spread my printouts before him. After scanning the images, he looked a question at me.

"Those are blowups of the cut marks on Palke's and Bonner's arm bones. They're labeled by victim name and specific bone."

"Got it." Going back through the stack, more slowly.

"Hacking is essentially blunt-force trauma inflicted by a sharp object."

"How about you don't go all sciency?" he asked, sounding exactly like Claudel. Or my sometime investigative partner Skinny Slidell back in North Carolina.

"Research on such trauma has established two things. First, when cutting bone, sharp tools leave behind both individual and class characteristics. Second, no two tools produce the exact same marks."

Monck's attention to the printouts suggested genuine interest. Or that the pictures were more engaging than what I was saying. Either way, he didn't interrupt me again.

"With both Palke and Bonner, the wrist end of each left radius and ulna was severed cleanly. The blow caused no crushing, no breakage, no triangular fragmentation at the blade's exit point."

"The exit point is here?" He raised an image and pointed.

"Yes."

"What does that mean?"

"The unknown implement was *not* an axe."

"An axe is not subtle."

"Exactly. With both victims, the blade's entry points are also clean. No fracturing or chattering."

"Chattering?"

"Tiny jumpy steps in the vertical wall of the cut. Look at images two, four, and six. A machete often leaves chattering. You'll notice there's none."

Monck studied the photos. Then, "Musgrove suspected a machete, but you don't think so."

"I don't. The lack of fracturing and fragmentation at both the blade's entrance and exit sites is characteristic of a much sharper tool." Oversimplifying greatly.

"Like what?"

"Like a cleaver."

"You're saying it was a cleaver?"

"Or a tool resembling a cleaver."

"Go on."

"With a machete, the width of the blade entry site is approximately 3.5 millimeters. With a cleaver, it's closer to 1.5 millimeters. The cuts I measured fell toward the narrower end of that range. You can see the measurements superimposed on several of the images."

"Not an axe, not a machete." Monck's eyes met mine, sparking with the same excitement I was feeling. His lips parted and the bionic hand rose to emphasize a point.

The quick move upended Monck's mug, sending coffee spewing in all directions.

"Shit!"

"Crap!"

Monck sprang to his feet and bulleted from the room, returned in seconds with a roll of paper towels. While he blotted first the desktop, then his dizzying tie, I shook coffee from the prints.

"My bad," he said.

"May I spread these across the other desk?"

"Let me help."

When we'd done that, Monck resumed his seat.

"Uri Stribbe." I could see the fire of the hunt burning in his gaze. In his blood. "The slaughterer."

"A *shochet* uses a *shechita*," I said.

"A fucking cleaver."

"There are additional features I've yet to observe."

"Does a *shechita* fit with what you're seeing so far?"

"It does. And there's something else."

Mock raised both brows in question.

I told him about the fragment with its Hebrew lettering.

"What does it say?"

"I don't know."

"We need a translation."

"We do."

Monck leaned back in his chair. Tapped his fleshed fingertips to his chin. "Uri Stribbe." Mumbled more to himself than to me. "This Jamaican boy is coming for your ass."

A thought sat up in my id.

What?

The thought rolled over and resumed dozing.

"You're feeling pretty solid about Stribbe?" I asked.

"As the rock of Gibraltar."

"Is he still in jail?"

"Mama lawyered up. I've got no physical evidence to tie him to the murders, so I had to cut him loose."

I sipped my coffee. Found it as bad as I'd feared. Then, "You mentioned other updates. Make any headway with Musgrove's ex?"

"Willis is still in the wind. But don't worry, we're going all out on this." Voice filled with loathing. "When we nail the bastard he'll wish he'd never been born."

I waited.

"I've been taking a deeper run at Cloke."

"The FBI agent?" I asked, wondering if Monck had shifted focus to Cloke to keep his mind off his boss's murder.

"*Special* agent," he corrected. That sarcasm again.

"And?" Truncating what I suspected would be another Claudel-*esque* quip.

"Cloke was working at the operational technology division at FBI headquarters in Washington, DC. Prying that much loose was like asking for the director's home telephone number."

"The OTD does what?" I asked. *Operational technology* sounded like it could be anything.

"According to Special Agent Lyle Carmichael, the guy I was finally bounced to"—Monck flipped pages in a legal pad lying on the desktop—"'the division develops technologies that enable and enhance the intelligence, national security, and law enforcement operations of the agency.'"

"Why dispatch a computer nerd to Provo?"

"Carmichael was not at liberty to say. And refused to confirm that Cloke was actually 'dispatched,' as you put it."

"Might Cloke have come here concerning the dead boaters?

Maybe the government is worried about the impact of a potential incident in international waters?"

"That's a stretch."

I didn't disagree.

"Here's some intel that set me buzzing," he said. "I checked with immigration and customs enforcement. Over the last seven years Cloke has made eight trips to Provo, each time flying coach, billing the ticket to his personal Mastercard, and not identifying himself as law enforcement upon departure or arrival. Each trip he left and returned to DCA," he added, using the acronym for Washington's Ronald Reagan Airport.

"Except for the last."

"Except for that one."

"Is Cloke married? Maybe he was coming to Provo to vacation with the missus?"

Monck sighed. "Carmichael preferred not to say."

"Girlfriend? Boyfriend?"

"Carmichael wouldn't comment. But I did my own digging. No repeat names showed up on any of the dates Cloke checked through passport control. Or on his flight manifests or those of the adjacent days."

"Did he always stay at the same place?"

"The Ocean Paradise? No. I'm looking into that."

"Did Carmichael know why Cloke phoned down here about Uri Stribbe?"

"He did not. Or—"

"Refused to say."

"You've got it."

"Cloke was asking about Uri Stribbe. Might he have been looking into the murders?"

Monck shrugged. "Why send an E-geek to investigate a serial?"

Good point.

"Might Cloke be a victim?" I was posing questions stream-of-thought style. "Maybe he came to Provo for whatever reason, was randomly grabbed by this psycho. Like the others."

"The guy's thirty-six. Too old for the known victimology."

"Did you request a photo?"

"Carmichael promised to get right on that." Sarcastic as hell.

"Did you explai—"

"Screw those pricks. I got a pic on my own."

Monck dug a printout from his file and handed it to me.

The image was blurry, as though the subject had moved just as the photo was snapped. It showed a young man with a straight nose, arching brows, and a lot of dark hair slicked back from his face. A young man who was Marine Corps poster good-looking.

"This was taken as Cloke passed through passport control."

Monck placed his palms on the blotter, preparing to rise.

A sudden thought struck me.

"*Is* he?"

"Is he what?" Monck held position.

"Outside the victim profile? He looks young."

Monck said nothing.

"Or maybe we're going at this all wrong. Maybe there are other victims we've missed."

Monck gave me a look I couldn't interpret.

"I *will* find Cloke," he said. "But right now, Uri Stribbe is out there and I'm going hot on his ass."

"But—"

"I appreciate your coming, doc." Monck pushed to his feet. "But how about you do your bones and leave the sleuthing to me? At least for one day?"

A day is not what he got.

26

The rest of the day was a study in disappointment.

I'd been in the autopsy room less than an hour when the door swung open.

Startled, I turned from the scope.

Monck looked like he'd just come from an all-you-can-eat buffet of frustration.

"I finally caught up to Willis. The jackass claims he was in Houston when Musgrove died."

"Milo Willis?" Focused on cut marks, my mind was scrambling to make connections. "Musgrove's ex?"

Monck nodded. "Willis says he was teeing off with buddies Wednesday through Sunday."

"He was at a golf resort?"

"Yep. According to him and his three fairway pals he never left."

"You don't sound convinced."

"Let's just say I plan to corroborate. I'll check his credit card charges, airline tickets, talk to the clubhouse manager, the restaurant staff, the guys in the caddy shack, border patrol on both ends, you know the routine."

"If Willis wasn't in Provo he couldn't have killed his wife."

"That"—Monck shot a flesh finger at me—"is what I like about you."

Surprised that he valued any of my character traits, I raised questioning brows.

"Your bullet-quick thinking."

"Bite me."

Monck scowled. I could have scowled back, wasn't in the mood. Hell, the guy had just complimented me.

"Now what?" I asked.

"Good question."

"As I said. Maybe we're going at this all wrong." Maybe *you're* going at this all wrong.

Monck spread his feet and chest-crossed his arms.

"Let's assume for now Willis didn't kill Musgrove," I said. "Then who did? Throw out some ideas."

"Willis hired a hitman to do her while he was away?"

"Would Willis benefit from the death of his ex?"

"I'll look into that, too."

"Is he capable of that type of premeditated violence?"

"Who knows? I've always thought he's the 'get wasted and give the old lady a beat down' type."

"Another theory?"

Monck thought. "Well, suppose it was the same sicko who's been murdering tourists."

"Musgrove doesn't fit the serial's victim profile." I was playing devil's advocate. "Galloway, Palke, and Bonner were all young males."

"Maybe she was getting too close, the perp got spooked, and popped her."

"Maybe."

Monck was getting into it. "Maybe it was a rando B and E gone bad. Like the one at your condo."

"*If* that was a random B and E. Perhaps Musgrove and I were both targeted."

"By the serial?"

"It's possible."

"Why?"

"Same reason," I said, shrugging. "We made him nervous."

"Why now?"

Sudden flashback. "Musgrove received a text while we were having dinner Friday night. Her demeanor suggested that the info was surprising, but she wouldn't elaborate."

"What kind of info?"

"That's a question for a cop."

"So," said Monck, uncrossing his arms and hip-jamming both hands. "Who is this psycho prick?"

"I thought you were liking Uri Stribbe."

"I am."

Again, that wee rustle in my subconscious. "Something about Stribbe bothers me," I said.

"What?"

"I'm not sure. For the most part in that interrogation you did he seemed like a wimp. But now and then I'd detect a flare of—" Of what? "I don't know. It was hard to get a take on the guy."

"Ever see that docudrama on Jeff Dahmer?"

Monck had a point.

"Musgrove was cop-trained, and she was fit," I said. "Whoever attacked her must have been strong."

"Or wily and quick."

"Maybe we're trying to fit Stribbe into a mold we expect."

"What's that supposed to mean?"

Unsure, I said nothing.

"Okay, doc. Let's play your game. If the serial isn't Stribbe—the guy who speaks Hebrew and has masterful cleaver skills—then who?"

"What about the brother?"

"Dovid?"

"He seemed angry. And volatile. And had access to cleavers."

"Uh-huh."

Second flashback to a comment Musgrove had made.

"What about Glen Wall?" I asked.

Monck looked lost for a moment. Then, "The bartender at Polly's Tiki Shack?"

I nodded.

"According to Musgrove's notes, Wall had a solid alibi for the period Palke went missing."

"Provided by his brother and cousins."

Monk raised his brows.

I raised mine.

"I'll recheck him, too."

"What about Cloke?" Now I was reaching. "Why did Cloke travel to Provo repeatedly? People at FBI headquarters knew noth—"

"Or refused to say."

"Cloke and Musgrove are both law enforcement."

"Were." Bitter.

"Might that be a connection?"

"Meaning Musgrove lied about not knowing the guy?"

"It's possible."

"Why?"

I ignored his very valid question.

"Did Cloke's trips to TCI coincide with the dates of the murders?" I asked.

Monck gave me a look that suggested I may have raised a good point. Still, his next questions, and his tone, suggested serious skepticism.

"You're thinking Cloke traveled here to use Provo as a hunting ground? That Musgrove was an accomplice?"

"Or maybe she was on to him and didn't want to say anything until she had proof. In case she was wrong. Maybe that text she received was about him."

"Why has Cloke vanished?"

I had no answer to that.

"*Where* has Cloke vanished?"

Or to that.

"I'll do a deep dive into all of this."

"Maybe go back at Uri?"

"Adeera's Rottweiler lawyer has him shrink-wrapped tighter than a frozen pizza." Monck did not sound hopeful.

"What else could break wrong?" I asked.

A lot.

By the end of that day, it was a whole new ball game.

Before leaving the hospital, I phoned Monck. Was rolled to voice mail. Of course, I was.

I packaged the bones, returned to the morgue, and signed both sets of remains back over to Iggie. He seemed uncertain what to do with them. I suggested he seek counsel from the coroner.

Though troubled, and a bit confused, I was certain of my conclusion. Wondered how the Merry Monckster would react.

The sun was low when I headed out, a fuzzy peach kissing an apricot horizon. The world around me was glowing a soft coppery pink.

My work was done. I was eager to reunite with Ryan and Birdie. But Montreal's subdued northern sunsets offered nothing so vivid. I'd miss Provo's spectacular fruit salad dusks.

Back at the Villa Renaissance, thinking it would be my last opportunity, I went for a beach walk, then an ocean swim. More like a clumsy try-to-maintain-my-balance frolic in the surf.

The brief respite was as soothing as I'd hoped. I was on my laptop, eating Caribbean jerk fish salad from Turks Kabob, and checking flights from Provo to Montreal, when my mobile sounded.

"Brennan."

"Two in one cockwomble day."

Monck's tone caused my recently sun-warmed scalp to prickle. Abandoning the takeout I asked, "Two?"

"Looks like Willis could be telling the truth. Now Stribbe may be in the clear, too."

A beat, as disparate data bytes joined in my head.

"Uri Stribbe has an alibi?"

"Stribbe was at a service Friday night. I forget what the thing's called. More than thirty people saw him."

"That's what he said in the interview."

"Afterward, he attended some sort of dinner at the synagogue. Dovid and Adeera were at his side the whole time. They swear he never left the condo after returning home around ten."

"If it's true, that rules Stribbe out for Musgrove. But he might still—"

"According to Adeera, on February 25, 2022, Stribbe was in Brooklyn celebrating something called Purim."

"New York?"

"No, Uzbekistan." Pause. "Of course, New York. Again, big brother and mama vouch for him."

"That's the date Quentin Bonner went missing."

"Yes."

"If it's true, Uri couldn't have done Bonner."

"How can you be so perceptive?"

"A question I ask myself daily."

"You keep saying 'if it's true.'" I could picture Monck hooking air quotes.

"They're family. A family dominated by a hard-as-nails matriarch."

"Meaning you think they might lie?"

I said nothing.

"Here's another factoid," Monck said. "Shared by mama. Uri is mildly autistic."

Audio replay.

Mental head slap.

"That's what Adeera yelled as I ran from their condo. She wasn't threatening a fiery cataclysm. She was saying that Uri's on the spectrum."

"It doesn't matter how much head shrinking this animal slicer needs. My gut still tells me—"

"Autism isn't that kind of illness." Though I didn't disagree with Monck's gut.

A heavy silence filled the line. I gave it to him. Gave him time for his thoughts. Eventually, they circled to my afternoon call.

"You left me a message saying you've made progress with the cut marks."

"I have."

"Roll it out."

"By phone?"

"No. By—"

Not in the mood for further derision, I launched in. "As I've explained, different types of blades leave different marks in bone. One of the characterist—"

"Make this quick."

After a censorious pause, I gave the briefest of synopses.

"The blade was extremely narrow and sharp, but slightly damaged."

"Damaged?"

"The cutting edge had a very small nick."

"A feature you could use to ID the thing?"

"Yes."

"Why didn't you see it before?"

"I needed magnification and couldn't get access to a microscope."

"Could it be a slaughterer's *chalet*?"

"*Chalef*. Maybe. But a *shochet* is duty-bound to keep his blade perfect. So that the animals—"

"Don't suffer. Right."

Monck thought about the nick. So had I since discovering it.

"What about Dovid?" I tossed out. "Maybe Uri's brother grabs discarded cleavers that no longer make the grade?"

"Or maybe your hunch is right."

"I wouldn't call it a hun—"

"Maybe mama and big bro *are* both lying. Like you, I got the vibe Adeera would do anything to protect her boys."

"And that her boys would do anything she demanded."

"Either scenario ticks," Monck said.

"Like a bug on a screen."

I listened to a full minute of agitated breathing. Then,

"Can you meet me at Chalk Bay station tomorrow at nine?"

"I've finished my analysis and plan to fly home. Remember? You do the sleuthing, I do the bones?"

"I'd appreciate your insight."

Had I heard correctly?

"A memorial service is in the works for SIO Musgrove for Friday or Saturday. You wouldn't want to miss that."

"Sure," I said. "What's one more day."

"Bring your files."

Three beeps, and he was gone.

Monck's call left me more edgy than before my sand and surf outing.

What the hell?

Locating Harry's email, I ran through the names of the meditation programs baby sister had sent. Liked one called *Smiling Mind.* How could that be bad?

After downloading the app, I created an account, and chose a program.

I tried my best to concentrate on mindfulness. To ban all the worries of the past few days.

Images kept breaking through, one uglier than the next. Galloway. Palke. Bonner. Musgrove.

I lasted five minutes.

27

While driving, I made a mental note to ask Monck about the Honda. To whom did the car belong? To whom should I return it when leaving the island?

The self-reminder caused a brief twinge of melancholy. Seemed I'd grown fond of the trusty old beater.

It also triggered a sharp stab of pain. Musgrove had arranged for my wheels. Musgrove was dead.

Focus, Brennan.

Arriving at the Grace Bay station, I went straight to the squad room. The whiteboard had been pulled forward and cleaned of all previous notes. Pictures of Galloway, Palke, and Bonner had been taped in a row across the top. The same shots Musgrove had taken to Montreal.

Monck stood before the board, spindly in teal and gray today. He held a rag in his prosthetic hand.

"Java's ready." Flapping the bionic arm at a Mr. Coffee perking spiritedly beside the file cabinet conch.

229

"Thanks."

I filled a mug. Added powdered creamer that looked like it might have been purchased that decade. Sat in the same chair I'd occupied the previous day.

"Thanks for coming."

That surprised me.

"I've been considering a comment you made."

That surprised me even more.

"Let's suppose that the perp isn't Uri Stribbe. Let's suppose we're trying to fit him into a mold we expect."

I had said that.

"Tunnel vision can be counterproductive."

"It can," I agreed.

"Perhaps we should refine the mold."

"You're talking about profiling."

"Yes."

"There are experts for that."

"Not in Provo. But we can construct a rough sketch using what we know."

"I suppose it can't hurt," I said.

Grabbing a Sharpie, Monck drew a line down the middle of the board. Labeled the space on the left *Victims*, that on the right, *Perp/Motive*.

"Toss out anything that comes to mind. I'll start."

I nodded.

"All three vics are white males between the ages of eighteen and twenty-two." Monck wrote their names to the left of the vertical divider: Robert Galloway. Ryder Palke. Quentin Bonner.

"All *known* vics."

Monck tipped his head to acknowledge that I'd made a valid point.

"Unless you include Cloke," I added.

"There's no proof Cloke is dead. For now, let's stick to established facts."

"Right."

"All three were killed in the past seven years."

After checking his files, Monck jotted the dates. April 16, 2017. August 5, 2020. February 25, 2022.

Three-year gap. Two-year gap. Spring, summer, late winter. No patterns there.

"All were tourists," I said. "All came by air and disappeared shortly after landing in Provo."

Monck listed the carriers, the airline codes, and wheels-down time of each flight.

American. Delta. United.

"They all landed between ten a.m. and two p.m.," I said.

"Good one," Monck said.

It wasn't. It was lame.

"Each victim rented a car."

Monck added the companies. Three different outfits.

"Only Galloway's vehicle was recovered," I said.

"In the airport parking lot."

"Two of the three were seen at a place that employed a very sketchy bartender."

Monck added Polly's Tiki Shack and the name Glen Wall.

"Have you learned anything new on Wall?" I asked.

"I'm working on it."

"Each victim was shot in the chest," I tossed out, redirecting a bit.

Monck wrote COD: GSW beside each name. Cause of death: gunshot wound.

"No bullet or casing was found with any set of remains." Monck.

"Each victim's left hand was hacked off." Brennan.

"Hands not recovered." Monck.

The scribbling expanded as we both pulled data from our files.

Height. Weight. Eye color. Hair color. Ancestry. Hometowns. Occupations. Accommodations in Provo. Restaurants or businesses visited, as documented by credit card bills or witness accounts. Last-known sightings. Times of disappearance. Body locations. State of decomp. Patterns of dismemberment.

No matter how much minutiae we recorded, other than Polly's, nothing emerged to link any two victims. Except for the grim combo of murder and mutilation.

"Time to think about the perp," I said. "His MO. His motive."

"Let it fly."

That triggered an idea.

"All the victims arrived by air. Maybe the killer stalks the airport. Maybe that's his hunting ground. Maybe he has access to the terminal. To the tarmac. To flight manifests."

Monck began a catalog to the right of the vertical line.

"Wait." I sat forward. "We're both saying 'he.' But we don't know that."

Monck pivoted, brows dipping low.

"Who says the killer can't be a woman?" I asked.

"Females use guns," he said slowly.

"And have skills with cutlery."

"Okay. Let's unpack that. Why would a chick shoot a guy, then lop off his hand?"

"It's symbolic? Maybe she suffered trauma at the hands of a man? No pun intended."

"Daddy?"

"Or her hubby, her ex, her pimp."

"So she hates men?"

"Yes. But maybe she doesn't want her victims to suffer. She's driven to kill but does it humanely—a quick bullet to the chest—then removes the hand as cleanly and painlessly as possible."

"Why keep the hands?" As usual, Monck sounded dubious.

"We don't know that's the case."

A mechanical finger circled impatiently. "We're speculating now."

"Maybe it's part of the psychosis. Part of the fantasy that must play out."

"Uh-huh."

I swept my gaze across the row of young faces topping the board. Had the same reaction as when Musgrove first showed me the photos.

"All three vics were extraordinarily good-looking," I said. "Maybe she was—"

"Agreed. They were hot. But I'm not feeling a female vibe. Let's go back to thinking the perp is male."

I lifted a palm, indicating he should continue.

"Maybe the guy's not a looker. He's the sad little loser who never gets the girl. Maybe he sees himself as a victim, perpetually eclipsed by more attractive dudes."

"Or maybe he's gay. Maybe he views handsome men as unattainable. Resents them. Or he resents those smooth enough to be able to hook up."

We were both into it now, spewing ideas without thinking them through.

"Maybe he desires hot dudes and wants to control them." Now the titanium digit jabbed my way. "Maybe killing them is his way of scoring."

"He can't have them as lovers, so he keeps their hands to use later in some sort of ritual."

Neither of us wanted to visualize that.

"Three grown men disappear in broad daylight. No one witnesses any of the grabs." Now Monck was shifting gears. "Forget motivation. Where does he do it? How?"

"The old tried and true? A spiked drink in a bar?"

"Musgrove floated those pics past every bouncer and barkeep in Provo. No go."

"Including Glen Wall at Polly's?"

Monck's expression registered that my point had landed.

"Here's a question," I said. "Does he shoot his vics right away? Or does he hold them somewhere and murder them later?"

"Galloway's body was discovered two days after his buddies reported him missing. Decomp was minimal, so for him the answer is probably no. With the others, time between the snatch and the killing is anyone's guess."

I tried another tack.

"Palke and Bonner were found in close proximity to each other. By then, the perp had established a dumping ground. But why leave your victims where they'll eventually turn up? Why not bury them? Drop them far out to sea? Grind them in a wood chipper? Dissolve them in acid? There are dozens of ways to get rid of a corpse."

"Disposal at sea would require a boat, maybe a secluded dock," Monck said.

"Good point. So probably no boat."

"But the perp definitely has a vehicle."

"Agreed. But that doesn't answer my question."

Monck thought a moment, then his brows angled up. "He wants the bodies found."

"Why?" I asked.

"He craves media attention? His fifteen minutes of fame?"

"If so, wouldn't he leave his kills in more obvious places?"

My gaze returned to the lineup topping our notes. My thoughts shifted to the victims' final moments on earth. Galloway, sweat-slicked and pumped on endorphins coming off a run. Bonner, absorbed with F-stops and lenses and light. Palke, high on flashbacks of parrotfish, jacks, and tangs.

Monck's voice brought me back.

"—maybe he's acting out against a specific man in his life. A man he hates."

"Or a man he loves. Or loved." I jumped back in. "Maybe someone who disappointed or betrayed him. That's why he kills kindly then leaves the bodies where they'll be found. But not right away."

"So, he's bat-shit nuts but cunning."

"He doesn't mutilate his victims—"

"Except for the hands."

"But even that he does mercifully, with a single quick, sharp blow. Why?"

"He's proud of his bladesmanship?"

"Is that a word?" I asked.

"If not, it should be."

"After Galloway, he found a dumping ground he thinks is secure. He must also have a hunting ground where he feels safe. Where he thinks he blends in."

"So, the guy must be a local," Monck said.

"Or someone familiar with the island."

"Probably single. If he did hold Bonner and Palke for any length of time he'd need privacy."

"A setting secluded enough not to draw attention."

"Could be a home that he owns or rents."

"Or a place where he works. A warehouse. A barn. A storage facility of some sort."

We both fell silent, studying the scrawled mess on the board. Digging for that single link that could create the tiniest crack.

Emitting a throaty grunt of frustration, Monck dug a folded sheet from his bag, opened and taped it over the notices blanketing the adjacent corkboard. I recognized the lacey, asymmetric map of Provo.

"Let's plot every goddam site any vic ever touched."

Back to the files.

As I cherry-picked location info, Monck pushed pins with his real thumb. Blue for Galloway, red for Palke, yellow for Bonner.

Bobby Galloway and his friends had a rented condo at the Sunset Beach Villas. He left there heading for Taylor Bay Beach. Two days later, his body turned up in the Frenchman's Creek Nature Reserve, his car in the airport parking lot.

Ryder Palke and his girlfriend were at the Royal West Indies Resort. From there, he went diving with Caicos Adventures. Four years later his skeletonized remains were found near the Wheeland Settlement, at the end of a road accessing the TCI waste disposal facility.

Quentin Bonner was staying at the Sibonné Beach Hotel on Grace Bay Beach. He set out to photograph shorebirds on Parrot Cay. Two years later his bones were found in the same wooded area as Palke's.

We added pins for the three rental car companies. For any restaurant or business at which any victim's credit card had made a charge. For every witness sighting recorded due to police canvassing.

Two hours later, dozens of pins formed a rainbow quilt covering most, but not all, of the island. Satisfied we'd marked every location mentioned in Musgrove's and Monck's files, he and I studied our creation.

"Bonner and Palke were both sighted at Polly's," Monck said. "Musgrove ruled Wall out, but it can't hurt to give the toad another poke."

"Galloway and Palke both ate at Grace's Cottage," I said, feeling a flutter of excitement at seeing a second pair of side-by-side pins.

"As does every tourist coming to Provo."

We studied it some more.

"He doesn't display the bodies," I said, picturing the recovery sites I'd worked. "He's not making a statement with his victims."

Monck said nothing.

"Maybe we're reading the whole thing wrong. Why leave his victims at a dead end beyond a waste treatment plant? Why so far out of the way?"

"I'll bite. Why?"

"Maybe he *doesn't* want his victims found."

Monck said nothing.

At length, I stated the discouragingly obvious.

"Besides the bar, the restaurant, and the body dump site, there are no overlaps."

"This was a total waste of time. We've got jackshit."

Monck yanked his mobile from his pocket and checked for messages.

"Gotta go."

With that, he strode from the room.

Ignoring Monck's rudeness, I refocused on the map. At the pins dotting every sector save the far northwestern end of the island.

Was I viewing the killer's hunting ground? If so, his territory was a damn big one. Did he live within it? Far enough out of it to avoid suspicion?

What *did* we have?

The killer was probably single, knew Provo, and killed handsome men.

Monck was right.

We had jackshit.

28

I was brushing my teeth, thinking about breakfast, when my mobile sounded.

"Good morning, Detective Monck."

"Good morning. I just got word. Musgrove's memorial service will be at four Sunday afternoon at Our Lady of Divine Providence Catholic Church."

Crap. Stuck for two more days.

"Where is it?"

"On the Leeward Highway. Across from—"

"Cheshire Hall Plantation."

Christ. I'd been here so long I was learning the landmarks.

"It's cool if you'd rather not hang."

"I can compose a report here as well as back home," I said, resigned.

"Right."

I waited out a pause.

Monck cleared his throat and dove in: "Compelled by yesterday's spectacularly fruitless exercise, and desperate to jog something loose, I went fracking through Musgrove's file again, rereading everything in it. Seven years' worth of shit."

"And?"

"First, let me explain, Musgrove had a process. After talking to a witness or a POI—"

"Person of interest."

"—she'd jot her impressions right away. You know, while the interview was still hot in her mind. She'd do a full write-up later."

Monck inhaled, blew out the breath, then continued: "Way at the back of the file, crumpled and stuck to another page, I found a Post-it with a scribbled note about someone she refs only as JR. She'd jotted *BS* and *sus* beside the initials."

"Bullshit? Suspicious?" I guessed.

"Or suspect."

"That's it?" Seemed thin.

"JR's address was on the Post-it. He, or she, lives at the end of a spur shooting off Malcolm's Road."

"That means nothing to me," I said, leaning in to see if I'd missed anything with my toothbrush.

"Near the Wheeland Settlement."

"Sorry."

"By the dump."

That snapped me back from the mirror.

"And the road running past the waste disposal facility?" I asked.

"Fuckin-A."

"Did Musgrove reinterview this JR person?"

"That's the other thing that caught my attention. The note was dated two days before her death."

"Holy shit."

"I'm on my way out there now. Once I find this JR character, the two of us will have a nice little chat."

"Keep me looped in."

"I just did that."

Dead air.

I sat a moment, heart thumping in my chest. Questions rocketing in my head.

What had Musgrove discovered? Why hadn't she mentioned JR? Was Monck about to confront her killer? A multimurder predator?"

The phone rang in my hand. Time for a change. The *Law & Order* bit was getting old.

After checking the screen, I answered.

"Hey, Harry."

"'Sup, big sis?"

"I'm still in the islands."

"Poor, baby."

"I know. It's a tropical paradise. But I've been here over a week."

"Hear that noise?"

"What noise?"

"A sort of high-pitched keening?"

I heard motor sounds. Emmylou Harris singing about two more bottles of wine.

"No," I said. "What is it?"

"My heart breaking for you."

"Why are you calling? And why did you call last time?"

"I want to know if you and your lovely daughter will join us in Texas for Thanksgiving."

"What do you have in mind?" While Harry has sundry talents, cooking is not among them.

"A surprise."

"I'll talk to Katy."

"How goes it with the serial killer?" She seemed genuinely concerned.

"The main suspect may have alibied out, but the cops are running a new lead." No need to mention Musgrove's murder and Monck's assumption of duties as head detective.

"What are *you* doing?"

"I've finished with the bones, so right now I'm sitting on my ass."

"Well, don't."

"Don't what?"

"Sit on your ass."

"Thanks for the input."

"There must be some other bitsy part you can play."

"Maybe." I told her about the fragment and the need of a Hebrew translation.

"You know lots of Jews."

"Not here in Provo."

Harry thought a moment. The sound of her gum chewing set me on edge.

"Is there a synagogue on the island?" she asked.

"I called. The rabbi's wife declined to get involved in a police matter."

"Go anyway. What can she do, shoot you?"

"I'll think about it."

"Think about Thanksgiving."

"Will do."

I wouldn't. Harry's plans would change a dozen times between then and November.

"Listen. I've been debating whether to say something. If it was me, I'd want to know."

Oh, boy.

"You can never divulge your source on this." Voice lowered to a conspiratorial whisper.

"Cut the drama, Harry. Just tell me."

"Ryan's flying down there. He's planning some sort of romantic *assignation*. It's supposed to be a surprise."

"When?" Mixed emotions having a whale of a time inside me.

"Late Saturday night. I sure as hell wouldn't want the love of my life popping in unannounced. Roots, nails, clean underwear. It's high maintenance keeping the merchandise fresh."

"How does he know I'll still be here?"

"Don't you two love birds talk every day?"

"Not *every* day."

"When he calls tomorrow he'll probably ask questions all casual-like. Only if you say you're leaving will he fess up about what he's planning."

"Thanks for the tip."

When we'd disconnected, I tried Ryan.

Got his voice mail.

I hopped online and checked flights from YUL to PLS. There were two nonstops on Air Canada, one landing around three p.m., the other just past midnight.

Agitated, I considered alternatives.

I could stay in the condo. Write my report on Palke and Bonner. Knock that out before the assignation.

I could have a nice lunch by the pool. Book a mani-pedi. I don't dye my hair, so my roots were good. Why not? I deserved a break now that my part in the case was finished.

But that's not how my brain rolls.

When stressed, I must either exercise or work.

I could run on the beach. Swim. Work out. I thought the complex had a gym.

I yanked my hair into a loose pony. Pulled on jeans and a tee. Went to the kitchen to brew coffee.

I could walk to Graceway Gourmet. Buy fish to cook for dinner. Pick up frozen yogurt at Turkberry.

Even as I considered options, my dreamtime visitors kept demanding attention. Galloway. Palke. Bonner.

Given the light show taking place in my head, I doubted I'd be able to concentrate on a report. Still, I opened the living room's glass doors and sat down at the dining room table.

Sipped the coffee. Shockingly, it wasn't awful.

I booted my Mac Air. Created a blank document. Stared at the screen.

Save for the steady *thrum* of the distant surf, the silence in the condo was so loud it shrieked.

Unbidden, my fingers typed a single word. *Jackshit.*

Screw it.

Closing the laptop, I stuffed the hard-copy file into my purse, and bolted.

Rabbi Zev Abrams and his wife, Leah, lived at Caribbean Chabad House of Provo. I knew that from Monday's conversation with Adeera Stribbe.

I used Google Maps to navigate, keeping a close eye on the suggested directions. I was still clueless about what had gone so wrong the previous Tuesday.

Ten minutes after leaving Villa Renaissance, I pulled to the curb outside the building I'd noticed from the Stribbe condo. Killing the engine, I took a moment to assess.

The place was a one-story contemporary with an angled roof and an addition that didn't come close to honoring the original architect's vision. A large, covered patio stretched across the back. A swing set, plastic sandbox, and vegetable garden shared space on the far side.

Other, smaller homes lined the street. I saw no signs of activity at any.

The Abramses' front door was offset to one side. I got out and crossed to it. A glass-encased sign listed details about services in terms I didn't fully understand: *kabbalat shabbat, shabbat, kiddush, kaddish, minyan, mincha/maariv.*

I rang the bell. A muted bonging sounded deep in the interior.

Already the day was warm and muggy. Not the faintest hint of a breeze stirred the palm fronds overhead.

In less than a minute, a tiny woman opened the door. I figured she couldn't have topped five feet. The woman's eyes were large and almond-shaped, with irises the pale green of Riesling grapes.

Though decades younger than Adeera Stribbe, this woman's style of dress was similar. She wore an ankle-skimming navy skirt, loose white blouse, and a heather cardigan that, in her case, hung all the way to her knees.

Unlike her uphill neighbor, this woman did not cover her head. Her chestnut hair was center-parted and cascading down around her shoulders.

The Riesling eyes widened on seeing a stranger, dropped to my sandals, ran up my jeans and tee, and settled on my face.

"Yes?"

"Leah Abrams?" I asked.

"And you are?" Not unfriendly, but cautious.

"Temperance Brennan. I called to request a translation of a Hebrew inscription."

"You're with the police."

"I'm a forensic consultant."

"I'm sorry, Ms. Brennan. I did ask my husband, and he agrees with my initial response. It's better we remain aloof."

"The lettering is quite short. It would take only a mom—"

"It's not the time. We're happy to give that."

"I don't understand."

"Suppose our input were to implicate a member of this congregation? A member of our community? What then? What if that person was hurting? Would he or she feel comfortable coming to Zev for counsel?"

"Are you thinking of someone in particular?" I asked.

A beat. Then, "Surely we're not the only Jews you know."

"Of course not. But I trust your—"

"The government must have us all on some database."

"It's not like that." I suspected it was.

"Isn't it?"

"I'm sorry if I offended you. I'm simply trying to get to the bottom—"

"*Shabbat Shalom.*"

Leah Abrams gently but firmly closed the door.

Returning to the car, I again kicked into self-castigation mode.

Good job, Brennan. You picked the exact wrong thing to say.

I *wheep-wheeped* the Honda's locks.

And Friday? Really? You came on a Friday? The eve of Sabbath?

I slid behind the wheel and started the engine. Waited a minute for the AC to emit a hint of coolness.

Abrams was right. I had to know other Jewish people in Provo.

Think, Tempe, think.

Suddenly, a notion occurred to me.

The man was friendly enough. Had probably studied Hebrew. Wasn't likely to be a congregant.

I shifted into gear.

One last try.

29

The landscaping hadn't improved since Monck and I visited on Monday. The morning was inching from warm to hot and, if anything, the lawn looked even more pitiful than it had. The shed was still there. The doghouse. The motorcycle.

This time I hadn't called ahead. My target was either home or he wasn't.

I parked at the head of the drive and crunched along the path. Felt the irritating grit of crushed oyster shells invading my sandals.

Arriving at the front entrance, I could hear music blasting inside the house. Above the music, what sounded like quarreling. Perhaps a TV?

I thumbed the bell.

Betty went bonkers.

The voices went still.

The music cut off.

A period of homicidal barking, then Joe Benjamin opened the chartreuse door. The hooded eyes narrowed, suggesting that their owner was either confused or unhappy to see me.

I spoke through the screen. Loudly, to be heard over the yapping.

"I don't know if you remember Detect—"

"Where's the cop?" Benjamin peered past me, scanning down the drive.

"Detective Monck is busy with another matter."

"Did you talk to Uri Stribbe?"

"We did, sir."

"The guy's an odd duck, eh?" Benjamin's hand stayed tight on the knob, his thumb bobbing like a botfly testing the air. "What's up now?"

I caught a flicker of movement in my peripheral vision. Turning, I saw sunlight glint off the window in the door of the backyard shed.

A bird? A reflection of shifting palm fronds?

"I wonder, sir. Do you read Hebrew?"

"What the heck kind of question is that? Of course, I read Hebrew."

"I have an inscription I need translated."

"Maybe ask the rabbi?"

"I did. The Abramses feel it would not be appropriate for them to get involved."

"Big surprise."

"I'm sure the rabbi understands what's best for his congregation." Brennan, the peacemaker. "As they say, good judgment comes from experience."

"Yeah. And experience often comes from bad judgment."

"You make a good point, sir." He did.

Betty continued her deafening protest.

"Betty!"

The dog took a break. Immediately reengaged.

"God dang it!" Sharp with annoyance. "Hold on."

Benjamin bent, grabbed Betty's collar, and dragged her away from the entrance. I watched their tug-of-war withdrawal play out below the framed black-and-white prints.

At the end of the hall, dog and owner went left. A few seconds, then a door slammed and the barking recommenced, muffled, but equally wholehearted.

"I have to admire Betty's perseverance," I said when Benjamin returned.

"The dog's a jerkpot. But she's my jerkpot. Look, I'd like to help you, but I'm working today. I got a deadline."

"One quick look?"

"Fine." Instead of asking me in, Benjamin palmed open the screen door and stepped outside.

"Thank you so much."

"No promises."

I pulled a microphotograph from my purse and handed it to him.

Benjamin glanced at the image. "Seriously? This is it?"

"That's all I have." No need to share details.

Benjamin squinted at the magnified dots Lindstrom had recognized as Hebrew letters.

Betty yapped from her place of captivity, zeal undiminished.

A drop of sweat broke free and rolled down my spine.

I was shifting my purse strap from one shoulder to the other when Benjamin spoke.

"It could be the beginning of the *hamotzi* blessing."

Benjamin's words snapped me back.

"The *hamotzi* blessing?"

"*Hamotzi Lechem Min Ha'aretz.*" The man's Hebrew sounded flawless. But what did I know?

"How does that translate?" I asked.

"Who brings forth bread from the earth. But like I said, you don't have much, and I'm no expert."

"I understand. Just a couple more questions?" Smiling my most beguiling smile.

Benjamin thrust the page at me but didn't leave.

Taking it, I asked, "When is this prayer said?"

"It's the third of the three traditional blessings recited by women on Friday night. Before the bread is cut."

"On what might the phrase be inscribed?" I asked.

Benjamin raised both palms and brows. "Where might *God Bless You* be inscribed? Take your pick."

"Might it be found on a *shochet*'s cleaver?"

"Unlikely. The blessing has to do with bread."

He reached out to grasp the screen door handle. Paused, as though struck by a possibility.

"I suppose it could be found on a challah knife."

"A challah knife?"

"They're used to cut the challah bread on Friday nights."

"Who might own a challah knife?" I asked.

"Any Jew on the planet."

"Where are they sold?" Excited. Thinking a Judaic specialty shop could be a good lead.

Benjamin snorted. An unpleasantly wet sound.

"Amazon. Target. The mom-and-pop kitchen store at the mall."

As we both fell silent, my eyes drifted to the shiny red and black motorcycle parked on the drive. Benjamin noticed.

"You into bikes?" he asked.

"I know that's a Kawasaki Ninja 250."

"I'm impressed."

"Don't be. I'm aware only because my sister owned one in college."

A brief hesitation, then, eyes on his sandals, Benjamin asked, "Want to go for a spin?"

Caught off guard, I answered with a total lack of grace.

"No way. I've seen too many dead bikers arrive at the morgue."

I followed through on the Graceway Gourmet and Turkberry idea. Deviated from the plan by eating the frozen yogurt on the spot. Then, I headed back to the condo, determined to continue with my report on the DOA boaters and to write ones on Bonner and Palke.

To fulfill my commitments to Musgrove.

I didn't phone Monck. What could I tell him? The inscription on the metal fragment had to do with bread.

It wasn't exactly intel to blow back your hair.

The visit with Benjamin was troublesome. Had the guy made a pass at me? If so, had I handled it badly?

No. It felt like the uneasiness resulted from more than an awkward social interaction. But what? What was bothering my hindbrain? Why couldn't I pull it to my higher centers? Something I'd seen? A comment Benjamin had made?

I wondered what Monck was learning about the mysterious JR. Was he or she a serious suspect?

And what about Cloke's frequent trips to Provo? Why did he come? Did the dates of his visits coincide in some way with those of the murders?

Was Milo Willis indeed innocent of his wife's murder? Would his golfing story pan out? If so, who killed Musgrove?

And what about this violent bartender, Glen Wall? Was he really off the island with his cousins and brother when Palke disappeared?

At five I gave up and went for a short run on the beach. Afterward, I showered, then called Katy. Ryan. Left messages for both.

At six, I fixed a salad and cooked the fish. Dined on the terrace watching a clementine sun sink through a musk melon sky.

Again and again, I checked my mobile. Pointless. Of course, the phone had signal. Of course, it was working.

Before returning to my laptop, I riffled through a mound of CDs I'd noticed in a kitchen cabinet. Though some dated to the eighties and nineties, the majority featured artists big in the sixties.

Perfect for mindless background accompaniment.

Choosing those showing the least number of scratches or nicks, I inserted the discs into a Bose Music Machine that looked older than they did. Hit play.

Billy Joel opened with "Piano Man." The sound quality was surprisingly good.

Two hours later, OD'd on Pink Floyd, Billy Joel, Bob Dylan, and Queen, I reread my report for the third time, made two final edits, and closed the computer.

Feeling smugly self-righteous, I checked every door, window, and lock in the condo, brushed my teeth, changed into a nightshirt, and crawled into bed, at long last free of Provo's serial killer.

Or so I thought.

After what seemed an eternity, I drifted off.

In my dream, I did the Palke and Bonner analyses again.

I was working outdoors under an ebony sky slashed by savage lightning. The bones sparked neon in the intermittent streaks.

I was arranging the second skeleton when Ti Musgrove joined me at the gurney.

Flash!

Musgrove's face went luminous in the electric sizzle. Her eyes and lips remained an eerie violet blue.

"You're getting it wrong." Musgrove's voice was high and warbly like a flute.

Getting what wrong?

I watched Musgrove reorganize the bones into circles, then center one skull in each.

That was wrong.

Moving quickly, Musgrove placed all the long bones in a row and swapped the positions of the two right ulnae.

No, I thought. That's not how you do it.

A jagged bolt ripped across the sky.

Flash!

In the blinding glare, I saw a figure, off to one side. Imposing height suggested it was a male. The figure's right arm rose, to beckon, to wave, or to warn me away.

I called out.

What? What do you want?

No sound left my lips.

The figure started in my direction, a one-armed cut-out against a black horizon.

Flash!

The figure wore a white shirt and orange pants. Darkness concealed its features.

I swiveled to see if Musgrove was noticing. She wasn't there.

I turned back.

The figure was now standing in the middle of a lush green field. No. Not a field. A soccer pitch. The sky was blue, the sun buttery yellow. The painted lines and center circle gleamed white as fresh snow on summer grass.

Other players jogged onto the pitch.

Faces blazed clear.

I recognized the one-armed figure as Delroy Monck. Monck moved to the left center forward position. Musgrove joined him at the right.

Quentin Bonner, Ryder Palke, and Bobby Galloway arranged themselves as midfielders. RTCIPF cops Rigby, Gardiner, Stubbs, and Kemp went to the backfield. Oddly, the fifth defender was SPVM Constable Plante.

Each team member was uniformed in blood red. Except for the goalie. Instead of a crimson jersey and shorts, he or she wore a neon green and yellow tee with a striped emblem on the front. There would be no confusing that player's position.

I was now sitting with other spectators high up on steep bleachers. I turned to the man beside me to ask a question. The man was Ryan.

Le gardien est la clé, he said. The goalkeeper is the key.

Since the goalie's face was obscured, I asked who it was.

La clé.

Out on the pitch, Monck crossed to speak to Musgrove. She threw up her hands and strode off the field.

What's happening? I asked.

"Decoy run," Ryan said in English.

30

This would be one of the longest Saturdays in my life.

8:00 A.M.

The day commenced with my amateur psychoanalysis the minute I opened my eyes.

Not sure why I bothered. Habit, mostly. My dreams are disappointingly dull.

Typically, my subconscious takes a handoff from my higher centers and does a remix of current events. Occasionally, the id crew throws in a sketchily scripted theatrical twist.

Obviously, I'd absorbed more than I'd realized from the previous weekend's soccer broadcasts. No Freudian breakthrough there.

The actors weren't phantoms from some traumatic childhood event or random adolescent experience. All were persons with whom I'd recently interacted. It was natural that the TCI cops and vics were on my mind. Musgrove leaving the field needed no explanation.

The only riddle was Ryan's enigmatic comment about the goalie.

But enigmas exist no more in the age of Google. Grabbing my iPhone, I entered the phrase Ryan had used. Was linked to a glossary of soccer terms.

Decoy run: When a soccer player executes a run to draw attention away from the intended play.

I lay back against the pillows and thought about that. About the goalie's neon green and yellow jersey. I'd recently encountered a similarly vertiginous garment. Where?

Holy moly!

I replayed Monday's interview. My conversation from the previous day.

Suddenly, I was *en fuego* to talk to Monck.

10:00 A.M.

I was spooning a second round of grounds into the coffeemaker when my mobile rang.

"You found Cloke?" I guessed, too amped for a proper greeting.

"I did not find Cloke."

Engine sounds told me Monck was already wheels to the pavement.

"But I did kick loose some curious facts."

I ran tap water into the pot.

"When I checked Cloke's dates in Provo against the dates the vics disappeared, only one coincided. Bonner."

"So Cloke isn't your guy." Already I'd switched from "our" to "your."

"Not likely."

"Unless he has an accomplice."

"Killing duos are rare."

"But they do happen. Lake and Ng. Bernardo and Homolka. Lucas and Toole."

"Bonnie and Clyde. Leopold and Loeb. I get it. Count me as still skeptical."

I placed the pot on its coil and thumbed the on button.

"I rang Carmichael again," Monck continued. "Demanded to know why a feeb was on my patch. As expected, I got another blow off. I pressed him about Cloke's previous visits to Provo. Carmichael seemed surprised."

"That Cloke had made so many trips? Or that you knew about them?"

"Hard to tell with these mooks. He was about to disconnect when I dropped the S-bomb."

"Serial killer." Though eager to share my own breakthrough— maybe breakthrough—I was also curious about what Monck had learned.

"I briefed Carmichael on the facts—the gunshot CODs, the severed hands, the vics all being good-lookers and newly arrived on the island. I explained that his boy has been in the wind since landing here last—"

"That got his attention?"

"After sitting on hold long enough to smoke a brisket, I was bounced up the chain to a guy named Rossiter."

"Probably an SSA." Supervisory special agent.

"Rossiter sounded about as engaged as a DOA on Ambien, but his interest perked up as I went through the whole shitspiel again. He asked questions. Was maybe taking notes."

"Oh?"

"While prohibited from divulging classified intel, Rossiter was willing to share that Cloke was assigned to a group overseeing assets such as power grids, radar systems, and navigational programs."

"Sounds like most of the OTD."

"I pointed that out. Rossiter didn't disagree."

"Did he say why Cloke made multiple trips to Provo?"

"He had no comment."

"Did he know why Cloke was interested in Uri Stribbe?"

"No comment."

"Did he know why Cloke phoned Joe Benjamin?"

"Same answer."

"Did the jackass say *anything* useful?"

Crank it down, Brennan.

"According to Rossiter, his underling has aspirations."

"Meaning Cloke is ambitious?"

"Or the guy chafes the boss's balls."

"What about JR?"

Monck snorted air through his nose. "JR is a toothless, seventy-six-year-old hag who builds bed swings using sustainable materials. Juniper Rose. No last name."

"Musgrove was ordering a bed swing?"

"A white one with blue cushions."

"*Sus* was an abbreviation for sustainable, not suspect. *BS* was code for bed swing."

"Affirmative."

"What about Glen Wall?"

"He's still on the island. But I'm finding that no one wants to talk about the guy."

"Milo Willis?"

"Still working it."

"Uri Stribbe?"

"Same answer."

I allowed a heartbeat of silence, then took the plunge: "Joe Benjamin. What do you know about him?"

"You asked me that on Monday."

"I'm asking again."

"When did you talk to Benjamin?"

"Yesterday."

"Why?"

"I've got time on my hands, so I took a shot at getting the Hebrew inscription translated. The rabbi and his wife refused to get involved. I thought Benjamin might be willing to help."

"Was he?"

"Yes."

I told Monck about the *hamotzi* blessing.

"The fragment came from a bread knife?"

"It could have."

"Does that square with the marks you saw in the bone?"

"No."

More silence as we both chewed on that.

"Something's off with Benjamin," I said.

"And this insightful character analysis is based on—?"

"He lied to me. To us."

"I'm listening."

I decided not to mention the odd invite for a spin on the bike.

"Benjamin claimed he hadn't interacted with the Stribbes in ages. When we talked to Adeera later that day, remember what she said?"

Monck shook his head.

"'That *chazer* is only helpful when he wants something. Then he has no shame.' That comment bothered me, so I called Adeera to ask the last time Joe had been in the presence of either her or Uri."

Monck said nothing.

"Benjamin had been to their condo two weeks earlier."

"Your point?"

"It's a decoy run."

More nothing.

"An attempt to mislead us."

"I'm fluent in soccer. Why would Benjamin want to mislead us?"

"He's hiding something."

"What?"

"I don't know. But I spotted another tell. Benjamin listed reasons his father grew to hate New York. Snow. Lumpy sidewalks—"

"I was present."

"Pretty boys." Hooking finger quotes Monck couldn't see. "That seems an odd irritant for an old man. Also, while talking to him, I had the feeling another person was there."

"So, what? The dude's not allowed to have a life?"

"There's something else."

I stole another calming moment before putting it into words.

"When we arrived at Benjamin's house, an old Dylan song was blasting. 'Mr. Tambourine Man.'"

"Big deal. It's a classic."

"The same track was playing yesterday."

"So the guy—"

"I keep bumping on this one line in the lyrics."

Monck waited as I recited the words.

Yes, to dance beneath the diamond sky with one hand waving free.

4:00 P.M.

Monck came to the condo at four, goofy hair an unresolved spat. He looked as wired as I felt. And by then I was bursting out of my skin.

I offered coffee, the last thing my sizzling nerves needed. Monck accepted. We drank it on the terrace as he briefed me on the latest.

The usual legal pad was covered with the usual scribbles. He consulted it now and then, checking a name or date.

"A man named Avner Binjamin bought the home on Karst Way in 2013. In 2017, when Avner kicked, title transferred to Yosef Binjamin."

"Joe Benjamin. He altered his name."

"Yes. There's no record of the property changing hands again. Utilities have been in Joe Benjamin's name since shortly after his assumption of ownership."

"What's his story?"

"Here in Provo, he hasn't one."

Monck raised fleshed fingers to emphasize points.

"Benjamin has no jacket. He pays his taxes. He's never been involved in a dispute. He's never filed or been the subject of a complaint."

"Any record of a nine-one-one call to the address?"

Monck wagged his head. "Since living here, Benjamin's been a model citizen."

Were my instincts so wildly off base?

"Further back, the story sprouts interesting legs." Monck drank half his mug. Set it on the table between us. "Benjamin said he and his old man moved to Provo from Crown Heights."

"You did another deep dive, this one in Brooklyn?"

"I'll spare you the details. My informant, one Uncle Shlomo, probably toothless and a hundred years old, was exceedingly forthcoming. Once we'd connected, I couldn't get the old codger off the phone. I suspect he's lonely."

I twirled an impatient wrist. Stick to the point.

"According to Uncle Shlomo, Avner had two sons. Yaakov, older by five years, was the bad son. Josef was the good son."

"What? Were they cops?"

Monck ignored my lame attempt at humor.

"Between his sophomore and junior years in college, Yaakov brought shame upon the family and disgrace upon himself." Delivered with what I suspected were Shlomo theatrics.

"Can we skip the drama?"

"If you skip the jokes."

"Done."

"While summering in Israel, Yaakov blew off a hand building a bomb meant to kill a Palestinian activist."

"Holy shit."

"Yep."

"Did he go to prison?"

"Due to the kid's ineptitude, no crime was committed. Also, Daddy whisked the little cretin back to New York as soon as the docs stitched what remained of his arm back together."

"Which arm?"

"His left."

My pulse kicked into hyperdrive.

"According to Uncle Shlomo, after Yaakov's disfigurement, life with Avner revolved solely around son number one. Yaakov had always been the golden boy, smarter, better looking—"

"Do you have a photo?"

Monck slipped a folded sheet from the tablet and handed it to me.

I unfolded the paper.

My breath caught in my throat.

I was holding hard copy of a printed email. Centered on the page was a single image, probably a recent iPhone retake of an old snap-shot. Two young men stood shoulder to shoulder, heads tilted and almost touching.

The man on the right had heavy brows, wild corkscrew hair, and John Denver glasses. The man on the left had heart-stopping indigo eyes, thick black hair, and features that would have scored a month on any calendar featuring hot Jewish men. Hot men. Period.

Someone had scrawled a name and date in Sharpie below Hottie's very square jaw. *Y. Binjamin. June 12, 2004.*

"That was taken shortly before golden boy's mishap with explosives," Monck said.

"Where's Yaakov now?"

"Apparently, being disabled did not agree with him. He killed himself in 2012."

"Yaakov was twenty-eight. Joe was twenty-three."

"That tallies," Monck said, looking thoughtful about what the intel meant.

"It *all* tallies." Facts were body-slamming in my brain like protons in a supercollider. "For years Joe is ignored by his father. He holds his brother responsible. His *handsome* brother. His *handsome* brother who lost his *left hand*."

Monck allowed me my rant.

"Eventually, Yaakov kills himself. Guilt eats Avner up. The year after the suicide, Avner and Joe move to Provo. Four years after that, Avner dies."

Totally pumped, I air-jabbed a finger in Monck's direction.

"Avner's death is the trigger. The first killing goes down in 2017."

"Bobby Galloway."

"It's *him*, Monck. It's Benjamin. You need to get a warrant to search his home."

"Based on what? This is all speculation."

"Pretty freakin' good speculation."

"I know the judges here. Every one will require more. Besides, the more I poke at this guy Wall, the more I find questions I want answered."

"So we wait until another vic dies?" Fear and frustration were turning me churlish. "Maybe Cloke?"

"Take a deep inhale."

"You sound like a yogi," I said, sighing.

I knew Monck was right. But he was here, so he was taking the hit.

"I'll put round-the-clock eyes on this freak," Monck said.

"And in the meantime?"

Palming both knees, Monck pushed to his feet. "In the meantime, I keep digging."

31

Partly caffeine. Mostly anxiety.

Every neuron in my brain was firing at warp speed.

I couldn't concentrate. Couldn't sit still. Would have preferred a crawl through razor wire to a computer session.

By sheer force of will, I made myself settle at the keyboard. Finished with the dead boaters by five-thirty.

I was starting the Palke report when titanium knuckles whacked my door. Welcoming any excuse for a break, and eager for news, I answered the knock.

"How did you get upstairs without a key?"

"I'm a cop."

I let Monck in. Pointedly offered no coffee.

We took the same plastic chairs out on the terrace.

"You found something?" I asked.

"A shit ton."

"Enough for a warrant?"

"I've got a guy working that."

"How long will it take?"

265

"Do you want to hear this?"

I leaned back and assumed my listening face.

"First, more backstory."

"Is it relevant?"

"Could be."

I said nothing.

"Avner Binjamin only allowed Yosef to attend college locally." Monck glanced at his notes. "New York City College of Technology. In Brooklyn. The kid—I'll stick with Joe—earned a degree in computer systems and technology."

"He said he's into cyber tech. Web design."

"Which explains the big-ass WiFi booster on his roof."

"This info comes from Shlomo?"

"The old coot and I are now best buds."

I couldn't help rolling my eyes.

"Like big brother, Joe made his obligatory youth pilgrimage to Israel. He was older, already out of school. Apparently, it took years to persuade the old man to grant permission."

"Given that things went so well there for Yaakov."

"After bouncing around a bit, Joe ended up at an agricultural cooperative outside Tel Aviv. A place called Bnai Zion. At a chicken farm."

"A chicken farm."

"A chicken coop, actually. With its own colorful saga."

I offered no snarky quip.

"Around 2010, the building's owner apparently ditched raising poultry, renovated, and began renting to technology start-ups looking for cheap space."

"Joe worked for one of those start-ups," I guessed.

"He did."

"Which one?"

"Shlomo couldn't recall."

Monck glanced at his watch.

"You have boots at the courthouse as we speak?" I asked.

"Either there or out dogging his honor's whereabouts."

"Will a judge give a cold crap about Joe's boyhood woes?"

"Uncertain. But the next little goody should grab his attention."

I refolded my hands in my lap and leaned back. The chair didn't like it.

"Joe told us he had a night gig answering phones."

"To pay the bills."

"Phones at night. I kept weighing that, ran a check of the obvious. He's not a nine-one-one operator or one of our dispatchers. Didn't work for the fire service or an ER. But further expert sleuthing uncovered a tantalizing service in Provo. *VVV. Vannie's Virtual Voices.*"

"Nice alliteration."

"You ever call an office or a business and get corkscrewed through a mind-bogglingly irritating maze of choices?"

"All the time."

"Or call after closing and get a recorded voice that cares nothing about your problem?"

I nodded.

"The experience can make you furious, yes?"

"To say the least."

"Vannie's schtick is that a real live human answers every call coming into her clients' switchboards. Twenty-four/seven."

"Remotely."

"Yes. Her employees act like front-office receptionists, greeting those who phone, patching callers through when they're available, taking messages when they're not. They're friendly as shit and live only to solve your problem."

"Let me guess. Joe works for Vannie."

"He does."

I waited for the judge-grabber.

"Persuaded by a casual allusion to a potential audit, Vannie produced a list of clients going back five years. I ran the name of every outfit on the list against calls made from Palke's room at the Royal West Indies Resort and Bonner's room at the Sibonné Beach Hotel."

"Why would they use the room phones?"

"Depending on their cellular plans, tourists often use landlines for local calls to avoid international charges."

That made sense.

"Musgrove had the phone dumps in her file?" I asked.

"She did. Unfortunately, there were no cell phone records for Palke and Bonner. And no records of any kind for Bobby Galloway, mobile or landline."

"Okay."

"On August 4, 2020, at 9:42 p.m., Palke phoned Reef Dive and Water Sports, a local outfitter for SCUBA, snorkeling, and such."

"Palke or the girlfriend."

"Agreed."

"On February 25, 2022, at 7:27 a.m. Bonner rang Bert's Photo and More, a camera and electronics store on the Leeward Highway."

Monck raised expectant brows in my direction.

The agitated neurons grasped it in a nanosecond.

"The calls were made outside business hours, so they were rolled to an answering service. To VVV."

"There's that lightning insight that so impresses me."

"Jesus, Monck!" In my enthusiasm, I shot forward in my chair, which compromised its sketchy arrangement with gravity. "That's how he finds his victims!"

"Vannie's proxy receptionists take names, phone numbers, and addresses in Provo. They're encouraged to chat up the caller to assuage any disappointment at not getting through."

"Vannie's is Joe's virtual hunting ground." I was literally on the chair's edge. "Later, he does a drive-by to see if the guy meets his standards." Sudden insight. "Don't you see? His sick game involves a three-stage hunt. First, there's the audio spotting by phone of potential prey. Then there's the visual tracking. Finally, there's the capture and kill."

"Cowabunga."

"Did you say cow—"

Monck's phone buzzed.

He yanked it from his pocket.

I held totally still.

The voice was male, his words too muffled for me to catch. His message was brief.

Monck answered two queries with the same clipped response. "Affirmative." Asked, "Single vehicle?" Then, "Ten-twenty?"

As Monck listened, his droopy eyes narrowed, and his thin lips tightened.

"We've got paper," he said upon disconnecting.

Eureka! A warrant to search Benjamin's place.

"You're heading there now?"

"Affirmative."

Monck rose.

I rose.

"I'm going with you."

"Fuck that."

"Why not?"

"I won't have adequate backup."

"Why not?"

"Half the unit is tied up at an accident scene. The other half is laser focused on nailing Musgrove's killer."

Monck strode toward the glass doors. I spoke to his back.

"I've been to Joe's home twice." Too loud. Too aggressive. "I can find my own way."

Monck turned, face the color of claret.

"Fine. But you stay in—"

"The vehicle."

Years with Claudel and Slidell had honed the response.

6:30 P.M.

We took Monck's Jeep. Sporadic *brrrpp*s from its siren cut us through traffic like a scythe through hay.

While driving, Monck shared what he knew of the incident

sapping half his pool for backup. It wasn't much. A single vehicle wreck with a possible 10-55. Intoxicated driver.

Staticky radio transmissions supplied only one additional detail.

The accident had taken place on Karst Way, where Joe Benjamin lived.

The name sent adrenaline jolting through me. Coincidence? I don't believe in coincidence.

We arrived at the turn off in fourteen minutes flat. From the highway, all looked normal save for a trio of vultures looping low in the sky. Wending upward, it became clear that wasn't the case.

A half mile along the precipice, a cruiser blocked the pavement. One look at Monck and the guard waved us through.

The throbbing lights became visible at fifty yards out. The closer we drew, the brighter they painted the asphalt, the limestone, and the vegetation. Red-blue. Red-blue. Red-blue.

The action was off to the left, on the road's uphill side. I counted three cruisers, an ambulance, a hook-and-chain tow truck, and an unmarked car.

A stretch of ground along the shoulder was already cordoned off, the yellow tape following the gentle slope of the hillside, then suddenly seeming to drop off the earth. The optimistic vultures circled high above the flimsy barricade.

Two cops stood inside the cordon, both wearing the usual RTCIPF striped pants, shirt, and red-banded cap. Though their backs were to us, I thought I recognized Constables Gardiner and Rigby from our rendezvous with the *Cod Bless Us* and its ill-fated passengers.

A third cop stood outside the tape, two teens beside him, one maybe thirteen, the other a few years older. Both wore cutoff jeans, faded tees, and grim expressions. The younger of the pair looked like he might toss his lunch.

A woman in civvies was squatting on the pavement, measuring whatever one measures at accident scenes. Not tire tracks or skid marks. I saw no sign of either.

Monck added his Jeep to the cluster of vehicles and turned to me.

I cocked a brow.

"You touch nothing, you say nothing."

"Yes, kemosabe."

We got out and headed for the tape.

No one stopped us to request ID. Either Monck was recognized again, or no one was keeping a scene attendance log. Or both.

A few stern words for his charges, then the third uniform broke away and crossed to us. His tag said *Const. E. Lightbourne.*

"What have we got?" Monck asked.

"Pickup thought it could fly."

Monck did not look amused.

"Toyota Tacoma, maybe a 2011 model." Lightbourne was all business now. "Solo driver, no passenger. Looks like the truck left the pavement at high speed."

I felt a fast pulse in my temples, my palms, my throat.

"Black?" I asked, thinking of the truck I'd seen parked at Benjamin's place.

"Maybe."

"The driver?" Monck asked.

Lightbourne wagged his head slowly.

"When?"

"Two kids called it in." Lightbourne gestured toward the teens. "Their story is that everything was hunky-dory when they went by at two. The truck was ass-up when they returned around four."

"Why were they poking around the hole?"

"They saw vultures, looked down hoping to see a dead critter."

By reflex, Monck and I checked our watches. The accident had happened just hours earlier.

Someone had died while I was hosting a pity party over having to write reports.

In my heart I knew who that someone was.

"Are your witnesses reliable?" Monck asked.

"Neither of these boneheads will be winning a free ride to Oxford."

"The truck got a tag?"

"Yeah. Talk to Gardiner. She ran it."

"Roger that."

"Feel free to have a gander."

As Monck and I stepped forward, I realized I was about to stare at death yet again on this beautiful island. The steady procession of corpses requiring my attention wasn't what I'd signed up for, but I couldn't back out now.

I kept on Monck's heels as we headed for the pit.

32

There are countless sinkholes, blue holes, and caves throughout the Turks and Caicos archipelago, almost all created by the karst process. That is, by the slow action of acidic rainwater dissolving soft limestone, which in turn produces carbonic acid, which further feeds the erosion.

TCI's most famous gaper, The Hole, is in the Long Bay Hills area of Provo. The cavernous pit is roughly fifty feet across and plunges approximately sixty feet to a brackish pond below. Water depth is estimated at an additional twenty-five feet.

Geologists believe The Hole was initially an enclosed cave system whose ceiling collapsed one thunderous day far in the past. They also think the water's semi-tidal nature suggests a partial connection to the ocean or to the marine ponds of Juba Sound.

I learned all this later through a website geared toward TCI tourism, another operated by the National Park Service. That late July afternoon, I had no jargon for, nor explanation of, the bizarre feature I was about to observe.

Immediately after speaking with Lightbourne, Monck and I beelined toward the action. Closing in, I noted that my guess about those present had been spot-on.

I recognized the pear-shaped form of Constable Gardiner and the bulk and blond bun of Constable Rigby. Both were inside the cordon, about five yards off the road, the former slightly uphill from the latter.

Rigby turned at the sound of our steps. Offering no greeting, she trudged to the perimeter and lifted the tape. Monck and I ducked under.

"Detective."

"Officer."

Monck and Rigby exchanged nods. Though no one was looking, I added mine to the mix.

"Constable Lightbourne tells me there's a fatality."

"Yes, sir." Face cop-neutral.

"May we approach?"

"Yes, sir. But don't be stepping too close. You don't want to tumble over the edge."

"I do not."

"Ground creepers is flattened some. You'll see the track."

"Roger that."

Monck set off, long-stepping like a mantis stalking a moth.

I followed, weaving through jagged rocks that repeatedly threatened a piece of my skin. Some lay loose, others thrust upward from sedimentary roots deep underground. The thrusters made me think of whales breaching at sea.

I moved cautiously, thankful I'd changed from sandals to sneakers. Every few steps, one foot or the other skidded on the layer of sand blanketing the ground.

A few paces out from the asphalt, I noted a rusty plaque on a telephone pole. *Little Hole. No path. No handrail. Extreme danger.*

Heeding the warning, and Rigby's caveat about taking a tumble, I picked my way carefully.

Monck stopped at the point where the tape disappeared abruptly. Spread his feet. Hip-planted his real and prosthetic hands. Above his head, the vultures maintained their grim vigil.

I drew up at his side. Almost gasped.

The sign's admonition wasn't hyperbole.

We stood at the edge of a yawning crater; its craggy walls composed of crumbling limestone. I estimated its diameter to be thirty feet, its depth fifty.

Unlike its Long Bay neighbor, about which I would later educate myself, Little Hole enjoyed no link to the sea. Its base was dry and contained no water.

What it held was far worse.

The Tacoma lay "ass-up" about thirty feet down. Even at our high elevation on the hillside, the smell of scorched metal and burnt flesh was unmistakable.

I re-created the crash in my mind.

The truck's impact against the wall face had sparked a fire and sent shards of limestone blasting upward. The billowing smoke and shower of chalky sediment had turned the vehicle's exterior the color of a ghostly dawn.

I swallowed. Found my mouth short on saliva. Forced myself to focus on details.

The pickup had two doors. The force of the impact had blown both open, accordioned the engine, and bent the cargo bed twenty degrees off kilter. The windshield had spiderwebbed on the passenger side, exploded outward in a starburst pattern in front of the steering wheel.

Newton's First Law of Motion: an object in motion stays in motion. That's why we wear seat belts.

I studied the moving object that had blown through the glass.

The driver lay half in and half out of the starburst, clothing scorched and seared to his or her blackened flesh. I noted clawed fingers, joints flexed into the pugilistic position typical of fire victims.

"Close-up and personal?" Monck proffered a small pair of Bushnells I hadn't noticed him slip from a pocket.

"Thanks."

I brought the binoculars to my eyes and adjusted the knob. Wanting to see. Not wanting to see.

The scene crystallized into grisly focus.

The driver's skull was distorted, its occipital bone protruding at an impossible angle, its frontal bone mashed down into its orbits. The exposed brain was a scorched hamburger mess, dotted with bone chips and crawling with flies.

Tiny glass cubes peppered both the body and the truck. Here and there a shard winked orange in the few rays managing to slice into the hole from the low-hanging sun.

My gut was telling me who had died in this wreck. Still, I couldn't be certain. The driver remained half inside the cab. The fire and trauma had rendered his or her face unrecognizable.

Almost invisible, even when magnified, a minute detail told a heartbreaking story.

"I think there's expectorated blood around the lips." I handed back the glasses. "On a strip of unburned skin where one hand may have protected the mouth."

"Meaning?"

"Death wasn't immediate."

Monck peered down another very long moment. Lowered the glasses and started to speak.

"Nasty one, eh?"

We both turned.

Constable Gardiner had crossed the cordon to join us.

"We're finished with what we can do here. The tow crew is itching to get on with their bit. You okay with that?"

"Is anyone going down there?"

"Chief says no can do. Too dangerous. Ordered us to lug the whole kit and kaboodle up and process topside. Hauler boys say they have a plan."

"Have you spotted anything suspicious?" Monck asked.

Gardiner blew out a breath.

"Guy runs off the road on a clear sunny day? Leaves no rubber on the pavement?" He pantomimed drinking from a bottle. "CSU's on the way. But I'm guessing the coroner will dot the I and cross the T on this one."

"You ran the tag?"

"Yes, sir." Gardiner whipped the ubiquitous cop spiral from his ill-fitting pants. "The vehicle is registered to a Joe Benjamin. Joe, not Joseph, no middle name or initial. Lives right up the road." Thumb-jabbing the two lane at his back.

My scalp tingled as he read off the address.

Monck spoke to me as Gardiner waddled away.

"Thoughts?"

"We're closing in on Benjamin for three homicides, maybe four. The day after my second drop-by, he goes off-road into"—I pointed at the pit—"whatever that is."

"Little Hole."

"He's lived on Karst Way for ten years. Surely, he knew the sink-hole was here."

"You're thinking the bastard offed himself?"

I shrugged. Who knows?

"Or maybe karma reached out and grabbed him by the balls," Monck said.

"Maybe."

"Too bad I don't believe in karma." Monck said nothing for several seconds. Then, "Let's go."

"Where?"

"This warrant allows me to toss Benjamin's house." Tapping his pocket. "I aim to do that."

6:50 P.M.

The crows still cawed. The sole palm still swished overhead. The shells still crunched under our tires.

Two things had changed.

A VW Jetta sat where the driveway cut from the asphalt. Silver, with local plates. A sticker identified the car as a Budget rental. There was no one inside.

Monck's back and shoulders tensed as his eyes darted the scene. A brief pause then, hand cocked toward the Glock on his belt, he strode across the path to the front of the house.

I followed, expecting to be ordered to return to the car. Perhaps nerves made him forget I was there, but there was no command to hang back.

Monck thumbed the bell, anticipating only canine fury.

Not a peep from the aggressively bellicose Betty.

"Police!"

Silence.

Monck rang again.

More silence.

Our eyes met.

"Old Rinty should be all bowed up at us being here."

Unfamiliar with Monck's expression but inferring its meaning from his tone, I said, "Maybe Benjamin locked the dog in the shed?"

"Hmm."

Monck rapped again, hard, with his titanium knuckles.

Hearing no indication of a presence, human or canine, he jerked back the screen, turned the inner handle, and pushed open the chartreuse door.

Unlocked. No Nazi dog.

Something was definitely wrong.

Monck was about to cross the threshold when a bellowed command stopped him in his tracks.

"Halt!"

We both whipped around.

Two men were trotting up from the road.

One was a squat, square block of a guy. The other looked like a scowl on legs. Both wore black pants, white shirts, and ties the belligerent gray of a winter storm.

My first thought was LDS missionaries. Until they reached us.

Scowl held out a credentials case with an ID on one side, a badge on the other. I recognized the bald eagle on top, the blindfolded Lady Justice beneath it, the words "Federal Bureau of Investigation" and "Department of Justice" arcing above and below her.

"FBI," Scowl barked, in case we remained unclear.

"You can buy those on eBay." Monck chin-cocked the gold shield.

"You've gotta be Monck." Scowl's scowl deepened. "Word is, you find yourself funny."

"And I'm playing here every Saturday this month."

"You're the forensic anthro?" Directed to me.

"Temperance Brennan." Cool. "Let me guess. You two are very special agents?"

Scowl turned to Square Block. "We got Abbot and Costello here. Better call for a bus, Ross. I may die from laughing."

"No need for incivility." Square Block's smile projected an overload of charm. "I'm Ellis Rossiter. The humor-challenged gentleman with me is Alfie Reid."

"You're the SAA," I said, recalling the name. "Cloke's boss."

"Indirectly."

"You've come to Provo looking for your lost boy?" Monck asked, his tone glacial.

Rossiter shot Reid a quick sidelong glance.

"You know anything about that?" he asked, the smile never faltering.

"At the moment, Cloke's not the focus of my concern."

"May I ask what is?"

"I briefed you by phone on the Provo serial," Monck said.

"And you were thorough, indeed, sir."

"The owner of this home, one Joe Benjamin, is our primary suspect. The guy just said the big adios in a single car wreck. I have a warrant to search his property."

Rossiter's eyes again skidded to those of his partner.

"Benjamin's dead?"

"He is."

"What do you know about him?"

"We think the asshole clipped four people. That's why I'm about to toss his place."

"And Special Agent Cloke?"

"AWOL since landing."

"That's it?"

"That's it."

"You think Benjamin may have grabbed Cloke?"

Before Monck could respond, a crow kamikazeed down while screeching an earsplitting series of *caws*.

Startled, we all ducked.

While straightening, Monck shifted a bit to his right, allowing me a clear view of the hallway arrowing inward from the chartreuse door. I saw the white tile, the framed prints, the arched opening giving onto the orange living room.

Again, my pulse went ballistic.

On the floor, wedged against the faux wood, were two brown paws. Beneath the paws, pooled blood fast congealing at the edges.

"Holy shit, Monck. He killed his dog."

As before, Monck yanked open the screen.

"Stop!"

We both whirled.

"Please hold." Rossiter's gaze had gone stony.

"Fuck that."

Monck charged over the threshold.

33

Most of the blood had come from Betty's nose and mouth. The potcake lay on her side, hind limbs flexed, fore-limbs stretched, head twisted back and pressed to her shoulder. Deep gashes on her muzzle and thorax suggested a vicious attack.

Wordlessly, I reached out to Monck. He dug gloves from his shoulder satchel and handed them to me. Pulling them on, I crossed to the dog.

Betty's eyes were open and vacant, her pupils dilated. No need to hold a finger to her throat searching for a pulse, or a mirror to her nostrils testing for breath.

"Looks like someone really hammered this pooch," I said, a tad flippant to hide my emotion. I hadn't liked Betty much. But cruelty to any animal sends something ugly darting into my soul. And boils my anger.

"The divot-like lacerations suggest a boot."

My gaze swept the wall and the woodwork.

"Low-level blood spatter indicates the kicks kept coming after the dog was down, maybe already dead."

"Jesus," Monck said.

The special agents behind him remained silent.

I laid a hand on Betty's thigh. Her body felt cool but only slightly stiff.

"Rigor is minimal," I said. "I'm no expert on doggie decomp but, given Betty's size and the ambient temperature, I'd say she's been dead four hours tops."

"The timeline clicks," said Monck, shrugging. "The freak ices his dog, then takes off in the Tacoma to do himself."

I rose, knees unhappy with their renewed responsibility.

"Why would he do that? Betty was a jerk, but Benjamin seemed genuinely fond of her."

"He didn't want the mutt to suffer? Knew no one would take her?"

"So he beats her to death?"

"Benjamin has killed four people." Monck sounded as amped as I felt. "He's insane."

"Now what?" I asked, not really buying the explanation.

"Now I toss this place from here to tomorrow." He yanked more gloves from the satchel.

"I can't let you do that."

We turned. Rossiter was well into the hall. Reid was by the door, limbs and face in vigilant cop mode.

"I'm sure you didn't mean that the way it came out," said Monck, lips barely moving.

"I'm afraid I did," Rossiter said.

"You have no authority here."

"You're poking into business way over your pay grade, detective."

"Is that so, *special asshole.*" Monck was no longer bothering to conceal his fury. "Here's how this plays going forward. You and the people's princess over there"—jabbing a thumb toward Reid—"focus on your lost agent. You leave me to my serial."

"Or?"

"Your situation on this island becomes very difficult."

"Is that a threat?"

"That's a fact."

Reid's jaw muscles bulged and his fingers curled into fists. Rossiter pooched out his lips but said nothing.

Seconds passed.

A floorboard creaked. An appliance hummed in the kitchen. Beyond the screen door, the crows called to each other, perhaps opining on the absurdity of jurisdictional squabbles.

Having considered his options, which were limited, Rossiter spoke. "I'm going to have to ask the lady to leave."

The lady?

"No."

Monck's shotgun retort surprised and pleased me.

Rossiter sighed.

"You have a point, sir. We are on your turf. Therefore, I am willing to divulge limited intel on a need-to-know basis. Needless to mention, anything I say goes no further than the four of us."

"Needless to mention," Monck said.

Annoyed by Rossiter's "lady" reference, I merely glared.

"We believe our two investigations are linked."

"The Provo killer and Cloke's disappearance."

"Yes."

"You think Benjamin offed your guy."

Rossiter slid another sidelong glance to his partner. Reid's jaw tightened and he gave a tight shake of his head.

Despite the negative input, Rossiter continued. "We feel the stakes are much higher than some deranged psychopath knocking off tourists."

"And those stakes are?" asked Monck, dubious as hell.

"Benjamin had expertise in coding. Computer programming."

"There's a hot news flash."

"And you know what about that?" Clearly, Rossiter's tactic was to elicit more info than he shared.

Monck didn't fall for the ploy. "Get to the point."

Again, the hesitation. The careful choosing of words.

"You've had some unexplained incidents involving transport, am I correct?"

"Explain that."

"Planes—"

"Ross, you can't—" Reid started to object.

Silencing his partner with a sharply raised hand, Rossiter looked a question at Monck.

Monck's brows dipped, but he said nothing.

I felt a sudden nudge from my subconscious.

Pssst!

What?

Unguided, my eyes drifted to the hall at Monck's back.

To the row of framed prints.

A previously ignored detail registered.

A synapse fired up a casual comment made over lunch.

Boom.

Two neurons reached out and joined hands.

"Are you referring to the Piaggio P.180 that went down off TCI a couple years back?"

"And you know what about that?"

"Tail number N774KZ."

Both feds stared as though I'd named the Zodiac killer.

"And you know what about that?" Apparently, Rossiter's pet phrasing.

"The pilot and passenger were both DOA. Analysts found nothing wrong with the plane."

Reid's face went red enough to goad a bull to charge.

Rossiter kept his voice even. His eyes on Monck.

"Please." Gesturing toward the sofa beyond Betty. "The time for petty bickering is over."

"Not another step." Monck's tone went granite hard. "I'm declaring this a crime scene."

"Then I'd like you both to come with us."

"And why would we do that?"

"To prevent the loss of thousands of innocent lives. Trust me. There is no time to lose."

7:10 P.M.

While driving, Monck called his unit, asked for a constable named Sith. Stoked on anger and adrenaline, he didn't even try for polite.

"I've got a BOLO riding for a white male, late thirties, name Calvin Cloke. FBI special agent. Any eyes on this guy?"

"Not yet, sir."

"No credit card charge? Cell phone use? Nothing?"

"No, sir. The guy's ghosting big-time."

"Shake the goddam bushes and find him! Anyone even suspects they've seen a hair of Cloke's ass, I want to know."

"Yes, sir."

"And I need a deep toss of a home on Karst Way." Monck provided the address. "Owner is one Joe Benjamin."

"Looking for what?" Sith's uncertain voice sputtered back over the speaker.

"Signs of Cloke. Signs of Galloway, Palke, Bonner. Signs that a goddam serial killer lived in the dump!"

"Yes, sir."

"Then we lock the place down. No one in, no one out except CSU. Got it?"

"Got it."

Glancing sideways, he twirled a bionic finger at my phone. "Maybe someone will stop by to pick up the dog."

"Dog? Should the team take precautions?"

"No."

Understanding Monck's directive, I searched for then dialed the number for the potcake center to request collection and disposal of the canine corpse. I figured no one would answer at that hour, but that I could leave a message.

I was wrong. The operator who picked up was extremely obliging. And devastated to learn of the dear dog's passing. I suspected the woman had never met Betty.

7:30 P.M.

Twenty minutes after leaving Karst Way we joined Rossiter and Reid in a second-floor mini-suite at the Sea Breeze Resort on Sand-castle Road. Though not oceanfront, the place boasted a pool and free beach shuttle. And had flourishing populations of mildew and mold.

More important, the place had an FBI-friendly price point. As Rossiter had quipped upon our arrival, the bureau rolls three-star all the way.

We entered a portion of the "suite" containing two queen beds, a bureau and matching nightstand, a Lilliputian flat screen, and a lamp with mounded conch shells forming its base. Dingy gray tile on the floor.

An open door to the far right revealed a minuscule bath. I spotted no Speed Stick, Brylcreem, or Gillette foamy on the counter. No bottle of the Dior Sauvage in which Rossiter must have bathed.

I wondered if special and special were forced to be roomies. Didn't ask. Didn't care.

A frosted glass panel separated a small sitting area on the left from the footage devoted to sleeping. In it, a side counter held a mini-fridge and microwave that might have been new in the eighties.

The hotel's decorator was exceedingly fond of lime green. And dark wicker. Monck and I settled on a couch featuring both. Ditto the chairs taken by our hosts.

The HVAC below the window at my side was noisy but effective, keeping the room temperature near that of shaved ice. Within seconds, goosebumps covered my arms.

"Sorry, but there's no time to order up coffee." Rossiter's apology masked a tension he was trying to hide.

"I can see you're shattered." Monck sounded like a man craving caffeine. And looked like a man who really didn't need it.

I expected the interview to focus on Cloke. I was wrong.

"Tell us what you know about Joe Benjamin." Rossiter sounded as if he actually expected compliance with his opener.

Cupping his prosthetic hand in his real palm, Monck frowned. "Your dance. You lead."

A low wicker table occupied the space between the sofa and chairs. A beat, then Rossiter pulled a brown file folder from a briefcase beneath it and laid it on the glass.

I expected drama. Bold red warnings. *Top Secret. Confidential. For Your Eyes Only.*

I was wrong again. The only thing printed on the dossier's cover was a signature grid. A single name on the top line.

"There's no time to be coy. I'm going to put it right out there. We think our agent has gone rogue."

"Cloke."

"Yes. And we suspect he's working with Joe Benjamin."

"Working on what?"

Wordlessly, Rossiter added a MacBook Air to the tabletop. Booted it and began typing.

Reid jerked his right ankle up onto his left knee. Hiked and lowered his shoulders. Though his eyes remained glued to the raised shoe, the man's disapproval was palpable.

Rossiter spoke after hitting a bazillion keys. "The data I'm about to share is encrypted. To gain access, I'm entering a passcode known solely to me. It will work only once. The file cannot be copied, downloaded, or printed."

My eyes met Monck's. I could tell that his anger was still in high gear. And that, like me, he was anxious. And curious as hell.

"What you will see is part of a communiqué delivered to the FAA, TCCA, CAA, and EASA."

At Monck's blank look, Rossiter elaborated.

"The Federal Aviation Administration, Transport Canada Civil Aviation, the Civil Aviation Authority, and the European Union Aviation Safety Agency."

"The bodies that regulate air travel in the US, Canada, the UK, and Europe," I clarified, feeling a chill not coming from the raucous unit at my side.

"Yes."

Rossiter rotated the laptop.

Monck and I leaned toward the screen.

Read.

My breath froze.

34

"It's a ransom demand," I said, somewhat disbelievingly, nerves vibrating like plucked fiddle strings. "For one hundred million dollars US?"

"Yes."

"Who sent it?"

"We believe it's from Cloke."

"You *believe*?"

"Our people are working to verify."

I refocused on the screen.

The full amount must be transferred at precisely 10 p.m. EDT, July 20. An encrypted link will be provided five minutes in advance, a password simultaneously by separate email. If funds have not been deposited within five minutes of transmission, four commercial airliners will be seized in midair. Should these flights be canceled, others will be chosen. Doubt our sincerity? Train your eyes on the friendly skies of Chicago. More to follow at 8 p.m. EDT.

My gaze flew to Rossiter. "Where was this received?"

"A computer at OTD." I had to think for a second about the acronym, then remembered: Operational Technology Division.

"When?"

"Noon today."

"Is the threat credible?"

"Affirmative. Cloke provided a little *demo*"—hard with sarcasm—"by circumventing FBI security and jamming our WiFi for almost fifteen minutes. An action that took exceptional cyber chops."

Rossiter's gaze slid to his partner. Reid gave a tight shake of his head. Not subtle. Clearly, the two were holding back.

"How could Cloke have the expertise to hack your system?" I asked.

"We really don't have time—"

"How?" Monck barked.

Rossiter glanced at his watch. Swallowed. "That's where Joe Benjamin comes in."

"Go on."

"Ever hear of NSO?"

"It's an Israeli software company." Pretty much the extent of my knowledge.

"Pegasus?"

"It's spyware." Then, baffled. "I don't see the relevance of your questions."

Rossiter's eyes again shifted to his partner. Then, "Nothing I say leaves—"

"This room," Monck snapped. "Got it."

Rossiter drew a deep breath. Exhaled.

"Pegasus is widely regarded as the world's most potent spyware," he began.

"Why?" Monck asked.

"The software can crack encrypted communications on both iPhones and Androids. Pegasus is produced by NSO and has been used to track terrorists and drug cartel members."

I reached down into my mind. Where had I read about this? A *New York Times* article. Snippets began filtering back.

"Pegasus has also been used against journalists, dissidents, and human rights activists," I said.

"There may have been instances." Terse.

"What was that quote from the NSO sales brochure? Something about the software enabling law enforcement and spy agencies to"—I hooked air quotes—"'turn their target's smartphone into an intelligence gold mine'?"

"That pitch referred to a program called Phantom."

"Big difference. I read a lengthy exposé on NSO. Two investigative journalists found that the American government has some very cozy history with the company."

Rossiter and Reid seemed to be looking to each other for help in getting the conversation back on track. And moving more quickly.

I was surprising even myself with how much I was recalling from that article I'd read. It must have made an impression. "Didn't the FBI also purchase the system, planning to use it for domestic surveillance?"

"That didn't happen." Rossiter's forehead now glistened like a sidewalk after a rain. The man was clearly uncomfortable.

More snippets from the *Times* piece reconvened in my head.

"To demonstrate a 'zero click' version of the spyware, FBI personnel were instructed to buy smartphones and set them up with dummy accounts using SIM cards from outside the US. Pegasus engineers then opened their interface, entered the phone numbers, and began an attack."

"Zero click?" Monck asked.

"Meaning the program didn't require a user to open a malicious link or attachment. So the agents monitoring the phones couldn't see the Pegasus computers connecting to a global network of servers, hacking the phones, then connecting back to equipment in a US facility. They saw no sign of a breach."

Rossiter tried to interrupt, but I was on a roll.

"What they *could* see, minutes later, was every piece of data stored on any of those phones unspooling into the Pegasus computers. Every email, photo, text thread, personal contact, whatever. They could also see the location of each phone, and even take control of their cameras and microphones."

"Echoes of Edward Snowden," Monck said. "Governments transforming personal devices into surveillance tools to spy on their own citizens."

"Exactly. But there was a hitch. To placate the Americans, the Israeli government required NSO to make Pegasus incapable of targeting US numbers."

"Let me guess," said Monck. "Some genius came up with a workaround."

"Phantom, a system that could hack any US device."

"Wasn't NSO eventually blacklisted by the Biden administratio—"

"Enough!"

Rossiter's vehemence startled us both into silence.

"First of all, the FBI decided to never deploy Pegasus. Second, and more important, the *morality* of the spyware is not the point!"

"What *is* the point," I pressed.

"I can't go into that now."

"Do it or we walk," Monck insisted.

"You're not grasping the urgency of the situation."

"Help us understand," I said.

"Jesus. Fine. The CliffsNotes version of NSO's origin."

"We're listening."

"NSO traces its roots to an agricultural co-op outside Tel Aviv. A place called Bnai Zion."

My gaze met Monck's.

"Sonofabitch," he muttered, barely audible.

"A chicken coop repurposed for rental back in the day. Space for technology start-ups," I said.

"Yes," said Rossiter, eyeing me strangely.

Monck and I exchanged a "holy shit" glance. Rossiter's "tale" was tracking with Uncle Shlomo's account.

"Among the tenants were two former school friends, Shalev Hulio and Omri Lavie. Long story short, after several flops, Hulio and Lavie launched a company called CommuniTake, offering software that allowed tech-support workers to take control of their customers' devices." Rossiter raised an index finger. "But only with permission."

Rossiter was speaking so quickly I had to concentrate to follow.

"As with their prior efforts, CommuniTake also fell flat. Ever the entrepreneurs, Hulio and Lavie pivoted away from phone maintenance to a different potential market: law enforcement and intelligence agencies. They knew that cops and spies had long been able to intercept transmissions. They also knew that newly developed encryption techniques were rendering those captured messages unreadable.

"If one could control the device itself, they reasoned, data could be collected *prior* to encryption. CommuniTake was already able to grab control of iPhones and Androids. All they needed was a modification to allow that to happen"—the finger came back up—"without permission."

"What does this have to do with Joe Benjamin?" Monck demanded. I could tell his patience was close to depleted.

"You asked for this."

We had.

After checking his watch once more, Rossiter resumed. "Lacking contacts in the intelligence community, Hulio and Lavie recruited a third partner, Niv Karmi. Karmi had served in both the military and the Mossad."

"Niv, Shalev, and Omri." Monck toggled the initials with lightning speed. "NSO."

I couldn't help playing the A student: "Didn't NSO catch its first break when Pegasus managed to bust into encrypted BlackBerrys used by Guzmán's Sinaloa cartel in Mexico?"

"Again, ma'am," Rossiter chastised in his best let's-move-this-along voice. "The success or morality of Pegasus isn't the point."

The reprimand sent my molars reaching for each other. But I said nothing.

"Seeing expansion as essential to their business plan, Hulio, Lavie, and Karmi began hiring like mad," Rossiter resumed.

"Joe Benjamin was one of those hires?" I ventured.

"He was. For several years, Benjamin worked closely with the three partners, expanding and honing his already impressive arsenal of cyber skills. In late 2012, he returned stateside to care for his aging father."

I heard the *thuck* of titanium knuckles slamming flesh. Felt my own hands begin to sweat.

"We believe Benjamin took the knowledge he acquired at NSO and went on to develop a zero click program with a unique twist. This new program was designed to hack into and take control of navigational systems."

Rossiter again checked the time. I fought the impulse to reach out and throttle the guy.

"What kind of navigational systems?" Monck asked.

"Pretty much any kind. And the implications go far beyond cars and trucks. We're talking boats, choppers, planes."

"How do you know this isn't all bullshit?" Monck's voice held enough rancor for me to know he'd run out of patience. Rossiter was smart enough to read the room.

"At two-thirty-four this afternoon the pilot of a United Airlines flight en route from Chicago to Punta Cana radioed that he was experiencing a potentially catastrophic system failure. The plane was diverting off course and his manual-override attempts were ineffective. In his words: it was as if someone had taken control of the plane."

Rossiter's look was long and meaningful. "Keep your eyes on the friendly skies of Chicago."

"Jesus God. What happened?"

"Eight minutes later all systems returned to normal."

A pair of images blasted into my brain. Five corpses on a vessel adrift at sea. A black-and-white print of a twin turbo prop plane.

"The Sea Ray SDX 270 found six hundred miles off course last week?" I prompted, speaking with as much calm as I could muster. "You think Benjamin was responsible for that?"

"Yes, we do."

"The Piaggio P.180 that went down near Provo a few years back?"

Rossiter nodded glumly.

"A framed photo of that aircraft hangs in Joe Benjamin's home," I said.

If Rossiter was surprised, he hid it well. A beat, then, "It's apparent that the two of you were already aware of some of the intel I've just shared. May I ask your source?"

Monck told Rossiter about Uncle Shlomo. About Avner and his two sons. About Yaakov's injury and subsequent suicide. About Joe, né Yosef.

When finished, Monck asked, "How long have you known about Cloke's connection to Benjamin?"

Rossiter's eyes again went to his partner. Reid's body language made it obvious he didn't like the openness with us. Not at all.

"A while," Rossiter said.

"A while," Monck repeated, caustic. "How'd they hook up?"

"In the interest of national security, I cannot disclose the means by which our special agent learned of Benjamin's proficiency in coding."

"Did Cloke know about brother Yaakov's wee bomb incident?"

Reid made an odd noise in his throat.

"No comment," Rossiter said.

"You come on to my turf, tell me a local is planning to blow planes out of the air, and say no comment?" Monck spit back, sharp, angry.

"We believe Cloke tracked Benjamin for some time, eventually traveled to Provo to propose his get-rich-scheme in person."

"I'm hearing a lot of *we believes*. What is it you *know*?"

"Back off, detective," Reid snapped. "The clock is ticking, and Special Agent Rossiter has shared what he can."

No need to be a psychologist to know Reid didn't like us. I was mulling what his principal beef was when another image detonated in my overstimulated brain.

A serpentine track on a rainy ridge.

"I think Benjamin may have targeted *my* phone," I said quietly.

"What?" Monck's eyes went wide.

I described my aborted drive to the synagogue. The rain. The Google Maps directions that sent me high onto a spiny ridge.

"How could he have accessed your phone?" Monck asked.

"Remember? I called him on our way to his house."

"Sonofabitch!"

"Unbelievable," Rossiter said after a moment. "Your serial killer is running with our cyber terrorist."

Now it was Monck who looked at his watch.

7:55 p.m.

Five minutes until Cloke's follow-up communiqué.

Four hours until Ryan's "surprise" arrival?

We waited as this unending Saturday waned, the room so silent I was certain the others could hear my heart pounding.

The email landed on the OTD computer precisely at eight. Rossiter had it on his MacBook Air four minutes later.

Rossiter did the zillion key thing, then he and Reid leaned into the screen.

Looking like a man just given a cancer diagnosis, Rossiter swiveled the laptop toward us.

Fear hit like a bazooka round to the chest.

35

Cloke's second email consisted of a coded list.

> DL 1313 ATL 6:15 STT 10:26 Boeing 757
> BA 2113 LGW 5:40 ANU 10:08 Boeing 777
> AF 0009 CDG 4:40 SXM 10:19 A330
> AC 2107 YUL 7:55 PLS 11:44 A220-300

"These are the planes this asshole is threatening to hijack?" asked Monck, voice masking his horror.

"Yes."

"All are flights coming into the Caribbean. Delta from Atlanta to Saint Thomas, British Airways from London Gatwick to Antigua, Air France from Paris to St. Martin, Air Canada from Montreal to Provo. All landing between ten and midnight tonight."

"All in the air right now." Monck.

"I know a passenger on AC 2107." My chest was ice, my lips barely able to form the words.

Three faces swiveled toward me.

"I have to warn him." Reaching for my phone.

"We can't allow you to do that," Reid said.

"Allow me!?"

"One leak could compromise our whole operation."

"You have an *operation*? You can't even manage to find your own agent! You can't trace his goddam emails!"

"We have people on it."

"Jesus! You're the freaking FBI!"

"Hysteria won't help."

Hysteria?

But Reid wasn't wrong. And Ryan had probably disabled his phone for takeoff.

Tamping down my emotions, I said, "The AC passenger is a detective with the Sûreté du Québec, the Quebec provincial police. The man understands security and would never cause a leak. Get word to him."

Reid narrowed his eyes toward his partner.

"Let me explain why these emails are so hard to track," said Rossiter, soothing as an EMT talking a jumper from a ledge. "Then I will share—"

"I want my friend off that plane!"

"Please. Bear with us. That flight has just taken off. One call and we can have the plane diverted."

"Seriously?"

"Seriously. I understand your concern. But hundreds of lives could be at stake here."

"Talk fast." Hating that he was right.

Rossiter resumed his explanation.

"Cloke and Benjamin have been communicating with each other and with the various agencies using a VPN."

"Do *not* play me with jargon," Monck snapped.

"A virtual private network." I interceded, sensing the tension in the room escalating to match my own. "A VPN encrypts internet traffic and disguises a sender's online identity so third parties can't track any activities or steal any data. Especially since the encryption takes place in real time. Don't ask me how it works."

Monck looked at me like I'd spoken Macedonian.

Rossiter continued.

"If you surf online with a VPN, the VPN server becomes the source of your data. Your ISP—internet service provider—and other third parties can't see which websites you visit or what data you send and receive. A VPN works like a blender, turning your transmissions into gibberish. Is that clear, detective?"

"Clear as Pickapeppa sauce." Wired on adrenaline and piqued by Rossiter's condescending tone. "Why the fuck is this relevant?"

"And why are we sitting in this room doing nothing?" I demanded.

"Those are my orders. For now."

"They sure as hell aren't mine," Monck exploded.

Rossiter lifted a placating palm. I noted that it trembled slightly.

"You asked why we couldn't trace the sender of the ransom demand," he said. "The answer is that the message was probably pre-programmed as to time of dispatch, then routed through a dozen anonymous servers all over the globe. The same will be true of the link they'll provide for deposit of the money. The funds will go through a scrambling process, into an untraceable account, then be instantaneously transferred into the vapor."

Monck shot to his feet. "Enough, for Chrissake. I'm hitting the street. Obviously, you can't flush your maniac agent, so my officers will."

"Please, detective." Rossiter's hand rose higher. "Hold on."

"No way. I'm done."

Monck strode for the door.

"Several days ago, the OTD intercepted a phone conversation they believe took place between Cloke and Benjamin."

Monck froze.

"What?" Too strident, my brain still in high-voltage mode. "How is that possible? They were being so careful."

Reid fired Rossiter one of his spy-versus-spy squints.

"Sorry. Classified." Rossiter did not seem sorry. "Suffice it to say one of them got sloppy."

"What kind of bullshit answer is that?" Monck barked.

"Could your *people* pinpoint the origin of the call?" I asked.

"Useless. The connection was made burner to burner."

"What was said?"

"I'll paraphrase." Rossiter took a nanosecond to choreograph that in his head. "Cloke and Benjamin were pointedly unspecific about their plans, simply referred throughout to 'the op.' Benjamin was having second thoughts. At first Cloke was encouraging, eventually threatening."

"And you're just now disclosing this?" Angry heat was turning Monck's cheeks poinsettia red.

"We needed to verify the nature of their activities."

"Thus, your unannounced presence on my patch," Monck, seething.

New images shaped up in my brain. A charred pickup crumpled against a limestone wall. A burned corpse impaled on a shattered windshield.

"Cloke murdered Benjamin," I said. "The crash wasn't an accident. Benjamin was familiar with that road and knew about that sinkhole. And suicide never made sense. Why ask for millions in ransom, then kill yourself?"

Monck was about to agree or disagree when his mobile sounded an incoming call. Snatching the phone from his pocket, he clicked on.

"Monck."

A voice sputtered, muted and unintelligible.

"When?" A flicker of something wild before Monck composed his face.

More sputtering.

"Four units. No bells, no cherries. I'm twelve minutes out. Do not apprehend until I'm ten-twenty-three. Repeat. Hold action until I arrive."

A questioning sputter.

"Affirmative. Suspect could be armed. Use force as required, but we need this asshole alive."

A brief sputter.

"Roger that. And a transport unit to the Sea Breeze."

Pocket-jamming the device, Monck pivoted to us.

"Cloke just used a credit card at Bugaloo's."

We all spoke at once.

"Booyah!" Reid.

"Where?" Rossiter.

"When?" I asked.

"Bugaloo's Conch Crawl, a bar and restaurant in Five Cays."

We all fired to our feet.

Monck asked the feds. "You guys carrying?"

Both nodded.

"Locked and loaded," Reid said.

Monck's tone to me allowed not a millimeter of wiggle room.

"Your ass goes back to your condo."

Fast as a heart attack, Monck was out the door.

9:00 P.M.

The uniforms dropped me at Villa Renaissance just past nine.

Sleep was out of the question.

I sat on the terrace, nerves on edge, willing my phone to ring. Hoping the steady *thrum* of the surf would calm me.

It didn't.

I felt angry that Monck had barred me from the action. Miffed that he was right. Totally useless.

And terrified for Ryan. On a flight that might be programmed for disaster.

I'd agreed not to warn Ryan. Anyway, how could I? By the time the ransom email landed Ryan's plane was already in the air. And if I could have gotten word to him, would my action have been morally defensible? Could I have justified placing hundreds of other lives in danger?

Thinking of Ryan made me think of tea.

I went to the kitchen to brew a cup. Back outside, I checked the screen of my iPhone.

No missed calls. Of course not. Less than thirty minutes had passed since Monck and the feds raced off to Bugaloo's.

I took a sip of tea—followed by several deep breaths.

A small, sand-colored bird circled low and close to the balcony, appraising. Its beak and legs were orange. Black feathers ringed its throat and ran in a narrow bar from eye to eye. I guessed it was a plover.

Seriously, Brennan? You're playing ornithologist while Ryan's life hangs in the balance and Monck and the feds are taking down Cloke?

Good with the appearance of the terrace, and with my presence on it, the maybe plover landed on the top of its low wall. Grateful for any distraction, I went as still as my shaky hands would allow and watched.

A full minute, then I whispered, "Would you like a treat, little guy?"

The bird cocked its head to eyeball me more closely. Stayed put as I slowly set down my mug and eased from my chair.

Back to the kitchen, this time for bread.

When I returned, the bird was still there. Ever so gently, I tossed a few morsels of crust toward his feet.

Hop-turning, he eyed me again, then my offering. Went for the latter.

I felt like Jane Goodall making her first breakthrough at Gombe.

I was doling and my avian pal was noshing when suddenly the bird startled and darted off in a flurry of wings.

I looked to see what had frightened the plover. Nothing down below. I turned toward the condo.

Soft yellow light was spilling through the sliding glass doors. A silhouette darkened the panel I'd left open. Not tall, not short. Holding a long, slender object with both hands.

My body began to mainline adrenaline.

Moving as gingerly as I had with the bird, I stepped toward my chair. Toward my mobile.

Suddenly, I was choking, hard steel pressing my throat. I felt myself lifted off the tile. Not much, maybe an inch. But enough. I couldn't inhale. Couldn't get traction under my bare feet.

"You and your friends have been busy," a voice whispered in my ear.

"Let me go," I rasped.

"Hurts, doesn't it?"

"Please."

"You'll have to do better than that."

I felt myself jerked upward and backward. Dragged inside and thrown onto the bed. My attacker's body fell heavy on my back.

It was *Groundhog Day*, island style.

"Go ahead. Scream for help." Did I recognize the voice? "Your friends aren't coming."

"I won't." Barely choked out.

"Good answer."

"Can't breathe."

The pressure on my trachea was replaced by the hard steel of a gun muzzle jammed to my temple.

"I'm going to step back and you're going to sit up. Don't try anything funny. I've got nothing more to lose by spraying your brains on that wall."

I nodded.

The weight shifted from my back.

Chest pounding, I palmed myself up and turned.

Unlike the night of the previous attack, this time I had light. Dim, but sufficient to recognize my assailant.

I forced myself to breathe evenly to slow my heartrate. To hide my shock.

Joe Benjamin was holding a Beretta 92 pistol in his right hand, a slender, curved sword in his left, the smaller of the Samurai pair I'd seen on his shelf.

Throat on fire, I forced myself to swallow.

"The blade of your wakizashi is damaged," I squeaked.

"What do you know about my Daisho?"

"You have the traditional duo, a large katana and a smaller wakizashi, the one you're holding. That one is damaged."

"How could you know that?" Benjamin asked, dumbfounded.

"I saw them on your shelf."

"How could you know my wakizashi is damaged?"

I needed to stall. To allow time for Monck to get to Bugaloo's and realize the credit card charge was a trick. To figure a way to escape?

"Why are you here?"

"What do you think?" Waggling the Beretta.

"Why would you want to hurt me?"

"You're just like all the rest. Can only spare attention for the pretty boys."

A part of me was incredulous. In the midst of it all, *this* was what he was focused on? "You're angry that I refused to ride on the Kawasaki with you?"

Benjamin's scowl deepened.

"You killed Bobby Galloway, Ryder Palke, and Quentin Bonner, then hacked off their hands with that," I said, nodding at the sword. "Somewhere along the way, you damaged the blade. After that you used a challah knife to open the flesh first. Only you broke that, too, leaving a fragment from the handle driven into Palke's left ulna."

"You're a mean but clever gal. A typical Stac—"

"Did you help me with the translation to throw more shade on Stribbe?"

Benjamin raised the pistol and cocked the hammer. I felt myself flinch.

Keep talking.

"I get why you did it," I said. "You were avenging your brother."

"What do *you* know about my brother?" he asked, spitting the words with contempt.

"Yaakov lost his hand—"

"I hated my brother!" Fingers squeezing the grip so tightly they blanched.

Wrong tack, Brennan.

"And who wouldn't?" Soothing as hell. "You tried so hard, and Yaakov got all the benefit."

Distant sirens? Wishful thinking?

"The world doesn't need all these pretty boys sucking its oxygen." Benjamin seemed oblivious to the faint wailing.

"Why kill Cloke?" I asked, realizing who'd died in the sinkhole. "Did he betray you?"

"Ah, you figured that out. Really hated to lose that truck. But my bike suits me for now."

In the hall, the soft swish of nylon.

Benjamin froze, muzzle level on my face. Had he heard it, too?

"How did you get Cloke into the pickup?" I asked quickly to cover the sound.

"With a little help from pharmaceuticals. That loser viewed himself as hot shit. Thought he was in charge." Derisive snort. "His op was dead in the water without my coding."

"Did you kill Detective Musgrove?"

"No way you're pinning that one on me."

"Did Cloke?"

"What do you think? The bastard kicked Betty to death. I'd say he has anger-control issues."

"Why did you agree to work with Cloke?"

Benjamin hiked one shoulder. "A chance to thumb my nose at karma. To tell the whole friggin' universe it underestimated me bigtime."

"A hundred million dollars is a lot of thumbing."

"It wasn't the money. God almighty, it was never the money."

"You told Cloke you were having second thoughts?"

A quick flicker in Benjamin's eyes, there then gone. He took a long moment to answer.

"There could be kids on those planes. Bubbies. Pets."

"You knew that from the outset."

"It didn't register at first. When we were setting it up, it was like some sort of video game."

Beyond the door, a soft tic. A heel kissing tile?

Benjamin turned this time. To bolt? Or shoot?

It all happened at once.

Gripping the quilt with both hands, I sent the tangle into his face, partially draping it over his head. Furious, he dropped the sword to brush aside the fabric. At that point, Monck thundered through the door and pushed Benjamin to the floor before he could raise the Beretta. In a series of lightning-quick motions, Monck pounded the gun from Benjamin's grasp, grabbed him by the hair, and smashed his face down hard.

Then again.

Then a third time.

Blood spread across the tile and trickled into the grout.

"Monck!" I shouted.

Monck slipped his real palm under Benjamin's chin, lifted, and placed his bionic wrist across the back of his neck. He could either choke the man out or snap his cervical vertebrae.

"Stop!" I screamed.

36

t was a day made of sapphires and diamonds, the sea and sky an unrelenting blue, the sunlight electric off the rolling surf.

I arrived late. For the first time, the Honda had showed attitude before firing up. Did the old heap sense we were about to part ways?

Spotting Monck seated in back, bionic limb draping the arm of the pew, I crossed to him. He looked gaunt and haggard. The black circles were back under his eyes.

Monck acknowledged my presence by sliding left to make room. I slipped in beside him, taking the last empty seat in the church.

I'd expected the usual high turnout of law enforcement, Musgrove's fellow soldiers in that thin blue line between order and chaos. They were there, of course, looking coiled and angry, livid over the murder of one of their own. They'd come from every jurisdiction in TCI, several islands throughout the Caribbean, the US, and the UK.

But it wasn't just cops filling Our Lady of Divine Providence. People from all walks of life had put on their Sunday finest to say their final good-byes.

I saw two waitresses from the Shay Café. A toothless old woman who had to be Juniper Rose, the bed swing builder. Iggie Bernadin. Harvey Lindstrom. Zev and Leah Abrams. Adeera, Dovid, and Uri Stribbe. Arthur, from Da Conch Shack. Surf bums. Fishermen. Shopkeepers. Several couples with kids in tow. And, of course, Musgrove's sister, Raina Ewing from Cockburn Town.

Fleeting thoughts of those *not* present skirted the edge of my mind. Musgrove's abusive husband, Milo Willis. Benjamin's victims, including Bobby Galloway, Ryder Palke, and Quentin Bonner. Musgrove's own killer.

Or was he? Monck's follow-up investigation had determined that Willis was, in fact, at a resort in Houston when Musgrove was murdered. So who strangled her?

The air in the church was syrupy warm, cloying with the aromas of jasmine, plumeria, oleander, and lily that hung in baskets and covered every horizontal surface. Cheap cologne and human sweat added extra ripeness to the perfumy mix. Fans rotating high among the ceiling beams had little effect.

The preacher was a young man with a bad comb-over and round horn-rimmed glasses, all smiles and handshakes and platitudes. At one point he ambushed my emotions by playing a Judy Collins recording of "Who Knows Where the Time Goes?," a song Gran had requested for her funeral. Otherwise, I couldn't fault his style. He sounded sincere and kept things moving.

At the end of the service, I watched Musgrove's sister lead the exit procession. No tears, but soul-deep grief was written on her face.

My heart ached for her. I understood. Nothing shatters lives like violent death.

As we'd agreed, I arrived at Danny Buoy's just past five. Monck was already there, fingers wrapping a Turk's Head lager. An empty bottle sat before him.

Upon entering, I paused to allow my eyes to adjust to the dimness. To take in Monck. A full week together and the man remained an enigma. A skeleton with a titanium hand and size thirteen suede loafers.

In the scores of hours we'd spent together, Monck had never mentioned his Irish-Jamaican heritage. His ancestor, the second Duke of Marlboro. Never shared one detail about his personal life. Was he married? Single? Divorced? Gay? Did he live in a condo? On a boat? In a shack by the sea? Did he prefer soccer or hoops? Pepsi or Coke? Did he like being tagged The Monk? I knew nothing.

Which suited me. Gutted by the heartbreak of Musgrove's death, I'd needed a cop not a buddy. What was it Aristotle said? "My friends, there are no friends"? Perhaps the chill had come from my side.

The pub was uncrowded late on a Sunday afternoon. But customers were trickling in. I recognized the bed swing lady and a few other mourners from the church. Constable Gardiner.

I took the stool beside Monck and ordered a Perrier with lime. We'd barely spoken since the previous night's dramatic events. I'd been totally wrung out, and he'd been busy processing Benjamin. I was keen for an update.

No need to ask. Monck launched right in. Almost too eager. I wondered if the guy was already fogged over from the beer.

"Lindstrom will autopsy the sinkhole crisper tomorrow. He checked the corpse's mouth, has no doubt it's Cloke. Apparently, there are some doodle-dandy dental restorations—Lindstrom's phrasing."

"Benjamin said he drugged Cloke to get him into the truck."

"Lindstrom plans to run exhaustive tox screens. My money's on Special K. We found a vial in Benjamin's kitchen drawer."

"Ketamine."

"Yep." Monck finished the dregs of his brew, signaled to the bartender for another.

"Anything else in that house?"

"Two rental cars in the garage. Three mummified hands in the shed."

"Hot damn."

Monck held out his bottle. I clinked its neck with the rim of my glass.

"I should be able to match that wakizashi to the cut marks on the bones," I said. "The nick in the blade is quite distinct."

"How did you know what those things were?"

"Strictly curiosity. The swords didn't look Judaic, so after leaving Benjamin's house that first time, I googled a few images. Figured he was into Samurai artifacts, thought nothing of it."

Monck's beer arrived. I waited as he knocked back the top third.

"Benjamin's behind bars?" I asked.

"And willing to spill."

"Looking for a deal?"

"Oh, yeah. Plus, he seems anxious to unburden his soul, or whatever. All the time I spent talking to him, yesterday and again this morning, I couldn't get anything close to a clear read. I kept asking myself. What kind of psychosis prompts a guy to kill strangers just because they're attractive young men?"

Monck downed more brew.

"We've got Benjamin's computers at the station, so I had a tech take me on a stroll through his browsing history. The mope spent a lot of time in chatgroups or forums or whatever they're called where the main theme seemed to be bitching about women."

"Incel communities?"

Monck raised both brows.

"Involuntary celibates, men radicalized by their mistrust of women. Incels are misogynists, but they also resent the type of males they see as scoring all the sex."

A comment made during the attack at the condo suddenly made sense.

"Last night Benjamin called me a mean but clever gal, and started to say I was a typical Stacy."

The brows retraced their upward trajectory.

"Incels refer to good-looking guys as Chads and to attractive but unattainable women as Stacys." It was more complicated than that, but I kept it simple.

"They're pissed that the Chads monopolize the Stacys." As usual, Monck got it right away.

"Exactly. When you break it down, their main grievance is that women get to choose their own sexual partners."

"And they're not the ones getting chosen."

I nodded, gave a quick smile. "You were spot-on during our brainstorming session when you proposed that the perp could be a sad little loser who never gets the girl."

"I keep telling you, I'm a genius."

My eyes rolled without direction from me.

"What was the final word on Glen Wall?" I asked.

"Musgrove was correct to clear him. His story about being on a fishing boat checked out. The brother and one of the cousins are both pastors, and thus reliable witnesses. The other cousin is an ardent photographer. Lots of pics, lots of other proof that Wall was elsewhere when Palke went missing."

"Uri Stribbe?"

"Same deal. Adeera's claims about sonny's whereabouts were all corroborated."

"What's happening with Rossiter and Reid?"

"They're hot to extradite. Not gonna happen. Benjamin's staying here to face multiple counts of first-degree murder and a dozen other charges."

"He's owned up to Cloke," I pointed out. "The cut marks in the ulnae, and the rental cars and severed hands at his home should nail him as the serial. What about Musgrove?"

Monck frowned. "He's adamant he didn't do her. And she's a local cop and he's a local guy, and she didn't appear to be that close to tagging him."

"Seems more Cloke's style. After all, the bastard kicked a dog to death."

"Turned out the text Musgrove received while the two of you

were dining at Da Conch Shack contained intel pertaining to Cloke. Apparently, the inquiry she sent to the DC office landed with a buddy of Cloke's. What are the chances? Anyway, the buddy dropped a dime with a heads-up that a TCI cop was asking about him. Cloke got spooked, decided to take Musgrove out."

A moment of silence as we both thought about that.

"Have you questioned Benjamin about the airplane-hijacking scheme?" I asked.

"No need," Monck said with a snort. "During transport and booking, the guy wouldn't shut up. He maintained that he'd decided not to sabotage airliners. He claimed the caper started when Cloke was investigating a mysterious plane crash down here, and somehow tied that mishap to the software Benjamin had developed to hack into navigational systems."

"Cloke dug deep on Benjamin, learned of his past with NSO and Pegasus?"

"Yes, ma'am. Maybe to impress, who knows? Benjamin told Cloke all about his little hobby hacking cars and boats. The Piaggio P.180. The *Cod Bless Us*."

My own Google Maps misadventure. I didn't say it. Instead, I asked about a detail that had bothered me.

"Benjamin's program allowed him to sabotage the *Cod*'s satellite and radio systems?"

Monck nodded. "And the phones of those on board."

I pictured Doyle and his passengers, helplessly floundering in the open sea, losing hope, eventually dying of dehydration.

Monck's voice brought me back.

"Once Cloke was certain Benjamin was the real deal, he flew to Provo to persuade him to hijack commercial airliners for a big score."

"Did Cloke know about Benjamin's other extracurriculars?" I asked.

"Stalking, then capping good-looking male tourists? Negatory. Apparently, that's what caused things to go sideways. Cloke learned what Benjamin was up to and decided he needed to shut that down.

After all the hard work and planning, he couldn't allow Benjamin's craziness to bring Johnny Law down on their heads."

"Talk about choosing a partner with a messy sideline," I said, shaking my head.

"Toward the end Benjamin did appear to be having misgivings about the ransom caper," Monck said. "At least, that's the FBI read on that one sloppy phone call. Cloke may have come to Provo to cajole Benjamin back into compliance, maybe to blackmail him. But Benjamin wouldn't budge. The two ended up in a throw-down at the house on Karst Way. Cloke killed Betty. Incensed, Benjamin killed Cloke."

"With Cloke dead and Benjamin bailing on their 'op,' who was sending out the ransom demands?"

"Cloke had preprogrammed transmission times for the emails."

"Why?"

"Maybe to establish an alibi for himself? Who knows?"

Ice popped then fizzed in my glass. Monck chugged more beer, Adam's apple bobbing like a buoy in his throat.

"It's like a B-grade spy movie," I said. "Just in the nick of time, the villains are foiled, and the world is saved."

"No shit. We don't know whether the airlines were actually assembling the money, but by ten last night, while I was saving your sweet cheeks, Rossiter and Reid were shutting down every scrap of electronics in Benjamin's home—four phones, six laptops and desktops, seventeen storage devices, six external hard drives, the rooftop WiFi signal booster, the Ring doorbell system, and a second mother lode of hardware set up in the shed. In short order, the OTD accessed every one of Benjamin's networks and servers and deactivated his programs remotely."

"Jesus on a cyclone. How?"

"With Benjamin's help. The wackjob even provided passwords. Though with Cloke toast and Benjamin no longer playing, there may have been no one to activate the crash codes. Go figure."

"What are the chances, Monck?" I asked, slowly shaking my head. I still couldn't believe it. "Our village psycho partnered with the

FBI's international saboteur. Why? What *really* motivated Benjamin to throw in with Cloke?"

We fell silent a long moment thinking about that. I recalled snatches from the exchange I'd had with Benjamin the night before when he seemed furious with me. Suddenly it all made sense.

"It was about subservience and dominance," I said.

Monck looked at me. Eyes slightly fuzzy?

"The powerless, unattractive, repressed little man could play God by taking control of people and sending them to their deaths. Down a road to a killing ground. Out to sea. Into a fatal nosedive. Whatever. He was in charge. And in Cloke, he had a pretty boy essentially working for him, taking his orders. That would have been how Benjamin viewed it anyway."

Again, we went still. Then,

"Has Benjamin admitted to the first break-in at the Villa Renaissance?" I asked.

"Yes, ma'am."

"Why?"

"You and Musgrove seemed to be getting too close. He wanted to know what you had. She was a cop, so you were an easier target. He swears he meant to see your intel and scare you that time, not harm you."

"You believe him?"

"He's being up front with the rest."

"Why the second break-in?"

"He gives a somewhat darker explanation for that. You'd snubbed him, blah, blah, blah. As you've said, he got off on life and death control over people."

Neither of us followed up on that grim thought.

"How did you know I might be in trouble?"

"When we got to Bugaloo's, no one knew anything about a charge to Cloke's credit card. No one was aware of a phoned-in tip. That set fire bells ringing in the back of my mind. Figuring the stunt was a diversion from the real action, I raced to your place."

"I keep replaying those attacks in my head. How did he get into my condo? The first time it was my stupidity. But after that, I kept everything locked unless I was present."

"He hacked your hotel key."

My brows floated up.

"You know I'm no whiz with this computer stuff. But our tech guy explained it to me. The card has an RFID chip that stores data about your room number and other info that allows you access to certain areas of the building—elevators, pool, etc. When you swipe your room key over your door's lock, the computer recognizes the room number and lets you in. It also unlocks any latches inside."

"Like those on the windows and sliding glass panels."

I was about to comment when the bar door opened. I glanced over my shoulder. Backlit by the apricot rectangle of sunset slashing into the gloom was the form of another man built like a lanky Lego creation.

I turned back quickly. My smile must have been obvious.

"That your cop friend?" Monck asked.

I nodded. "He's unaware that I know he's coming. The visit is supposed to be a surprise."

"Who clued you?"

"My sister. Hair roots and nails and clean undies and all."

Monck gave me an odd look but said nothing.

"How does he know where you are right now?"

"He called earlier pretending to still be in Montreal."

"So he's up to speed on what's happened down here? Except for the sneak move by your sis?"

"And the fact that his was one of the targeted aircraft. He thinks his plane was diverted to Miami due to mechanical issues. He had to overnight there, and rebook today on an afternoon flight."

A brief scan—cop eyes—then Ryan made his way toward us.

I felt a hand on my shoulder. Turned. Did the whole wide-eyed *Omygodwhatareyoudoinghere?* thing.

Ryan wrapped me in his arms, pulled me close, held me to his chest a smidge longer than appropriate. Then he stepped back and extended a hand toward Monck.

"Andrew Ryan."

"Delroy Monck. Let me buy you a beer, sir."

Giving a thumbs-up, Ryan slid onto the stool beside me.

Seconds later, two more Turks Heads appeared.

"I understand the doc's looped you in on the serials and the cyber threats we've been chasing?"

"She has. And Detective Musgrove, of course. That one sucks big-time."

Monck nodded tightly. "You two plan to sneak in a vacation?"

"I've booked a few days at Wymara, if *ma chère* is good with that. But I'm also here to tie off a loose end on a case."

Both parts of Ryan's answer were unexpected.

"Deniz Been," he added, seeing my expression.

"He's the reason I'm in Provo," I explained to Monck. "Been was shot while watching fireworks from a bridge in Montreal. His body ended up in the St. Lawrence. I fished it out and IDed him."

"For a while, the thinking was that Been's death was gang-related," Ryan said. "That the kid was dealing on someone else's patch. That was wrong. Turned out Been had inserted himself into a violent three-way."

"The Québecoise girlfriend, Émilie Gaudreau, was seeing someone else?"

"A loser with a jacket going back to the stone age, who appeared to be safely out of circulation. Long story short, loverboy got paroled, got wind, got a gun, got it done. I'm here to break the news to Been's grandmother, his apparent next of kin."

"Henrietta Missick," Monck said without inflection.

"Do you know where I can find her?"

Monck nodded, glum. I suspected the beers were sending him to a dark place. "But not today. Too many reminders of death today."

Ryan's eyes crimped in puzzlement, but he didn't voice a question.

My gaze drifted past the men to a moth circling a faux Tiffany lamp overhanging the liquor bottles lining the bar. The beat of its wings matched the rhythm of the melancholy drumming in my soul.

Several moments passed.

Ryan took my hand and looked a question at me. Ready?

Thanking Monck for the drinks, we headed for the door. His parting words stopped us.

"You'll be going to her anyway."

We turned.

"Henrietta Missick is Tiersa Musgrove's first cousin. She owns the car you've been driving."

I left wondering if everyone in Provo knew everyone else.

That night Ryan and I dined alfresco at Grace's Cottage, then strolled the beach barefoot to Villa Renaissance. Once inside, we killed all the lights and opened the balcony doors wide.

We took our time making love. There was no hurry now, the only urgency the need for reassurance and release.

We rested a long time afterward, listening to the waves build and swell, crash and recede. Sex is like the ocean, I thought. Deep and endless and perpetually soothing.

Lying on my back, staring up into the darkness, one phrase kept rolling with the sound of the surf.

Yes, to dance beneath the diamond sky with one hand waving free.

Benjamin's victims would dance no more. Nor would Musgrove or the dead on the *Cod Bless Us*. But Benjamin and Cloke would not stop the music for anyone else.

I'd done my job.

I closed my eyes.

Felt content.

Wished Delroy Monck the same.

ACKNOWLEDGMENTS

I owe enormous thanks to Lisa Mitcheson, former superintendent of police, head of crime and public protection, Royal Turks and Caicos Islands Police Force.

The research done by criminologist Maria Mourani concerning the current gang situation in Montreal was very informative. Equally helpful was the work of professor and criminology researcher Marc Alain.

Hats off to Penny McCardle for her article on machete cut marks on bone. Same hats raised to Mark Mazzetti and Ronen Bergman for their *New York Times* series on NSO and Pegasus.

A heartfelt thank-you to my editors: Rick Horgan in the US, Katherine Armstrong in the UK, Anthea Bariamis in Australia, and Adrienne Kerr in Canada. You are the A team!

I am grateful to Courtney, Miles, and Cooper Mixon for including me on their expedition to the Turks and Caicos Islands.

Paul Reichs offered sound at-home editorial advice.

Skinny kept me company dozing in my office chair. Turk chose the rug. Roy mostly ran around in crazed puppy circles.

Melissa Fish was always there to check real-world facts and fictional details from earlier Temperance Brennan stories.

I appreciate the support of Deneen Howell, my legal representative at Williams & Connolly, LLP. Thanks for keeping me lawful.

I also want to acknowledge all those who work so very hard on my behalf. At home in the US, Nan Graham, Ashley Gilliam, Sophie Guimaraes, Jaya Miceli, Brian Belfiglio, Abigail Novak, Brianna Yamashita, and Katie Rizzo. On the other side of the pond, Ian Chapman, Suzanne Baboneau, Harriett Collins, and Rich Vlietstra. North of the border, Kevin Hanson, Nita Pronovost, Felicia Quon, Adria Iwasutiak, Jillian Levick, and Rebecca Snoddon.

There are many others too numerous to name. If I failed to mention you, I apologize.

My love goes out to all of Tempe's loyal followers. Hopefully, I will see many of you at this year's signings and other live events. Please continue to visit my website (KathyReichs.com), like me on Facebook (@kathyreichsbooks), and follow me on Instagram (@kathyreichs) and Twitter (@kathyreichs). You are the reason I write!

If this book contains errors, I own them.